E/
By

For Kerry, Alexana

&
In memory of Alfred Hull.

With special thanks to Brendan Gormley, my chief editor!

Contents

Prologue 3
Chapter One 3
Chapter Two 18
Chapter Three 33
Chapter Four 50
Chapter Five 66
Chapter Seven 91
Chapter Eight 102
Chapter Nine 113
Chapter Ten 146
Chapter Eleven 168
Chapter Twelve 194

Prologue

A starlit, infinite, deep indigo sea of nothingness gives way to a sky... of blue. Lights spinning, blue. green, yellow, orange, merging and diverging. No up, no down, no control. Seas and Land. Valleys and Rivers. Trees? Green, not like home. Will never go home. Crystal clear now, all vibration on hold. Crystal blue, red. Oscillating wildly and randomly. Hold the world in my hands, look back, too late, cannot go back. Have I chosen wisely? Is this really where my destiny lies? It is over......?

Chapter One

The mid-winter morning sky was just beginning to show the first signs of awakening from the darkness. The sun must now have just risen above the horizon, shrouded behind the endless grey cover that was a typical British winter's day. The sky's cold glow however, was as reassuring to Steve as the glow from a log fire. A very different sky to the one he had experienced less than a year ago, in his last days serving in the army overseas and a very different day ahead for him also. 'Morning Steve, early start as always?' asked Debra, who was office manager at the firm he had now been working at for about two months since leaving the army. 'Yes, old habits die hard.' he replied, like old soldiers he quipped to himself. Civvy Street took some getting used to. Thank god he was still relatively young and able to adapt more easily than he may have done, had he continued until his twenty fifth anniversary. Ten years in the Special Forces was long enough for any man.

'Ah, Fletcher, there you are...' David Lewis, a tall and slender man in his late forties who not only had a more than passing physical resemblance to *Death incarnate* but also possessed a manner that was friendly, condescending and mildly intimidating all at once, quite a feat to behold. 'We need to get the proposal out by mid-day to Hughes and Co, are we on track?' In particular, Steve was amused by Lewis' constant need to stamp his seniority over him on every occasion that they met or communicated. He'd had some demanding commanding officers in his time and this guy certainly had the right attitude to compete with them. 'Morning David' friendly and informal, two things that would immediately set the hairs on Lewis' neck tingling 'yes, I have the sign off on the commercials already, and just need the sales team's input on the executive summary before printing at ten and arranging for it to be delivered by hand.' And if you want I will arrange for your backside to be wiped at eleven twenty-three precisely, he thought to himself to help retain his sanity. This was the third time since yesterday afternoon he had been quizzed in some way, shape or form by his first boss outside of life in the forces. The status had hardly changed since the last update. 'Good, keep me posted, I want to know the minute it is delivered...' No goodbye or thank you. *Good* was indeed as good as it gets.

Steve was a solidly built, averagely tall man in his mid-thirties. He worked hard to retain his fitness, but had the slightest hint of an embryonic, developing, middle age spread around his abdomen. Running three times a week and rare visits to the gym were no substitute for life on a field operation. Oh, and Pizza and wine with his (for him) long-term girlfriend Sam, probably did not help matters all that much either. He took one final look at his profile reflection in the partly mirror-tinted windows of his company's offices and then sat down at his desk once more. Satisfied that no one was within sight, he slowly pulled out the envelope that had been delivered the previous evening to the small riverside flat he shared with Sam. He eyed the shape and size of the small paper rectangle. It was familiar to him, in a way he had never expected to see again yet alone twice in the past two months. Whatever it contained though, he mused to himself, could wait. He first had a very important deadline to hit, otherwise Lewis would have a nervous breakdown.

Inspector Hayes sat in the cluttered pig-sty that passed for his office. The case files piled in organised chaos around him, he flitted from one to another in a distracted manner, reminiscent of an artist trying with little success to create several masterpieces at the same time. The cases seemed, on the whole, unrelated and random events. Nevertheless, something was nagging at him and he couldn't put his finger on it. His little voice, his intuition was half whispering to him but he couldn't quite make out what it was saying. So he sat there, on his day off but in the office, using his own time to indulge his gut feel. His main focus was the *Houdini Gang*, a title afforded to them by the press which he thoroughly hated and could barely stand them being referred to as. However, even he now privately thought of them by that name, which served only to irritate him further. The moniker referred to a series of crimes that had caught the public imagination in a way probably never seen before. The only link appeared to be the seemingly impossible or implausible modus operandi and the increasingly outrageous rare and valuable targets successfully acquired.

The majority of the other files consisted of seemingly independent smaller robberies and a series of inexplicable robberies where only a number of selected DIY items, such as Silicone Sealant, were stolen from DIY or Hardware stores. The one thing that seemed similar across the total of these crimes was the lack of anything out of the ordinary on any CCTV footage, even a grainy half image at the edge of a screen. At most of the locations the cameras had been expertly disabled, simply powered off or destroyed without capturing an image of who had tampered with them. If they expanded to CCTV cameras in the vicinity no image that appeared to be taken around the time you would expect the criminals to have passed by vehicle or even by foot had revealed a lead. Any images at all had, almost spookily, unilaterally proven to be individuals with a legitimate, provable reason to be at that location at that point of time. Sure they had questioned a few, even carried out forensic tests on some linked to the higher profile cases (with what little evidence there was) but nothing. A blank was drawn without exception.

'Morning Guv, thought you were on leave?' DS Killen had never quite got the grasp of knocking before entering as opposed to entering whilst doing so.
'Yes I am,' then less irritably 'just reminiscing on the old ways of doing a copper's job…..' He looked up at the younger woman, now standing square to him in front of the faux mountain range of files. 'Something links these cases, apart from the lack of evidence or meaningful forensics. Something smells.' He paused, looking as if he were holding on to his next thought.
'Coffee?' his tiredness seemed to warrant her asking the question.
'Please, Helen, that might just kick start the thinking muscle.' The DS smiled and left for the machine, glancing back whilst thinking to herself that he would keel over one day if he didn't learn how to relax, or at least get a life outside of work.

Hayes was essentially grey. Grey haired with a skin complexion that had only the merest exposure to fresh air as well as a trademark, grey, pinstripe suit. The solitary bright splash of a red tie stood out from his dour exterior. In fact, only the fiery glow of his grey blue eyes hinted that there was the presence of something other than somebody counting down the days to his retirement. He drummed the one piece of desktop not covered by a file or computer as he re-opened the latest *Houdini* crime. This was one, however, the press had not speculated as being perpetrated by the same *gang*, their words not his, as the others. It was however conducted with a strikingly similar MO and shared the only piece of linked forensic evidence to any of the other crimes strewn across his desk. That was a single strand of black cotton fibre from the same source garment, which was most probably a sweatshirt. This rare and minor piece of evidence linked, with some increased level of certainty, only three of the assumed associated crimes. 'How are you pulling off these raids? And how are you managing to sell the items on undetected…?'

The rest of Steve's day had passed reasonably uneventfully. The bid had been delivered successfully on time; he'd even got some level of thanks from David. "That's good" to be precise. Now he stood on a packed tube heading northwards, and home. The amber glow of London's streetlamps bounced off the low cloud ceiling, the odd black void of a gap in cloud cover smattering the image framed by the carriage's window, like a piece of abstract art. It was at that moment that he became aware of an odd sensation. It was the almost imperceptible feeling that he was being observed. He began to glance around at his fellow passengers. All he could see was the usual non-eye contact of a city commute. The feeling subsided, whoever or whatever had caused it was not immediately obvious and had seemed to cease observing him. "You're never alone with paranoia" he thought trying to contort his body's position to read the front page of a fellow commuter's newspaper. The headline was about the bloody *Houdini* Gang again.

The tabloids and free-papers had really gone overboard on the subject, to the point of hysteria. He almost longed for a story about a terrorist threat, or house prices crashing, just to break the monotony of the *mysterious, impossible* or *inexplicable* headlines. The smell of damp hung in the air as Steve briskly approached the entrance to the four-storey building in which his flat was located. As he slipped the key into the lock, he instinctively looked around once more just as a car pulled out into the main street and drove off. The driver must have glanced his way as they checked for oncoming cars, he surmised. 'Hello?' She was obviously still not home. To be fair, her route from the investment bank at which she worked was more problematic than his single tube line journey. He stuck the oven on, got out of his suit then switched on the telly. London news was reporting on some minor z list celebrity having a very public nervous breakdown. Very messy. His attention wandered for a moment to the letter still unopened in his suit jacket. He was in no hurry to read its contents, whatever they were. It, like the previous one, could wait.

Smoke and noise occupied every inch of space surrounding him. And dust, thick clouds of it, hung in the air like a gluey soup. The strange sensation of pain and numbness ebbed and flowed in competing claw strokes at his mid riff. Then sheer force, blasting him violently to the right in the opposite direction from which the pain emanated and he jolted, awake and alone in his lounge once more.

The moments silence was broken by his sharp exhalation and then a much more reassuring sound, the sound of another key in the lock. Sam burst into the lounge, oblivious to what he'd just experienced.
'Napping again?' She inquired whilst simultaneously switching off whatever drivel had been left playing on the television. 'I may have drifted off for five minutes.' He paused to look at the clock 'Oh sh....'
The word stifled as he concentrated on leaping up to the kitchen to check on dinner's progress. He came back into the room a moment later. 'Err, looks like another takeaway.' She rolled her brown eyes and smirked 'Oh well, as long as it's not pizza again.'

'Good morning and here are the main headlines today. Police continue to be baffled by the series of outrageous and bizarre robberies being carried out by the so-called *Houdini* gang. In what appears to be their latest attack yesterday evening the continual theme of seemingly impossible methods has been further extended by the theft, from an office on the twenty-second floor of the Gherkin Building, of a piece of art entitled "the Persistence of Memory" by world renowned artist Salvador Dali. The valuable art piece is estimated to be worth roughly Thirty-Five Million pounds. As you can see from the footage shot by our helicopter camera crew, somehow the entire external window of the office in which the painting hung has been ripped off, with the debris found disintegrated in the street directly below. Luckily, nobody was hurt in the incident. Police are refusing to confirm whether they consider this latest crime is in any way connected to the previous crimes attributed to the *Houdini* gang but are appealing for any witnesses to come forward...' <click>. 'Houdini gang huh?' The tall, blonde man chuckled somewhat mockingly to himself, placing down, with very precise, notably careful movements, the TV remote. 'That still makes me laugh.'

Six Thirty a.m. and he hit the snooze button on the radio alarm one last time, then turned to look at Samantha, lying inches from him with her back turned and the duvet tucked up below her chin despite the central heating having been on all night. It had been something of a whirlwind romance, with them having met soon after his "release" into normal life, almost a year previously. They had only lived together for a couple of months but neither of them was the right side of thirty so the need for taking their time seemed an irrelevant consideration. She slowly begun to stir properly, turning to face him once more. 'Mor...morning.' She half croaked, sleep still fogging both her mind and her speech. He simply smiled, kissed her then jumped up to get into the shower. The snooze on the alarm was purely for her, he'd been awake for over half an hour watching the rain gently tapping at the bedroom window, thinking.

He quickly washed and shaved whilst in the tiny shower cubicle, emerging just as Sam finished her breakfast. 'Are you not eating?' she inquired with a slight hint of concern in her voice. 'No, that Indian was more than enough calories for me until lunch time.' he retorted, gently patting his small but none the less present belly. As Steve dressed, he emptied the pockets of his suit from yesterday to transfer their contents to today's attire. He hardly acknowledged their contents as he did so, focused solely on making the station by oh seven hundred hours. 'You not in a rush then?' His faint East Midlands accent partially hidden by an acquired, ubiquitous, southern twang. 'Sarcasm this early? No, I have no meetings until half nine today so no rush but you go ahead, I know you don't like to waste your time.' She finished with a half-raised eyebrow, in her polished, nondescript, Grammar school educated Home Counties tone. 'Who's being sarcastic now?' they kissed for a prolonged time and smiled 'see you tonight.'

When Steve got to his office, he was faced with his usual clear desk, spoilt by a single rogue, yellow post-it note. "Come and see me when you are in – David." He raised both his eyebrows in surprise, for two reasons, not only at the note itself but also at the fact David was in before him. He carefully placed his briefcase next to his chair, hung up his coat, and then strode towards Lewis's office.

'Ahh, Steve, please come in.' Opening his office and gesturing for him to take a seat at his meeting table before he had even got to knock on the door.

'Good Morning David.' Hiding his continued state of mild surprise this morning, Steve noted that David was being overtly polite. He wasn't certain but in fact, it may have been the first time he had used the word please in his presence, let alone directed specifically towards him. He sat down, noticing that Lewis had momentarily waited for him to make contact with his seat before he did likewise. 'I saw the note and came straight in, is it with regards to the bid? Have we had some feedback?' The almost skeletal face cracked uneasily into something that resembled a smile, the thin skin creasing in ripples across his cheeks.

'No...no, we are waiting for the evaluation process to complete on that one as you know. No this is a new opportunity that has just arisen from a company called Enhancing Lifestyles UK. It's an exciting opportunity, and,' He paused again, hesitance was not a trait he'd associated with his manager before. 'They have asked that we involve you personally in progressing any further discussions.' The room fell momentarily silent, as the forced smile fell gratefully from David's face.

'That's... that's good to hear our reputation is growing?' Was the only reply that Fletcher could think of. What he really wanted to ask was how the hell had they heard of him? He felt that the commercial world would take him years to fully fathom out, if ever.

'Yes, it is, and if we agree to you running with,' purposely not saying leading, 'the negotiations then we will potentially have a sole partner status, which will mean we can hopefully win this business at a healthier profit margin than usual.' The unfamiliar smile returned, this time more naturally occurring at the thought of a juicy fat profit 'And that would be very good for us all.' Lewis finished, leaning forward in an attempt to add more weight to his assertion.

Steve sat back down at his desk, placing the three sheets of A4 paper David had handed to him out across the fake wood surface of his work area. His years of service had taught him to wear an effective mask in many situations, not least to wear one so that his would not betray any feelings of bewilderment or uncertainty in an alien situation. The previous meeting had just been such an occasion to hide his true feelings. The documentation provided a starting point from which to build a plan. He searched for

"*Enhancing Lifestyles UK*" via the internet. From their website it seemed they were an organisation set up to exploit the growing leisure pursuits market, covering all aspects from 'special red letter days' – one-off luxury indulgence packages such as driving an F1 car or hot air ballooning, through to on-going interests such as flying lessons or scuba diving courses. Lots of transactions and quite a few would be potentially high value. Steve could see how his company's expertise in integrating technology to deliver a secure cash management platform would be attractive to these guys at a minimum. He couldn't though help but feel something seemed a little artificial, almost plastic, about the company. Almost a bit too slick, if he had to put a finger on how it appeared to him. The feeling was probably due to the slight unease at being asked for in person. However, there was something about the letter that demanded further attention. Not so much the content but the way in which it finished. Managing Director. No name, an indistinguishable signature and a P.A.'s telephone number. It was almost like a letter depicted in a cartoon or a comic book. 'So, Mister nobody has asked for me in person!' he commented cynically to himself. 'This guy needs to get a sense of perspective.'

The carbon copied new build office block in West London resided comfortably next to its identical twin within the business park. To be fair the homogenous style of the architecture was one that could have been anywhere in the world. It had been a surprise how quickly the meeting had been arranged, that very same afternoon, almost as soon as he could make it across town to their "Global Headquarters" near Heathrow. The two-tone grey concrete and vast expanse of mirrored glass added to the faint allure of intrigue around what was turning out not to be another ordinary day at the office.
'Good afternoon sir, how can I help you?!' The young, blonde, girl on reception had almost inexplicably curly hair and exuded an air of extreme cheerfulness so out of place to appear almost anachronistic. She was straight out of a Nineties Disney movie. Actually, she had obviously joined the company straight after leaving a show on the Disney Channel. He was convinced of that as fact.
'Hi, I'm here to see Dr Gmitrowicz, at Enhancing Lifestyles UK?' The meeting was not with the Managing Director but his representative who would be his company's main interface during discussions, Steve had been told. And a doctor too no less, but in what field? Hang gliding?

'Ahh, are you Mr Fletcher?' If she was any more bright and breezy he felt sure her employers would be demanding a drugs test.
'Yes, that's me.' Not exactly military level security, he noted.
'Ok, I'll telephone through to let them know you are here, if you'd like to take a seat and they will come and escort you through.'

White marble floor and off white walls that appeared to be made of some kind of vinyl material merged into a blank canvas against which the steel, leather and glass furniture of the waiting area stood out boldly. He selected the desired seated position and eased gently into the black leather chair. Five minutes later the perky receptionist came over to where he was sitting. 'Ok Mr Fletcher, if you'd like to follow me I will show you through to the Doctors' office.' Was this a meeting or a check-up? A quick swipe of the security access ID card and they were in a long corridor. It seemed to stretch unfeasibly far into the distance, and vaguely reminded him of a military headquarters building he had visited many years ago, although the fresh newness of the building and the sparse framed photos which lined the route would have been out of place. Photos people indulging in hot air balloons, jet skis and other various and invariably expensive outdoor leisure pursuits. All interspersed with copies of the now familiar company logo and uniformly spaced office doors. All half filled with mirrored glass windows. Secrets were important in business, he thought to himself. Secrets could make the difference between success and failure. They reached the end of the long, neon-illuminated white corridor and turned right into... another corridor. This time they passed three doors on the left then stopped and paused outside the fourth. The receptionist was just about to say something through her perma-smile when a disembodied voice called out 'Please come in.' The mirrored glass was obviously only one way. She took a moment to regain her full smile after the abrupt interruption and then proceeded to open the door.

Inside, the office was a complete contrast to the all-encompassing blandness that had preceded it. A traditional looking mahogany desk occupied one side of the room, with a complementing bookcase on the opposite side, filled with uniformly stacked, bound books. It looked more like a university lecturer's office than resembling anything else he had seen in the corporate world.
'Steve Fletcher?' enquired the voice that had beckoned them in.
'Yes, good afternoon.' A firm handshake, which for some reason partly took him by surprise.

'Hi, I'm Jane Gmitrowicz, pleasure to meet you. Please, have a seat.' She gestured warmly towards the ornate leather Captain's chair at the front of her imposing desk. 'Did you find us Okay?' she enquired as she gracefully lowered herself into her notably slightly elevated leather chair.

'Yes, the wonders of internet maps!' Steve was about to launch into some light-hearted chit-chat to try and set the mood, but was compelled to remain silent for the moment as she suddenly fixed him with a concentrated, "this is a serious business" kind of stare. 'So tell me, why do you think we should use your services?' The meeting had officially begun.

The pace of discussions all the way through the meeting continued briskly, without too much time to think or ponder. However, every now and again he could not escape the feeling of being observed again. Not just by Dr Gmitrowicz. No, it was the feeling of being watched by someone unseen. It was a feeling linked to instincts that he had once used to great effect for his and his compatriots' survival. *Old habits die hard.*

'Well I think this has been very productive.' A warm smile accompanied the sentiment of the words. 'I think we will certainly move on to the next stage of *The Process*.' This was good to hear, he had felt a little confused and broadsided by the whole flow of the meeting, but if it had got the right result then none of that really mattered. 'One final piece of information gathering today though, hopefully you do not mind?' the doctor took from her top left drawer a folder already bearing his name. 'It's a psychometric test for you to complete. We like to make sure we really get to know our colleagues.'

Our colleagues? That was a bit of an odd choice of words. People often talked of working as one team with their partners in the business world, whether they were customers or suppliers. It was a rare experience to find an organisation that actually paid more than lip service to the notion though, in his opinion. 'Oh, and here is the agreement form from us to show that we will only use the information and subsequent results for the purposes outlined… And we will not share the information with any third parties etc. etc. Standard data protection stuff.' Once more, the hair on his neck tingled with the sensation of being watched. Steve nodded his approval not giving away his slight unease at the entire experience of the past hour. 'Shall I do this now?'

'Yes please, time is of the essence…..'

Despite the smoking ban having been in force for many years now, the dingy East End pub sported a yellowy beige hue reminiscent of the effect that years of exposure to nicotine smoke could produce. Grimes' was a little unsure as to whether the look was original or simply a colour scheme chosen to add an authentic "London boozer" ambience to the place. The clientele were certainly "authentic" in that regard. Nervously sipping his pint of warm beer and surveying his fellow drinkers as he awaited his associate Luke Dyer, who was late as always. Grimes thought to himself that he would never have frequented such a place before entering this little side-line business. The latent criminality hung almost perceptibly in the atmosphere like the smoke that would have once filled the middle ground between ceiling and floor. It made him instinctively uneasy. At that moment the main door flung open with a noticeably louder than normal thud. The doorway filled with the outline of a tall man with a triangular torso and cropped hair. After a brief pause, almost seemingly on purpose for dramatic effect, the figure stepped forward and properly entered the Pub. It was Dyer. Blonde hair a shade lighter, skin a shade darker than the last time they had met. Some of his ill-gotten gains had obviously been spent on some much needed "R and R". A couple of confident, no cocky strides later he arrived at the bar next to the middle-aged man who was still nervously gulping his pint.

'A little early for you Grimes?' commenting without making eye contact, nodding approval for the pint of export lager being delivered dutifully to him. Even in this day and age bar staff knew the best way to avoid any aggro from their punters was to keep the ones most likely to start it happy.
'Well, I think we both deserve it.' He retorted, handing over cash for his business associate's refreshment. 'So I understand the present has been delivered safely?' A more leisurely sip of the tepid brown liquid this time, the big man's presence making him feel more at home, or at least a little more secure.
'Yes, another satisfied customer.' A large, greedy glug of amber fizz taken down as if he'd not had liquid for days. 'I feel like I need a new challenge. These raids are proving all too easy.'
They finally turned to face each other.
'I'm glad you feel that way too. I think I have a project you are going to enjoy. It's a little different to what we have achieved so far....'.
"We", thought Dyer. Just like the press, his fat and balding business partner failed to recognise the singularity of his solo, successful efforts. One day he would tire of him and cut out the middle man altogether. For now though the arrangement suited. After all, why have a dog and bark yourself?

'Talk on, old friend, talk on.' He did seem to be able to find some interesting projects for Luke to work on, so maybe just a couple more "team" efforts before he would make the old boy redundant.

Grimes left the meeting and whilst he was pacing swiftly towards the relative safe haven of the tube line, a now familiar puzzle circulated around his mind. No objective he gave Luke seemed to faze him. Not one task, not one iota. On their first meeting he'd been challenged to come up with "the most audacious theft you could think of" and his imagination it would seem was found wanting, judging by the ease with which Dyer had succeeded to achieve the tasks set. After a number of projects had been completed, Grimes had begun to wonder how they were executed in seemingly near impossible fashion. When he enquired, he'd been fixed such an icy cold silent stare that its intent was communicated so clearly as to have been written in letters six foot high. Do not ask me that again, ever.

The crime scene was incredible, literally unbelievable. It was difficult to distinguish between any damage done by the initial raid or that which was caused simply by the fact that the elements, most notably the wind, had been given unfettered access to the small contained office unit on the twenty second floor. If it hadn't been for the fact that the damned painting had been displayed behind a secure glass screen (secure titanium-framed and clear Kevlar screen to be precise) there would have been no obvious certainty that it was the target of the raid. The wall on which it had been hung was left standing with the space it had occupied clearly visible. Investigation of the crime scene had been unavoidably delayed until a safe method of shielding the room from the sheer drop outside was decided, signed off and installed. Indeed, agreeing, planning and arranging the erection of the solid partitioning seemed to only further highlight the ludicrous requirements of any possible MO used to conduct this latest raid.

'Afternoon Hayes.' The stoic expression on the familiar forensic officer's face unerring, no matter the circumstances of the investigations presented to him.

'Hi, anything of note yet?' The Detective Inspector replied, surveying the utter carnage that surrounded them.

'If you are enquiring as to whether there are any familiar black fibres located then surprisingly yes.' The studious looking individual held up a clear plastic bag that must have contained the aforementioned items, despite ostensibly appearing empty to

the naked eye. 'Aside from that it is too early to tell. No prints but that's no shock hey?'
Hayes grunted his acknowledgement of the update, then moved over to view where the Salvador Dali artwork had once been displayed. It was a painting that notably depicted melting clocks. That surrealist art style had always given him the creeps. The content now seemed to sum up in microcosm the conundrum of the whole series of evidence-linked crimes, as well as those which he still felt sure must be linked somehow. It was like the normal rules of time and space simply did not apply to this gang.
'*Houdini Gang*? Try little green men.' He mumbled in a disparaging tone to himself just as DS Killen joined him.
'Sorry Sir?' She enquired, only half hearing him.
'Nothing... have we any idea how much was this painting worth?'
'Thirty Million, maybe more. You know art, its worth what someone will pay for it at the end of the day.'
'A nice little pay day for someone... all that for a picture you could never public admit to owning...' They both exchanged a glance that said exactly what they thought, what an absolutely crazy world it was.

These crimes seemed to be straight out of an alternate reality and were probably conducted on behalf of people who definitely lived in another world to the rest of us. It was at that moment the bespectacled forensic's demeanour caught Killen's attention. Carefully, she weaved her way through the wreckage to be able to observe the subject of his intense study.
'What does that look like to you?' he asked with a quizzical look on his face, the first time any hint of bewilderment had been shown.
'Err...well...crumpled concrete and exposed reinforced steel?...Iron?'
'No,' tapping the plastic stylus which he already held pointed just to the side of the subject of interest 'the outline, the shape. Can you not make it out?' The Detective Sergeant, unsure, shook her head, green eyes focused on the spot. 'See, four separate ridges...' now holding a hand out to roughly gauge the spacing, the similarity to it making Killen suddenly recognise what was evidently the rough outline of a splayed hand. 'It seems too convenient to be an accidental coincidence or an anomaly.' A rare moment of eye contact shared between the two. 'Can we take some tests and photos over here please?'

The psychometric tests had produced more or less the results predicted and desired, with few exceptions of any meaningful note. It was a better match than the previously gained results, even with the tweaks from the lessons learnt from the previously used, and now evidently error strewn, selection process. An internal call buzzed through. 'This is Jane.' she abruptly answered, pausing for the response, it was *The Boss*. 'Hello sir. Yes, as expected, better if anything.' He interjected with further questions. 'Absolutely, your suggested questions certainly made this info gathering session more productive than previously experienced.' *The Boss* unsubtly proving that he could add value. 'Definitely move to initiating *The Process* in my opinion...Yes, I haven't forgotten that we made a mistake last time but with respect... No, no I know you have the overall authority and responsibility... Okay, sending the report now, I will make a review call for oh eight hundred hours tomorrow.' Half swearing once she replaced the handset then remembering where she was and so regained her self-composure. They had definitely got the right result this time? Yes. Surely. There was no uneasy sensation in the back of her mind, or the pit of her stomach, no illogical question mark being suppressed by her professional persona. Looking into the small mounted mirror on the wall as if to better facilitate self-communication, she reaffirmed her certainty as if she were reciting a new age, confidence building, mantra chant.

One of the mysteries of public transport within the London area was that it was quicker and easier to travel via the centre of town, even if it added fifty per cent more distance to the journey, so geared to a "hub and spoke" design was the capital's transportation system even now. The meeting had taken longer than expected and for once Steve felt he had not just merely worked for his money but had grafted hard for it. What surprised him even more was how much of an exertion it had been. During longer days what were currently patches of darkness on the journey home were actually pleasant green vistas, calm interludes of nature amongst the grey man made edifices that made up the majority of the ride. He had a slight pang for the spring and the increased hours of daylight it would bring. Eventually he made it home, thankful for a rather uneventful, reliable and timely trip.
'Sam?' in almost astonished exclamation.
'Good Evening.' They both kissed. She pointed to the dinner table 'five minutes and it'll be ready. Guess they call that "timed to perfection".' Beaming her smile in a rather self-satisfied kind of way.

'Excellent, I'm famished. That leaves just enough time to get out of this suit.'

'That sounds a good idea.' Sam almost mock leered in a comical parody of what he may well have said if the tables were turned.

'Aha, very good.' One last peck. 'Back in a moment.' As Steve emptied his pockets he came across the envelope once more. He paused in reflection of what it may contain. 'It doesn't state urgent. If it is really anything important, they will write again.' He reasoned, thinking out loud. The rest of the suits contents were placed on the chest of drawers. The envelope and its contents were duly shredded and recycled. He felt he had finally moved on, there was no need to entertain anything that would set him back now.

Chapter Two

Doctor Gmitrowicz had been in the office since oh seven hundred hours that morning, determined to double check, triple check the report, if necessary (this was in addition to the numerous double checks she had carried out the day before). Jane had thought out every question, considered every objection and had typed out her answers, rehearsed every line. Professional pride at stake, with the sins of the past decision to be redeemed. She glanced at the small wooden crucifix on a pedestal her father had bought her as a little girl. This job, this vocation had tested her faith like never before. In the blackest hours, when she doubted most, she called it *his* faith. Without thinking she began to slowly rotate the diminutive idol. Acquired, learned behaviour passed on through the generations. The buzz of another internal telephone call interrupted her quiet meditation. It was the zero eight hundred hours conference call. *The Boss* started the meeting with haste.
'Ah Jane, good morning.'
'Morning Sir.'
'Thanks for sending through the report,' His deep, gravelly voice slightly echoed, talking hands free on speaker phone to further enforce his already considerable gravitas by sounding faintly distant. 'I have to say that it does sum up, as we thought, that we pretty much have a perfect candidate for the process. Especially in conjunction with what I managed to observe in your meeting....'
She glanced instinctively at the small mounted mirror. Being constantly monitored at the office was, after all, an unfortunate and unavoidable occupational hazard.
'Have your views changed at all?'
'No, Sir, no. I am certain we have the right profile here...' hesitating, unsure as to whether she should further qualify why she felt this way lest it prompt unwarranted, further questions. In fear of undermining her position she decided that the best policy was to keep her own counsel on her unscientific instinctual feelings. 'He has the benefit of being, well, that little bit older too... maturity is something we had not paid enough attention to previously, I feel.'
The Boss sounded his agreement with an almost guttural, low-pitched approving 'Mmmm... true, true.' The line fell silent momentarily. It would have been an awkward silence if this were a face-to-face meeting.
'Ok, I concur with your findings. Let's move forward and instigate *The Process*.' Jane allowed herself a faint victorious grin. Having

retained her composure however, she immediately moved the conversation on.
'When do we explain the reasons for our selection and the eventual...outcome? This selection is somewhat more of a complex situation than the last in that regard.' A clearing of the throat echoed over the line.
'I will do that, in person. Can I ask that you liaise with his employers to ensure that there are no added complications? Please do so face-to-face. Neither do we want a paper trail that can be found, retained, or indeed ignored for that matter.'

'Take...my...hand...Ste-.' A deafening, sickening thud. His compatriot was no longer in view. An unnatural calm fell and the scene faded from view. Out of the nothingness another hand reached for his. Pale, grey, almost lifeless and faintly scaly. 'Be calmed… you are still needed.' A sudden pang of fear gripped at his heart, jolting him back to consciousness.

'Wh..what's... wrong?' The involuntary spasm which had jolted across his body managed to wake Sam from her slumber. 'That...that's weird.' He exclaimed 'Two dreams about the attack so close together...I haven't had any dreams for months now.' Steve rolled to face her. 'And that one was just, well. It was just plain odd.' Visibly clammy, with the residue of cold sweat still on his brow. Sam lay there, staring back silently. Steve had never really talked about his life before they'd met. Sure the usual stuff, but never much about his time in the forces. She did not know how to react, so simply stayed silent, smilingly in a warm and reassuring way as best she could. His breathing quickly returned to a more normal rate and the fire that strangely filled his eyes subsided. In the shower, as shards of almost stingingly hot water pounded against his back, sluicing away the night's exertions, the memory of the dream kept returning to the front of his mind. Before now the visions had always been based on what he remembered from the incident. Rooted in fact. This last one, it had a surreal, ethereal quality and was not a true reflection at all. Like a childhood nightmare it was a collection of random snippets. It gave him the creeps and that was definitely not something he was used to.

For a change they both left for work together, enjoying the chance to talk as they made the short walk to their local station. It was one of those crisp and clear winter mornings, promising that there would be a clean, almost azure blue sky once the sun eventually fully rose above the horizon. It was a very different day indeed. Sam soon turned the conversation back to his rude awakening earlier.

'So, what is this... err... attack than you dreamt about?' Taking a direct and to the point approach.

'It was,' the old familiar feeling of being watched took his train of thought momentarily, instinctively causing him to scan his surroundings. 'It was during one of my last missions in Afghanistan. Deep in Helmand doing, well, let's just say it was a recovery and removal job.' When you'd been trained, to the point of almost programmed some would have said, to work on matters of national security, secrecy didn't end when you left the job. 'We were... on the return leg when my unit got hit by a mortar attack. Two out of our team died that day. A third lost his arm. If they hadn't have been beside me on the side of the blast...who knows.' Silence reigned for a long moment.

'What's wrong Steve?' Sam noticing that his attention had been drawn elsewhere for the second time in less than a minute.

'Hmm?' Acknowledging that he'd heard her speak but not fully listened to what was said. 'Hmm, nothing.' Putting his arm back round her shoulders whilst pulling her gently a little closer. 'Let's get a move on, we'll both be late at this rate.'

They just about made the tube on time, and fortuitously managed to get a seat together. The conversation had moved on to more pleasant topics. At the next stop, something made him glance along the carriage at those people now joining the train. There was something familiar about one man in particular. Not so much that he recognised his face from anywhere or any time previously, just the fact that he stood facing them with a clear view. Like he wanted to have a clear view of them, of him. Steve was sure he had half noticed the same guy every day that week. "Yes, you're definitely never alone with paranoia," he quipped to himself again. He got to the offices at about eight thirty that morning, later than normal but still fairly early in comparison to the majority of employees. He was greeted by the security guard who wore a countenance that could best be described as a face that evolution forgot. It was a very effective façade, serving no doubt as a deterrent. They half saluted each other in humorous recognition of their former careers. For the older man however, this was some time ago now. Steve pondered if that was the fate that awaited him a few years from now, if he could not make a success of his new-found career.

Lewis was already in his office, door shut as he conducted what appeared to be a teleconference. Whatever the discussion was

about, he appeared unnaturally (for him) animated. The sight caused Steve to involuntarily smirk.
'What's so funny?' quizzed Debra as he carefully placed his case by the workstation.
'I've never seen a skeleton dance before...' Gently nodding towards the direction of Lewis's door. They both momentarily giggled like schoolchildren before regaining composure. Ten minutes passed before the subject of the debate was finally over and David emerged still slightly flustered from his office, downing two cups of chilled water from the cooler.
'Steve, can I see you in my office in fifteen minutes please?'
'Sure, no problem.' Fifteen minutes? Was it related? Seemed an unnecessarily long wait if that was the case.

Precisely fifteen minutes later Lewis opened his office door expectantly and Steve was already there, as requested, literally just about to knock and request permission to enter. The expression on the rake thin man's face had returned to one of unflustered calm.
'I've had a conversation with our CEO.' Interesting... 'It appears you have done a pretty good job at the meeting yesterday. I can't say I like their methods but... it seems they wish to progress discussions at an aggressive pace.' Very interesting... 'To this end, they have requested you be assigned one hundred per cent to their account until further notice. They have also asked that you be the sole interface between our...' a small but noticeable hesitation, '*organisations*.' Steve silently signalled his understanding of the situation, taking a few moments to ponder what it entailed.
'So, I guess I'll need to hand over my other work commitments? What's the next step?' Having to consider these questions, and probably more so their answers, seemed to irritate Lewis.
'Yes, please prepare a report this morning and hand it over to Debra, she'll deal with distributing the workload later when it is convenient for us.' Ahh, that was the problem here, a lack of personal control. That made perfect sense to Steve, now. 'You need to be ready to meet at their offices again this afternoon, fourteen hundred sharp.' That didn't leave much time to get the report done and prepare for the meeting, Steve thought to himself realising he'd better tell Sam it was going to be a late one tonight.

The car sent specifically to ensure he made the meeting was a surprise. Arriving at twelve thirty it also seemed a little premature as the journey by car should only have taken an hour at the most.

The spectacle however gave the security guard something to grin about as he left. Once ensconced in the back seat, it headed off. The blacked-out glass partition between the driver and the passenger area added a further air of mystery to the proceedings. It was about ten minutes into the journey when Steve noticed that they were headed out of town in completely the wrong direction, heading towards the M11 motorway. As if noticing his sudden interest in where they were headed, the driver switched on the intercom.

'Are you Okay, sir?' very formal and received pronunciation. Almost a text book chauffeur performance.

'Err, yeah. Just wondered why we are taking this route, seems like we are headed in the opposite direction to where I thought we were going?'

'We are headed for *The Organisation's* facility in Suffolk, sir. Be about an hour and ten minutes from here. There is a paper in the pocket in front of you, if you would like to read.' The low buzz of the intercom's background noise clicked off. So there he was. Heading to an unspecified location, somewhere he didn't know, to have a meeting of which he had no real clue about the purpose or structure of. Today was just getting a little bit weirder by the minute.

He knew he liked a challenge but this latest "project" was even more left of field than the last one. The Target? A pharaoh's sarcophagus, from the British Museum. Okay, he wouldn't have to get twenty-two floors up the side of a prominent tower block in the centre of the city which had more closed circuit television cameras than any other city in the world but in a way this was logistically more difficult. Not least as the size of the object made it more problematic to extract swiftly and transport unobtrusively. Especially in an unharmed, pristine condition (as pristine as an ancient artefact could be anyhow). Today, Luke would simply be on a scouting mission. Scoping out the position of the target, the easiest access route, the best getaway route and pondering the best methodology to utilise. He also had to consider the best mode of getting the prize away from the scene, a safe interim storage place and the not too unimportant task of delivery post the extraction, without leaving himself, or the client, excessively open to detection. The challenge was great but so too was the reward. Another lottery win equalling fee, a Euro-millions multi-week rollover sized lottery win at that. This one would enable him to buy a yacht and moor it in Cannes. One more desired dream achieved. Oh yes, he was more than grateful to *The Organisation* for making his new career possible. Living under an assumed name and dying his hair were small prices to pay to ensure his continued anonymity. As was wearing shades and avoiding public transport wherever practical. Although to the mainstream it was a mystery how he was performing these daring feats of criminality he knew that *The Organisation* had undoubtedly spotted them as his handy work. As he strolled he glanced at the newsstand billboard. "Torn Apart" was the simple headline. He casually looked away. He hadn't meant to lose his temper with the girl but she just kept asking too many questions... tried too soon to get too close. He only wanted casual company for the odd evening. Luke wasn't the only one who knew what he was capable of. And if the *Organisation* had genuinely used the last remaining viable sample of *The Source* they also knew there was no way they could stop him. No way on earth. Power corrupts hey? Screw that. Playing by the rules was what his father had rammed down his throat, yet beating him red raw for every minor misdemeanour didn't every strike *him* as wrong. Instinctively and involuntarily Luke laughed out loud, causing a few people to look round bemusedly. He certainly got his just desserts, he thought. His father wouldn't be bothering anybody anymore.

'Your facility is on a military base?' he questioned the driver as he turned into RAF Lakenheath. This was one of the locations where the United Kingdom's air force shared with the American forces too. Silence was the only reply; the intercom was switched off and only now had he noticed there was no way that the passenger could turn it on to be heard. They pulled up outside a large grey concrete building. Its design was familiar to him. It could have been one of a number of military bases he'd visited in his time. Out of curiosity Steve tried the door. It was locked. Presently, the driver made his way to the rear passenger side door and opened it for him.. Why would they have child locks turned on in a car like this? As he stepped out from the vehicle, a door opened in the building and the more familiar face of Doctor Gmitrowicz greeted him.
'Good afternoon Steve,' checking the time, it was precisely two p.m. 'I hope the journey was comfortable?'
'Yes, if a little cloak and dagger.' He'd never known a private company have access to a military location, let alone one that was in parts effectively United States territory. 'How have..?' his question was cut short by the sudden roar of a passing jet on manoeuvres at low altitude. Jane laughed in surprise.
'Don't worry,' she said once the noise abated 'all will be revealed shortly, please come with me.'

Inside the building, they could easily have been back at the West London location. The décor, fixtures and fittings were all the same. Except for one noticeable difference. No photos on the walls. Not a single picture of what Enhancing Lifestyles was all about. Only another long corridor lined with mirrored glass doors. 'This is where we do our research.' Sensing his curiosity levels rising to a very high status. 'We take discretion very seriously throughout *The Organisation*.'

At the end of the seemingly eternal corridor was a small foyer area with unexpectedly a collection of lifts, one of which opened automatically as they drew near. They both entered and Dr Gmitrowicz swiped her plain, unmarked security card through the reader by the lift controls. The doors swiftly shut and they began to move. Steve felt his uneasiness slightly increase, they felt to him to be *descending*, and at quite a pace. Appearing calm, almost nonchalant, he glanced over at the lift controls this time taking in more of the detail than before. The lift floor buttons were unmarked, as blank as the doctor's pass card. To say something did not feel right was an understatement. What the hell were they doing *here*? After what felt like an age, but was in reality about twenty-five seconds, the lift came to a halt and the doors opened onto another, shorter, white corridor. Steve followed his host through to a small room two doors down on the left.

'Have a seat, Steve.' He'd not previously noticed how attractive she was before, her dark brown eyes almost glowed with the undoubted intelligence and confidence behind them. As she was about to speak again though, he noticed the confidence momentarily subside a little. 'OK, if you wait here I will see you a little bit later, *the Boss* will be in shortly to meet you and brief you on *the Process* face-to-face.' With that, a swift exit was made, interestingly with no further eye contact, as if avoiding giving any cue to ask questions.

The time alone gave Steve a chance to glance around the small meeting room he had been left in. Bland décor with no defining features whatsoever. It felt a bit like a police interview room, or at least how he imagined one would feel. Lonely, cold, stark and mildly intimidating if one was left in there after being arrested. In one of the ceiling corners there was a small curved fitting that resembled a home security alarm sensor. It was most likely some kind of closed circuit television device. His sense of being observed was obviously correct. Suddenly the door loudly flew open once more, and the silhouette of a large frame moved into the room. It was without doubt the gentleman who had only been referred to as *the Boss*. His presence made Steve automatically, instinctively rise to his feet. A large spade of a hand reached out to shake his.

'Steve Fletcher?' a brisk, military like air to the question which warranted a nod of confirmation, 'Good to meet you in person, please sit back down.' The distinct undertone of a polite order being given.

The Boss was clearly once a well-built man of action, six foot two and very, very wide. His silver flecked slicked back hair unmistakably once a jet black main atop a striking physique. Whatever activities had given him his physical prowess, the years had now allowed the slow but certain expanse of latent muscle to soften the lines of a once strictly angular, imposing torso. Before Steve could do anything more than return the salutation of 'Good to meet you too.' *The Boss* launched straight into the business of the meeting.

'I think at first I owe you an explanation of the unusual haste in organising this meeting.'

'That would be useful, yes, thank you.'

'Ok, please bear with me for the next five minutes. It will help you both understand fuller what we are trying to achieve but will... certainly leave you with more questions than answers. Can I ask that you leave any questions you have until I ask you for them?' In reality telling him when he can ask them more than a request. *The Boss* lent back steadily on his chair, the change in the angle of light on his head adding volume to the glinting silvery grey mane. 'Firstly, I can presume that you have chosen to ignore the latest letter sent to you from our sister *Organisation*?'

Steve pulled a face that said *hey?* Perplexed by the question he uttered a truncated 'Pardon?' almost without thinking.

'I'm referring to the letters from the MOD that have recently been sent to you?' Sister *Organisation*? What on earth did that mean? Enhancing Lifestyles was a military owned business? No, a part of the government?

'Err... I – I haven't opened them, shredded both that I have received.' Like a disgruntled headmaster who'd just discovered that his school budget had been wasted on superfluous play equipment that was not even being used, *the Boss* folded his arms in a disapproving manner. A small intake of breath, then through narrowed eyes he fixed Steve with an intense stare.

'Well if you had bothered to open one of these communications you may have felt inclined to contact us through more conventional communication channels and saved us the need for the charade of using our shadow company to make contact with you.' The man mountain's body language eased a little and his eyes returned to a less fierce gaze. 'Before we go on, I have to remind you of the fact that you are still security cleared to DV level, and that you are still bound by your contract to Queen and country.' The merest hint of a once broad northern English, possibly Yorkshire accent, long buried beneath a more refined delivery of spoken English with a more ambiguous pronunciation. At that moment, the lights dimmed as a screen simultaneously descended from the ceiling to the right of where they sat. The incredulity he felt about the situation bizarrely made Steve feel a little easier than he had for the past few hours. This was so left of field as to be almost pure comedy.

Something drew his attention to the headline other than the fact it was a ghastly, hideous scene described in the paper. That inner voice that his gut feel sometimes used to nag at him, constantly, until he took note was present once more. The article read:
Police today described in detail the horrific scene discovered by the south bank of the River at Shad Thames, near Tower Bridge. The body of a young woman, white with auburn hair and in her early twenties had been left seemingly "ripped into two parts". A spokeswoman for the Metropolitan Police stated that they were treating her death as murder but would not at this stage be revealing her identity.
'Torn Apart, how awful.' Hayes muttered as he put the article down. He drummed his fingers on the desk as he pensively looked at the phone. Finishing the out of time beat in roughly three bars, he grabbed the phone and dialled the desired extension. 'Hello, Ma'am? It's Philip, can I come and see you in a short while...'

The Super would not have seemed out of place in the houses of parliament. You had to be a political animal to achieve any sort of senior rank in the Met police these days, what with the Mayor, the Public and the various lobbyist groups all pulling in different directions and to different agendas. Oh, and the constant terrorist threat that had only really intensified and changed from a motives perspective in the space of a lifetime within a capital city that had lived with the reality of terrorist threats and acts for many, many decades. Hannah Jenkins was a relatively short, slim and immaculately presented middle aged woman with shoulder length fair hair. A warm smile greeted Hayes as he entered the room, a mutual respect for old fashioned policing values if not always the shared practical use and delivery of them.
'Thanks for seeing me a short notice.'
'That's fine Philip, what can I do for you?'

'Well, it's ... one of my hunches I'm afraid.' He gently dropped a copy of the article on her desk.

'Dreadful case this one,' she acknowledged 'I've just read the preliminary report on the crime scene. Blood stains, with a pool of blood and radiating splatter marks on the pavement just above where the body was found.' Then looking up from the page. 'What is your nose telling you on this one, then?'

Hayes slowly edged towards her office's window, the outlook giving him the perfect backdrop on which to focus his thoughts. 'Without seeing any more detail than that page, it's simply the tone of the report if that doesn't sound completely off with the fairies?' Turning to face Hannah, taking off his glasses whilst he did so. 'It made me think that this crime is pretty incredible. *Torn Apart?* By what? How? It makes no sense.' She briefly stuck out her bottom lip signalling her agreement to that statement. 'It reminds me, for that fact alone, of the robberies my team are investigating...' The super sat up a little straighter, visibly interested by the connection he had made.

'You're saying the *Houdini* Gang could be behind this also?' Even the Super was referring to them by *that* name now!

'I'm saying I feel there is a connection somewhere. I can smell it. That's all.' Face still slightly grimacing from the use of the popular press tag. 'Tell me how someone could have cut this girl in two and dumped both parts over the fence and got away without someone noticing? Tell me how they did it at all?' Green eyes stared unwaveringly at blue for a short while.

'She wasn't cut. The press have got it right with the description,' opening the file by her right hand, turning two pages over as she continued, '*The trauma to the victim's torso appears to be consistent with it having been removed by being wrenched in the opposite direction to the lower half under some considerable force.*' She closed the file and placed it at the edge of her desk near where Philip stood. 'I think you should take a look at this also, it is quite perplexing to say the least. I think the team could really do with your, unique, perspective on it.' He carefully, purposefully gathered the file in his hands.

'A little, light night time reading, hey?'

The first slide was entitled "Project *En*hance. Start Date: Tenth May Nineteen Eighty One." and had one other line of information present, a solitary figure of eight in the centre of the page. The slide looked like a scan of an original, grainy Xerox acetate slide. 'I know from your background Steve that you are aware that the task and ownership of defending of our realm is purposely distributed to many, many disparate organisations and departments under the Ministry of Defence. Some very publicly exist, others less so but are still in the public's consciousness. Ours is a very different organisation. We are essentially a single but extremely and deeply covert project. Think of it as the Trident Programme, but in *total* secrecy. Our desired and stated objective was to produce a single weapon, a single approach to ensuring we had a unique asset on the worldwide stage, a unique weapon in our countries defence system. Project *En*hance was set up to deliver a personnel capability at least eight times more efficient, more powerful than any ordinary personnel capability.' Steve had become accustomed to bullshit jargon through work, by personnel capability he presumed this *Organisation* and *the Boss* meant some kind of hi-tech equipped soldier. Very James Bond, he remarked to himself. *The Boss* moved on to the next slide by waving his hand over a small sensor in the table that had not been immediately noticeable to Steve.

'As the slides states, some clever bureaucrat worked out that the single point of failure on any manned operation was the man… the person,' correcting himself for these more Politically Correct times, 'and there were two options to either reduce or eradicate that fact.'

'Either replace the person with a machine or *en*hance them with technology?' interrupted Steve, feeling a little bored with the rudimentary lesson in "foot soldier" combat issues.

'Almost,' *the Boss* interpreting his interjection as interest not boredom. 'Replace the person and/or improve with technology versus… *En*hance the personnel's physical capabilities.' Pausing as if for dramatic effect and then moving to the next slide, which was an inserted film clip almost as grainy as the original slide. The short film appeared to show a single soldier in camouflage fatigues running through a training ground. Nothing remarkable until he appeared to hurdle a wall that was at least to head height, then compared what Steve assumed was meant to be the same individual easily keeping pace with a car along a disused runway at speed. The clip ultimately ended thirty seconds later, on the last frame of a five-second section seemingly viewing the same figure easily lifting the rear end of an articulated lorry clean off the ground to shoulder height.

'That looks remarkably like a viral marketing clip for an up and coming film from Hollywood.' Steve flippantly commented, then feeling increasingly irritated by the whole experience he leant forward, 'I know I signed up to say I would be available for recall in matters of national security but I fail to see why you need to show me this, this …. Fantasy project.' The big man's hand came down noticeably firmly on the table sensor, jerking the presentation to the next slide.

'I will get to the importance of this in due course but…' Taking a moment's breath as if to use a tried and tested self-help technique to calm down. 'If you could leave the questions to the end, we will get this part of *the Process* out of the way.' Pausing to take a slurp of water. 'That was actual footage of the eventual outcome of Project *En*hance… *The Organisation* took many years to perfect its objective, but by developing *the Process* of altering the body's chemistry to be based on not only carbon but in certain processes a silicon and carbon based chemistry, we managed to create an operative that was less vulnerable to injury, capable of feats of incredible strength and reaction times vastly improved over those reasonably expected from ordinary field personnel.'

The next bullet point appeared on the slide. Steve was still taking in the data download. That was real footage? Lifting a flipping juggernaut? Hopping over a six foot six wall? It was absolutely crazy; this was surely some kind of wind up that would be all over the internet by six o'clock that evening. The dulcet tones of his companion brought him back from his thoughts.

'Silicon is a relatively abundant element in the universe and shares a number of properties with carbon in terms of how it reacts, builds compounds and how it can react in chemical processes etc. One of the major differences however is its speed of reaction. Eight times faster than carbon. A soldier with that kind of reaction speed alone would have a significant advantage over the enemy.' The Boss fixed him with a steely, forceful gaze. 'The reality was even greater than expected in some areas. Aspects of strength, agility, healing all were increased between four times through to the power of eight times base normal human capability…' This time the hesitation was weighted with body language that suggested he expected a question to now be asked.

'You've…. Your *Organisation* have created a… a "Super-soldier"? What has this got to do with me?' A faint humourless smile came over the older man's face as Steve asked that question.

'This is no comic book or fantasy Mr Fletcher. *The Process* has not created an all-powerful, indestructible being. Simply one that is harder to disable or destroy.' There seemed a brief moment's almost poignant reflection on these words deep behind his battle hardened eyes. 'However, as you can imagine it was vitally important that any individual undergoing this process was of the right psychological profile and character to take the responsibility… honourably.' From *the Boss's perspective* honour was a much vaunted quality in the forces, and sadly a diminishing asset generally in society it seemed.

'You've got a renegade. The recipient of this, this process has gone AWOL, right?' Steve's intuition kicking in at a very timely moment. From *the Boss's* expression, the truth obviously hurt.

'Let's just say he's not on our payroll any more. And that gives us a very, very serious problem.'

Inside the Museum was like a maze. The thick slabs of Sandstone that made the exterior would prove a far more difficult proposition than the modern flimsy equivalent on the Gherkin. Not impossible but far riskier in terms of time and potential to fail in gaining entry at the first attempt. The windows were definitely weak spots in the outer façade and good potential points of entry, however getting the sarcophagus swiftly up and through could prove difficult. They were probably undoubtedly the best option Luke could identify though. Surreptitiously he placed a small highlighter marker dot on to the window nearest to the target. It was barely visible to the human eye from two feet away, but for him it would stick out like a sore thumb from the street at night. Both subtly and with studious attention to detail, he paced the distance between the window and the artefact one more time then made a swift exit from the building. Now there was just the small matter of planning the getaway route and method. He speed dialled his business partner on the mobile as he walked. 'Hi, scoped out the problem, I have most of the solution already formulated. Expect to be ready to deliver our product to the customer tomorrow. Given the…' Eyeing the gap between the second-floor window and ground level before he continued, 'the gravity of this package I better deliver it in person.' Oh yes, it was definitely better to be him now than it had ever been before. He took a small packet of white powder out of his pocket, which resembled rock salt in texture. In a single smooth motion he tore off the top of the small plastic covering and gulped down its contents. Mixing its contents with sugar certainly made the experience more pleasant than the raw desiccated material on its own. That small discomfort though was a small price to pay for all he had gained this past year.

'So, so I'll ask this question again, what has all this got to do with me?' Steve had already guessed they wanted to recall him for something, run a crack team to capture the renegade "asset" perhaps. He was simply playing ignorant, wanting this

Organisation to cut to the chase and spell it out for him. *The Boss* was as annoyed by his unsubtle attempt to irritate as he was by the fact his *Organisation* needed to recruit another person to solve the problem in the first place.

'Steve. Simply put I need to invoke your recall clause. We need you to lead the capture of this…this fugitive.' Now he had actually said it, the words echoed around Steve's mind. He had only really just started the transition to a "normal" life. What he'd experienced was good, it had left a desire to taste it even more. 'But I only agreed to a recall in matters of full national security, a serious threat to the mainland United Kingdom itself!' Steve protested vehemently. *The Boss* lent forward, his face lit with an ominous air. 'This is,' he replied flatly 'this is. And more.'

'Surely you have the personnel with the appropriate combat leadership skills to lead the team in capturing …him. There are plenty of good soldiers out there.'

'You'd think so, wouldn't you?' gesturing on the next slide, which was, simply put a scene of horrific carnage. Strewn bodies and generally a scene so wrecked that it was impossible to discern where it was. 'This is all that was left of the second team we sent to neutralise the threat. They had titanium bullets and restraints, with a stun gas strong enough to fell an elephant in less than a second. Not one team member survived ten seconds.' The man mountain then waived the screen to retract back into the ceiling, lights brightening as it did so. 'It's not just your skills we require Steve. It's you. Your service record is second to none, coupled to your age, maturity and psychological profile, it all makes you an ideal candidate for…' Steve made the final connection.

'You want me to take some potion or whatever it is that changes people into this, this human weapon? How do you know I'll not turn out the same?' The fire in *The Boss's* eyes returned.

'We don't, but you are the best match of experience and fit we can find. That kind of makes you our only choice to undergo *The Process*.' Steve let the words melt in, trying to see every angle around the problem he now found himself a part of.

'I'm guessing that I really have no choice in this now, no is not an option?' The big man leant forward once more to emphasise his next point. 'No is always an option, though probably not a very sensible one in this instance.' It was being positioned as very much a fait accompli. The overriding factor being that they needed him and that the cause was worth the sacrifice. Despite the wording, his words did not seem to be overtly threatening to Steve personally.

'So, why can't you take this, this *Process*?' *The Boss* glanced to his left momentarily, and then returned his gaze once more.

'You are the best fit for our requirements, there is no plan C.' His tone and expression inferred that age or health may well be an issue in taking this transformation on, which made perfect sense. The room fell silent for what seemed an extraordinarily long time. Steve finally broke the word vacuum.
'Then.... I guess I have no choice but to accept this fate. What are the next steps?'
'We will start *The Process* itself in the morning. Doctor Gmitrowicz will explain the details shortly. I suggest that you use the next half an hour to call home and explain that you are being kept away overnight... on business. We will deal with your employer. I don't have to remind you that this is not to be shared with anyone, at all?' He bowed and nodded his head to acknowledge his understanding. 'Good, welcome to the team, Mr Fletcher.'

Chapter Three

It was a long way, deep into the complex before they reached *the Organisation's* ring fenced facility. Large, double steel doors stood out awkwardly against the otherwise anodyne blankness of the rest of the complex. Next to their almost gothic appearance, the biometric scanner entry system seemed entirely out of place. Doctor Gmitrowicz gained the appropriate security authorisation and the monolithic leviathans duly obliged, sliding gracefully back and away to allow them to proceed into the hall. Inside was unmistakably a laboratory, a cacophony of bizarre gadgetry and instrumentation filled the immense space with a constant hum, occasional random bleeps and other electronically generated sounds. Exactly what "experiments" were being conducted though was unclear as all the machinery was facing away from the main thoroughfare. Jane looked across at the man who would become the next recipient of *the Process*. He was, understandably, visibly nervous. She placed a reassuring hand on his shoulder and smiled.
'Are you ready?' an almost completely pointless question. 'No.' was the honest reply.
One could hardly imagine how Steve felt, barely anything more complex than a frog had to naturally experience the kind of mid-life rebirth and metamorphosis he was about to undergo. Humanity's ancestors had lost the instincts to deal with this kind of change hundreds of millions of generations ago.
'It's funny,' Steve let out a muted nervous laugh, 'I've always been against genetically modified products...' She laughed loudly. A deep, genuine reaction to his perfectly timed act of humorous bravado. She gave him a warm smile and removed her hand from his shoulder as they reached their destination.
'We can always delay this part until you are ready if necessary.' They both knew that wasn't strictly true, but Steve appreciated the sentiment.
'No, no. Why put off to tomorrow and all that. No let's get underway, if it has to be done. Then let's do it.'

The apparatus stood out, even in the surreal environment of the cavernous underground lab. At first glance it resembled a supercomputer, a gargantuan one at that. It was only on closer scrutiny that further details could be discerned to hint at the overall nature of the machine. The bottom left-front portion consisted of a hermetically sealed chamber accessed through an airtight door to maintain its integrity when in use, somewhat similar in appearance to an airliner's passenger door. Above this unit the motorised cover was slowly closing on two large glass containers, both of which were filled with a deep indigo-purple liquid that appeared to be a thicker viscosity than water, almost like a light engine oil. The front-right hand portion of the device was ablaze with light emitting diodes, meters, computer screens and controls. One monitoring screen looked very much like a hospital's "vital signs" display, still and quiet for the moment awaiting the next occupant to spring the various measures into life. With an almost solemn air, Doctor Gmitrowicz gestured towards the door. With some trepidation, Fletcher entered the small cavity behind the white portal.

The process had already started that evening, shortly after Steve had held the short, rather tense conversation with Samantha. It was difficult for him to deliver what was essentially a lie about his whereabouts, albeit not for any nefarious or other reason that she was possibly likely to imagine was the real reason for his absence. It was after this unpleasant task that the initial course of injections occurred, along with digesting what would best be described as a chemical soup followed by a light, healthy if uninspiring meal of chicken and steamed vegetables. The injections were genetic exciters, they delivered the detailed blueprint of the altered state of Steve's DNA post *the Process* and their adhesion to his existing DNA would be delivered by the genetic accelerator the next day. The biochemical soup was important as it contained the necessary building blocks that the body required to deliver the metabolic and physical changes that would ensue for the following twenty-four hours.

The first cycle would be the last part he would remember. A sweet-smelling vapour induced a swift and deep unconsciousness. Reinforced titanium restraints extended from the chair to firmly secure all limbs and also the head. Once those were deployed, the first of twenty-five initial blasts of positively charged ions mixed with specific hadrons, pentaquarks to be precise, was set off whilst the first flask of silicon laced liquid was instantly vaporised in the intense, artificially created sub-atomic particle stream. The blasts intensified in their strength and frequency, as the second flask was deployed, via a small flexible metallic tube and hypodermic, directly into the base of the spine. The biochemical soup ingested the previous evening contained a semi-dormant synthetic virus that became active once its silicon based "twin" virus, which had just been injected into Steve's bloodstream, interacted with it. Together, they acted almost as microscopic DNA editors, sniping out old carbon-based code and inserting silicon-based replicated coding.

Finally, a mixture of low resonance sound waves and continued bursts of an additional ten blasts of ionic energy activated the microscopic 'Nano-spheres' which were also injected into the bloodstream moments earlier. Each sphere released a precise, intense but non-lethal dosage of radiation which remained significant for a matter of seconds before, like the devices that emitted them, they faded into mere memories. The radiation significantly increased the efficacy of the genetic modification process as well as significantly reducing the time it would have otherwise taken to complete the change. There, in this artificial cocoon, Steve would remain in a medically induced stasis for twelve hours, being constantly monitored as *the Process* completed, permanently altering his biological structure and metabolism into something more than human.

Void, immense and immeasurable. Except it was not empty. All that ever was, has or will be in one instant, or so it seemed. Not enough senses to comprehend it in its entirety. Slowly it began to coalesce into form and substance, what had been a void was not at all, it was just how it appeared. Union. Connected. Pin pricks of light could be seen both at a distance yet also as if they were near. These stars were more than just balls of gas. Connected. Conscious. Amidst it all, three others stood out to varying degrees. Shrouded from view, yet they felt as clear and bright as a summer sky. Neither dreaming nor awake, merely aware.

Jane continued to monitor his vital signs periodically. They all seemed to be in line with expectations, performing similarly to the plotted, predicted paths the computer believed they should closely follow. Neurological activity signs were higher than expected though; something was going on in there that had not been the previous experience at this phase.
'Come and have a look at this.' She called over to one of her co-workers at the lab.
'Looks like readings consistent with dream activity in his synapses. That's one hell of a real experience for him right now.' Jane took in and digested her opinion.
'I'll want a full report on this type of activity compared to the previous recipient once *the Process* is complete.'
Three hours into the programme. Any time now a further injection of nutrients would be introduced directly into the bloodstream,

along with further Nano-spheres which would deliver, where needed, hybrid carbon-silicon compounds to ensure timely changes in metabolism were not rejected by his transitional state immune systems, as well as further support changes in molecular through to cellular structures. The advances in nanotechnology over the past few years had made the whole *Process* far easier, quicker and therefore less risky. The stasis phase previously would have lasted days. By now Fletcher's body would be covered in a thin biomechanical film, holding him in the protective state of suspended animation vital to his survival of this metamorphosis at this pace. The deployment of this film was originally inspired by the way that insect larvae develop into adult form whilst pupating.

Samantha was more annoyed than reassured by the early morning conversation she had had with Steve on her mobile as she travelled into the office. Why was he ringing so early to say he'd be away again that night? What was so important in his job that necessitated such a long and unexpected stay away? The past series of hours had made no sense whatsoever. It was, or so she would have thought, completely out of character for Steve to simply not come home. Sam didn't know whether to believe that he had been called away on business or to think the worst of the situation. Quite when he would have found the time to meet another woman she couldn't fathom out. Unless it was someone at work? Who did he sit near, Debbie? Debra? The urge to ring his switchboard and ask, no demand to be put through was overwhelming and powerful. She hovered over the green call icon on her phone screen, and then thought better of it at precisely the same time that a familiar number dialled in. Grimes. She glanced around as if to ensure nobody was watching her, as if there might be somebody tailing her. She then answered the call in a hushed tone.
'Hi there, I'm still on my way to the office can I call you back?'
Soon as you can was the answer, and had she seen the papers that morning? She had, the next package was ready for delivery and that meant a financial transaction. And that was where Sam took control.

There were very few things about the human condition that the process had left untouched. Hangovers were one of these rare reminders of life before Luke's metamorphosis, though they too were over far quicker than before. Although they did seem to be particularly stronger after the adrenalin rush of pulling off a job before drinking ten pints of brain death lager preceded by Tequila chasers (or rather doing so after whatever the correct scientific term was for the silicon infused version of adrenalin that pumped through his veins). The memory of the previous night was a momentary blur as he thought back to the latest escapade. In the end, the plan was executed more or less flawlessly...The small fluorescent marker previously left on the nearest window stood out like a bright star to his owl-like eyesight. After parking the plain white van with false plates acquired earlier that day approximately two and a half miles from the Museum grounds the next step was to effortlessly hurdle the perimeter fence, taking a small breath to perfect his aim then leaping clear through the target window in a single movement.

Within milliseconds he could almost feel the electrons whizzing their signal down the alarm wire to the central security processor from the motion sensors dotted around the building. It was a mere distraction as in not many more moments Dyer found himself by the ornate, ancient burial canister. The object was in the region of nine-foot-tall, similar in length and about half that in width. It probably weighed many tonnes. Lifting it would not be a problem, but getting it out of the building intact would prove awkward at the best of times, let alone with about two minutes before the police arrived. He spun around and rammed at full pelt the solid sandstone wall surrounding where the window had once been. Fifteen seconds gone. Now came the tricky part. With no inconsiderable amount of effort he heaved the prize into the air and, with more stealth this time, approached the gaping hole in the façade. Twenty-five seconds gone. He leapt from the building, landing square footed on the pavement outside, holding aloft the sarcophagus. Finally, the simple part, run like crazy back to his transport and drive like a maniac to the "safe house" where the latest package would stay until a drop off could be arranged. By the time he'd run the twenty miles back from the "storage facility" (an old ramshackle farm house rented out by Grimes since the start of their joint venture) it was one a.m., just about the time the West End really came to life. And boy did he have a thirst. So a quick (five seconds in total) shower and then straight to Leicester Square and time to celebrate another successful mission.

Luke turned towards the shrill sounding device that had awoken him. It was Grimes ringing his mobile. The piercing sound abruptly stopped as the call was discontinued. The phone display showing that the old man had rung five times so far that morning, this was obviously the first one to stir him from his slumber.

Slowly and with the carefulness of a bomb disposal worker handling an unexploded device Dyer picked up the handset; it was when he was not fully compos mentis that he would literally not know his own strength. Concentrating as much as his still partly alcohol impaired brain would allow, he gently dialled his business partner back.
'Where have you been?!' barked Grimes.
'The... land of <yawn> nod. Been a bit busy, sure the press are on it already. Left a bit of an impression behind.'
'Yes, getting a bit predictable tearing holes in the side of buildings. I hate to piss on your parade but there is the small matter of exchanging before we get paid? I've alerted our banker friend that their services are required once more. Bearing in mind the, *size*, of the package this time I think you will need to deliver it safely into our client's hands personally. I'm texting you the address of the handover site now, along with the scheduled exchange time. We'll meet in the usual location to swap our next mobile numbers and receive pay cheques. See you this evening.'
The irritating old git was good value for organising the detail of these deals, both pre and post the event. The next one though, Luke wanted to decide the target. Make his partner do some figuring out for a change, like figuring out who'd buy whatever it was that he'd dream up acquiring. Maybe he'd go for something with live guards this time, up the ante, make it a more *interactive* challenge this time. If he could think up the right target who knows, the *Houdini gang* could become a real global force to be reckoned with.

An amazing sunrise shone out across the vista. Deep red rays sprayed majestically and dramatically against the deep purple hue of the morning sky. A warm, tropical breeze gently caressed dark black vegetation. From the distant, almost razor sharp mountain range in the east, a flock of four winged birds gracefully swooped and glided ever closer. The indigo purple sea gently rippled, with the red and green fishers diving and rising as they caught their meals. The blood red sun full in the sky, sharing its path with the twin moons as they slowly circled each other in their eternal dance. It felt like home.

Six hours into *the Process* and Jane's attention was caught once more by the brain activity. It was completely unprecedented and unpredicted.
'It's almost like he is awake in there.' The technician remarked.
True, almost. It was more like a highly active and suggestive hypnotic state, like a distant repressed memory being brought

back in from the deepest, darkest realms of the subconscious. If only they could access the mind's eye, see what Steve could see right now. It was both fascinating and in a way a little worrying. In reality *The Organisation* were beyond the cutting edge of technology and scientific understanding here, had been for years. Each time they knew a little more but frustratingly never enough. And this time could be the last. *The Source* had deteriorated at an accelerated rate over the past few months and their efforts seemed futile to maintain its integrity, it was barely remaining alive in its coma like state. It seemed they were powerless in stopping the inevitable loss of this resource to their programme. That would then only leave distillation from a living recipient of *the Process* as a method of creating any further *En*hanced individuals and that had not proved previously successful. In the absence of the extremely unlikely or at minimum unpredictable event of uncovering an additional *Source*, Steve Fletcher was to all intents and purposes their last hope for success and continuity.

'I'll be in my office for the next few hours, patch the key diagnostics through to my screen so I can keep tabs on progress...'

In the solitude of her office Doctor Gmitrowicz could more objectively analyse the various data feeds. One in particular demanded attention, more so now than in the excitement of the lab itself, where Steve's vital signs and alpha and beta brainwave activity took priority. The Tachyon count was noticeably different when compared to predicted and previous trend lines, with the total reading being higher by almost ten per cent. It was believed that the theoretical faster-than-light particles were emitted as a by-product of the hadron bombardment, mixed with the rarefied environmental state within the stasis pod itself. Their emission, or rather the tell-tale traces they believe indicated their emission, normally faded within a half to one full hour maximum after the initiation of *The Process*. This time their traces had been less of a sharp spike and more of a continued significant burn, although it seemed to pulse regularly and constantly, with no detectable general sign of slowly fading to lower highs and lower lows.

'A constant trace... almost a self-replicating series of curves? Like a long wavelength?' Jane pulled out from her case the latest edition of New Scientist magazine. One of the sub headlines on the cover read "Life – Hypothesis on Unusual Self Replicating Systems. It's Life – but not as we know it". So little was known about Tachyons, in fact even in the very specialised circles she now frequented in the science community (working for a nonexistent, "non-part" of the MOD) it was still really conjecture that they were the reasons behind the effects she had attributed to them. No one had observed a Tachyon itself, in fact they probably never would. If they existed at all, it was in a realm outside of the observable universe. Theoretically existing beyond the speed of light meant they were impossible to physically spot, for obvious reasons. But the prospect that something existed in a world faster than light, of the same universe yet invisible to the sub-light speed world was... tantalising. Her father's cross, a constant travel companion when she moved between *Organisation* facilities, looked on over the scientific data. Jane shook her head, a mere coincidence of anomalous data appearing to tie in with her random choice of reading material. Synchronicity, that was all. Back to the task at hand. Five hours until *the Process* was complete. Then, Steve would be put through an "acclimatisation" programme to aide his adjustment to his new world view. Judging by *The Organisation's* intelligence on their former charge they had only a few days to complete what would normally take a month. It would appear he'd already murdered again, the only other previously known occasions had been as he escaped their employ or when he had evaded their attempts to capture him. This time it was a totally innocent member of the public. It could only be a matter of time before more innocent lives were harmed or lost. In hindsight, it was a surprise more had not already been taken.

For once, Hayes elected not to rush straight to the crime scene that morning. There was something escalatory about this latest robbery. Not only the size of the target (*Multiple Choice Question*? Which would be the hardest robbery to undertake? a) Stealing a painting via the outside of a building twenty odd floors up or b) Stealing a nigh on two ton sarcophagus two floors up from the outside of a solid stone walled building? *Discuss*) but also the proximity to the prior crime. Were the gang getting greedy? Or simply getting more orders to fulfil thanks to the intense, free, marketing publicity courtesy of the media machine? It was early afternoon before Philip decided to get Killen to take them both by car on the short trip across London to the British Museum. Unfortunately, in terms of managing his patience, the media circus evidently showed little sign of abating their feeding frenzy for these crimes in the near future. The twenty-four-hour news culture was tedious and on occasion quite self-referential, reporting back on its own analysis, simply to take up or maybe make up air time. In his opinion it also got in the way of controlled, balanced investigation by creating an opinion or a

theory where they perceived it was needed or a lack of detailed communication from the police left them struggling for something to report.
'Ready for the scrum, Guv?'
'No, Killen. I'll never be ready for it.'

Eventually they made it through to the cordoned off crime scene outside the now covered entry/exit wound in the side of the grand old building. The forensic was firmly ensconced at a desk in the site office hurriedly set up earlier that morning.
'Could you try and arrange a little more time between this and the next one please DI?' He dryly quipped as Hayes approached.
'Just be thankful. This increase in periodicity can only help ensure my budget and your budget doesn't get cut in the near future. What have you ascertained so far?' The merest glimmer of a friendly smile on both their lips.
'Well, aside from how they gained access,' pointing his trusted plastic probe in the general direction of what was once a window, 'this is by far the most interesting piece of evidence uncovered so far.' He pulled out a photo, enlarged to show the maximum detail. 'A trainer print, size ten I think.' The smirk evolved into a full-blown grin. 'In concrete Hayes, in concrete. Solid concrete.' He added just to remove any ambiguity in the fact that this was very unusual. The forensic got up and led the two detectives over to the actual print itself.
'How the hell did they make a two-inch-deep print in this pathway?' more an exclamation of shock from DS Killen than an actual question.
'If it wasn't so crazy, I'd say it's as if someone jumped from where the window once was, and bore the full weight of old Tut's burial case on one leg as they landed. Technically more of a leap than a jump I guess.' He looked straight at the ponytailed DS.
'This is crazier than that pattern in the Gherkin wall you reckoned looked like a hand print.' She remarked.
'Crazier and yet more conclusive in some respects. To my mind it is undoubtedly a trainer print, it is as clear as day.' The forensics' humorous expression faded. 'However, unless we can find something to corroborate this, to prove *why* there would be such a print, there's no way this evidence could feasibly be used as I see it? It's straight out of a comic book. We'd be laughed out of court.'

Finally, the twelve-hour period of stasis was coming to an end. The final half an hour was all about slowly bringing Steve back to consciousness. In many ways it was a similar concept to a diver going through decompression, if you were to bring a subject into consciousness too soon it could be catastrophic. It necessitated a managed approach. Measurement of all vital signs indicated that Fletcher's physiology was already significantly altered, as should be expected. The next twenty-four hours would be an extreme learning curve for him and they would also be critical in completing his successful transition to a hybrid carbon-silicon morphology. A final injection of further Nano-builders, micro robotic devices that would deliver modified hormones, mostly controlled releases of *sil-adrenaline* to bring him out of the controlled coma and into reality once more. The injection also included a final batch of modified synthetic virus that would finish off the process of modifying his immune system, so that it did not disastrously degenerate into a spiral of competing with and turning in on itself.

When the fog of unconsciousness finally lifted, Steve found himself lying, harnessed, in another square, bland room similar to the one in which he had slept the previous night. He felt extremely groggy, as if he'd awoken from a deep and drunken stupor. Doctor Gmitrowicz was also in the room and greeted him with a warm smile.
'Why... why am I strapped in?' each word seemingly taking his maximum concentration to utter.
'It's just for your own safety,' and mine, Jane thought to herself, 'as I mentioned in the brief, it will take some time to adjust your equilibrium to your new world. The restraints are there as a precaution in case you were to have suddenly jolted awake.' She signalled to the small observation camera in the corner and the titanium-alloy restraints were automatically uncoupled and retracted. The contents of the brief were slowly coming back to him, as were the memories of what had obviously been no more than extremely lucid and vivid dreams which he had experienced in his artificial comatose state. He edgily and carefully eased himself into a sitting position.
'I had some pretty weird dreams whilst in that cocoon.' He glibly commented.
'Really? That's never happened before. I could see there was brain activity but didn't understand how. It's meant to be impossible...'
'Tell the four winged birds that!' Jane looked quizzically at Fletcher as he slowly and repeatedly flexed his hands open and shut, as if checking part by part that he still had full control over his body in the same way as he had before undergoing *the Process*.

'How's the head?'
'Clearing, just about... I'm absolutely starving.' The process was still taking its full course and it was a very resource intensive task. The energy required in particular was extremely demanding calorie wise. 'What time is it?'
'Eight thirty. We have already notified your partner that you will not be home until tomorrow evening.' He raised his eyebrows in surprise.
'How... how did she sound?' How the hell was he going to explain the last few days?
'We'll give you a recording of the conversation to you to listen to. Especially as she thinks it is you she spoke to...'

They both headed down another anonymous corridor towards what Jane had described as the training and rehabilitation suite. Once through another biometric security door they found themselves in what essentially resembled a combined staff canteen and gymnasium. Two service areas were marked "non-*Process*" and "post-*Process*".
'I only normally eat organic sausages!' he joked, miming a comedic drum roll and accidently sending some plastic cutlery across the room with such force that it completely disintegrated on impact. It left a small mark where it had struck the wall.
'Be careful with your humour, it's so sharp you might kill someone.' Jane quipped back. 'No need to point out which food you need to eat then.' She gestured that he should go first into the self service area. 'Your need is greater than mine.'

The first thing Steve noticed was the taste. He had expected the silicon enriched food to somehow taste different, what he wasn't prepared for was the depth and breadth of flavour he could experience. The familiar tastes were somehow richer, more vibrant. There was also a whole spectrum of flavours that were just plain new to him. It sent his mind racing, much he thought like a small child experiencing chocolate for the first time. It created a positive loop which drove him to devour his meal at an accelerated rate. It was then he noticed the Doctor leaning back in astonishment as she watched what to her seemed like a blur of activity. Steve instantly stopped as suddenly as he had sprung into action.
'Uh, sorry, very hungry.'
After they had eaten, Jane spent approximately ten minutes going through, yet again, the new regime Steve had to live by. The silicon food additives, the exercise regime, the caution in doing simple tasks, the reinforced cutlery she had handed to him

to help ensure that he didn't keep breaking knives and forks whilst he learned to control his abilities, no driving until he passed the "Tactile Control" tests. They seemed to have, unsurprisingly, thought of everything.
'We have set up a large area of secure land as a training facility which we will show you tomorrow morning.' The rest of that day was free for him to do what he pleased, well as free as anyone was three hundred metres underground in a maximum-security facility that is...

Along with his heightened senses, heightened paranoia also appeared to exist. The drive from the safe house had taken him some thirty miles further than originally planned, as Dyer was convinced that somehow he'd been detected and followed despite "jogging" (at approximately seventy eight miles an hour) cross country from the outskirts of Reading, where he had purposely travelled by train just in case *the Organisation* had picked him up on CCTV and followed him (either in person or via the CCTV networks). His mobile had already rung twice. Grimes in an almost a constant state of panic attack no doubt induced by the middle-eastern buyers (they'd say re-claimers) of the ancient artefact. With his now customary stealth, he slowly approached the already parked van surrounded by at least ten men, some wearing long dark cashmere coats. If they wore them to disguise the fact they carried fire arms it was doubly futile. It was both an obvious disguise, clichéd even, and also with his *enhanced* eyesight he could clearly make out the slight bulges the guns made, even from five hundred metres away. Eventually he pulled up just in front of the gaggle of men. Luke rang the old man. 'I'm here, has the money cleared?' his senses were telling him something was not as it should be.
'No, the customer said he'd call through the transaction as soon as his men see the package.' Luke let out a long groan that signalled his displeasure and mistrust very articulately, then cleared the call whilst cautiously opening the drivers' door.

The slightly built man wearing an all grey suit and overcoat strode purposefully towards the vehicle as Dyer closed the door. 'I will need to see the goods now.' Barking impatiently, without even a slight smile to signal something resembling courteous pleasantries at their first meeting.
'Sure, this way.' Luke noted the faint flinch of surprise in the small man's eyes and felt the quickening of his heart rate. The *gentleman* could obviously note from his demeanour that he was completely unthreatened by the blatant show of latent menace.

'Here you go, ready and available just in time for Christmas.' The poor attempt of humour brought a scowl and an increase in heart rate again. Was it his fight or flight mechanism or simply a hate reaction? Either way Luke was unbothered as long as they paid up. The weasel of a man's face broke into a wide beaming smile of exaltation. Almost as if welcoming back a long-lost brother from years of captivity as a hostage. He mumbled something completely unintelligible to Dyer in his own tongue and transferred a kiss from his lips, via his fingertips to the feet of the ancient relic.

'I believe right now a thank you would be in order.' Luke joked with more than an undertone of threat in his own voice. The weasel turned to face him once more.

'You will get your reward sure enough.' The half sour grimace returned and his heart rate dropped to a mildly agitated state. He brushed arrogantly passed Luke as he began to walk back towards his men.

'Git,' thought Dyer to himself 'I could break your scrawny little neck between two of my fingers, probably with even a simply flick.'

A brief nod of the head as the diminutive ring leader strode back brought a swift reaction in the gathered rent-a-mob that accompanied him. One made a brief phone call, whilst the rest seemed to transform from a loose gathering of men into a straight line. Heart beats all slightly elevated, they bore an uncanny resemblance to a firing squad. Luke felt his "Sil-adrenaline" react instantly to the point where the next few moments appeared to be played out in slow motion. The rake of a man exchanged a knowing glance with the telephone wielding heavy and then nodded at the newly organised ensemble. To a man, they immediately drew back their coats, all uniform battle-ship grey, then rapidly and seamlessly withdrew the various concealed firearms, took aim then fired. Dyer watched as, to his eyes, the bullets almost painfully slowly traced their way towards him. He had a split second to decide whether he would dive to avoid the brace of projectiles or simply take a direct hit. 'What the hell,' he thought 'looks like I'll be getting some action at last.' The bullets pierced and tore viciously through his clothes. The gathered throng of hit-men stood frozen in first disbelief then amazement as their target simply remained standing with a rather amused look on his face.

'That... is... rather more uncomfortable than I thought it would be...' The line of men slowly regained the use of their limbs and hesitantly backed away at the same pace with which Dyer staggered forward. 'Hadn't quite expected this as an outcome,' he thought out loud whilst slowly examining his right bicep around the entry points that had been left in his sleeve, just about making out the bullets perfectly embedded in his muscles, surrounded by his unbroken skin. Then it dawned on him what must have happened. 'Ah, must remember to tense my muscles before impact next time...' He looked up at the bemused gang of frightened men. 'I wonder what would happen if I flexed them now?' A half playful, half quizzical tone to the question accompanied by a faintly maniacal smirk. With split second reflexes he clenched every muscle in his upper torso, launching a blitzkrieg of extremely misshaped metal back at his would be assassins. It was a decidedly unfair contest, his opponents, even if they were even able to react, lacked the speed to avoid the onslaught and certainly lacked the physical resilience to withstand the inevitable impact. Like marionettes with their strings sequentially cut they fell to the floor, their diminutive leader left moaning in agony but still alive. Two others also twitched and writhed in pain, the rest were killed instantly. Dyer stood over the main protagonist then slowly crouched down to get a better face to face view.

'I really liked this jacket.' Placing a gentle slap to the face of the stricken man. 'You really have pissed me off.'
Slowly sticking a single finger into a nasty flesh wound and gradually, cruelly making it bigger, causing the man to yelp like a puppy. It was the protestations of the other survivors however that then drew Dyer's immediate attention. 'I am trying to think, will you please shut up!' Flicking with lethal velocity two small stone chippings clean through their skulls then returning focus to the newly appointed sole survivor. 'But, you know, I kinda like your bottle and attitude, so you can live... Someone needs to tell your bosses I'll be focusing all my efforts on them now... no one double crosses me and gets away with it.'
In a blur, Dyer retrieved the mobile from the ground where it had landed and placed it in front of the messenger. 'Better call them soon, Police will no doubt be on their way. Good choice of drop off site by the way. Easily accessible yet pretty secluded. Good to see you've done some research. I do prefer dealing with professionals.' Standing up to survey the surrounding area. 'Not a camera in sight. Tell your bosses I look forward to meeting with them very soon.' With that Dyer sprinted off cross country over the route he had already planned, covering hundreds of meters in a mere matter of seconds. The mobile began to ring; whoever

it was on the other end of the line had obviously expected a call back by now.

Grimes impatiently sat transfixed at his large, leather covered mahogany desk. A scene that was a in many ways a throwback to the eighteen hundreds yet dramatically at odds with the state of the art paper thin PC screen and laptop which sat upon it. Displayed on line were the details of the latest temporary offshore bank account, which was as yet unaltered since he first logged in. It still registered a zero balance. Something was up. He tried Dyer again, twice. The arrogant shit had gone back into ignoring all calls mode. At least that was what he hoped had happened. He had to try and find out what was happening, too much nervous energy pent up without release.
'I'll make another call, this time to the banker.' He thought to himself. Samantha answered nervously
'I thought we agreed, no calls during transaction time...' It was true; the less corroborating time bound evidence that they were communicating about anything other than legitimate business the better. They had pretty much got their communication and other interactions down to a bare and virtually untraceable minimum.
'I know, I know. But something is wrong. There is still no transaction for this call to coincide with. Not at my end at least. Is there a problem I should know about?' Samantha bristled, perceiving the question as an accusation that she'd diverted the payment elsewhere.
'No!' a whispered exclamation of annoyance. 'Still no movement on the feeder account. Have *you* spoken to the delivery boy?'
'No, not for five minutes, but I know he got the package to the drop off location.' Both paused thoughtfully.
'The Client?' she enquired, audibly a little calmer, accessing the logical side of her brain.
'Hmmm, wanted to avoid that route of enquiry if I could... They are the first client I have truly felt uncomfortable in dealing with.' At that moment Grimes' mobile began to vibrate across the leather. 'Ahh, call you back.' It was Dyer.
'What's happening, I-' Dyer, breathlessly, began to talk straight over him, voice incredibly animated as if high on an adrenaline rush after a bungie jump.
'They double crossed us! Tried to take the package by force... bastards.' Two rapid, deep breaths. 'Where are you now?'
'Just outside our usual meeting place. It might be better to talk through, face to face.' Breathing and voice returning to a more normal sounding state.

'You're outside the pub?!' That must be at least sixteen miles from the drop off zone. 'How the –'
Luke hung up before he could complete the question. Grimes shot back into his sumptuous chair, a gasp. How the hell? What the hell? Pulling himself together he got up, grabbed his coat and rushed out to meet his business partner.

When he finally got to the bar, it occurred to Grimes that he'd probably taken longer to travel five hundred yards than it had apparently taken Dyer to get there. He could feel his entire body trembling with either fear, expectation or was he just a little excited by the whole intrigue and unexpected passage of events that evening? He was only doing this for the money, right? With quite some trepidation he proceeded towards the silhouette of his business partner at the sparsely populated bar.
'Nice of you to pop in.' Luke pushed, with notable gentleness, the pint of warm beer he had pre-ordered for his rotund associate.
'I see your humour remains firmly rooted in the banal...' Grimes paused, anticipating a data download. He had to wait for a whole pint to be sunk in one before it was forthcoming.
'Woo, now that was a rush. Ten of them! Could have been a hundred for all the use they were.'
Grimes instinctively got his glasses out and placed them precariously on his nose as if to help him metaphorically focus.
'OK, so what actually happened?' The glasses provided a psychological barrier, a crutch which enabled the professional in him to take over and deal with this scarily bizarre situation. Dyer turned square to him, standing his full height and surveying the few other occupants of the pub. Satisfied that no unknown ears were listening he began to relay the events that had just occurred. The irritating ring leader. The heavies with guns. The double cross gone wrong. Behind their individual protective windows Grimes' eyes slowly grew wider. It was the part about the gunshots and what happened next that caused him to choke on his beer.
'Ugh.. you <cough> you what?' After being there for over five minutes it was only now that he noticed the smattering of holes in Dyer's clothing. 'That's... crazy...' in fear involuntarily taking half a step back.
'Yeah, completely mental... and pointless. But I guess they didn't really know who they were dealing with.' The situational contradiction of chatting calmly with his business partner in the familiar setting of the pub kept the older man from running out the door, stopped him from escaping the ludicrous and illogical situation he found himself in.

'I guess I owe you an explanation, Tony.' It was the first time Dyer had referred to Grimes by his first name in a long while. 'Yes you do, you could... I mean... Well firstly, how the hell did you get here so fast? You couldn't fly that quickly.' A mischievous grin flashed across Dyer's increasingly more relaxed face. 'Ahh... no, I didn't fly... this is real life after all not a super hero movie.' His attention momentarily shifted to the bar staff who briefly came within earshot before returning to the other end to serve. The grin broadened further. 'I ran.' Their eyes firmly fixed on each other, as if communicating on a subliminal level a hundred times more information than mere words could convey. Grimes broke the stare to study Dyers damaged clothing once more. He'd previously assumed that it was some kind of body armour that had prevented injury to his associate. Now he could see the faint flash of pinky-white unblemished skin through some of the holes and no visible bulkiness which such body armour would surely have entailed. 'Yeah, I could do with borrowing your over coat to get home in. Don't want to risk drawing attention to myself. Well, any further than I may already have.'

Grimes half nodded, face stuck in a disbelieving, gawping expression. 'You're serious aren't you, you actually ran. That's... impossible though?'

'Shhh... I think we better sit down, this could take some time...' There was a quiet table in the corner where this conversation was best continued, so Luke gently ushered Grimes towards it.

Chapter Four

The alarm clock went off at oh five thirty hours, which Steve instinctively slapped off instantly, shattering the device (obviously no specially designed alarm clocks allowed for in the Project Enhance budget, he thought to himself). He then sprang, more carefully, out of bed like a five-year-old on Christmas morning. He'd been looking forward to today despite the fact he was missing Samantha and dreaded returning home all at the same time. Entering the shower very gingerly, a reassuring sign notified that the mechanism was "reinforced" for enhanced personnel usage. Shower time was brief, dressing time swift and breakfast over in a flash. Keen was not nearly accurate enough to describe his state of mind at that moment. Doctor Gmitrowicz entered the briefing room at oh six oh two hours, only two minutes later than scheduled yet it seemed like an age to Fletcher's racing, expectation filled mind.

'Morning, apologies that I'm, oh, three minutes late.' Looking as pristine and professional as always, not a quick shower and pull on the nearest clothes for her this morning. 'I will never get used to these pre-dawn starts.' She could see from his body language that Steve was feeling the exact opposite of how she was feeling. Very alert, not a jaded, almost resembling jet lagged, lethargy. The lights dimmed again and the presentation on the day's planned events began. A lot of the information was a repeat of the "maintaining wellness" info already shared. Part of a plan to ensure the information struck home and stayed remembered. Next came the more interesting bits for Steve, an elaboration on what predicted capabilities should be and how they were going to train and test these throughout the coming day.

'So let me get this right. Essentially *the Process* may have increased say my strength between eight times and/or the power of eight?' Fletcher was keen to appear engaged in the presentation despite most of it being stuff he had already memorised.
'Yes basically it is not an – err – exact science.' The slight hesitation, perceptively nervous nature, betrayed the reality behind the statement, and how that didn't sit well with her. This was unpredictable and as erratic as nature itself.

'You... don't fully know, I mean understand, quite how the *Process* works?' sounding slightly less shocked than he actually was. Jane fixed a gaze framed with inquisitively raised eyebrows. 'Did Marie Curie fully understand what she was playing with?' instantly kicking herself as the words came out for picking possibly too accurate a parallel.

'I guess that is something you both share then... playing with fire having never fully experienced the burning side effects before doing so.' A tense paused ensued, broken by the robust, thumping entrance of *The Boss*.

'Just thought I'd check on how we are both doing this morning, how are you finding adjusting to the world post *the Process* Steve?' Both Fletcher and Dr Gmitrowicz had involuntarily straightened their spines on his entrance, such was the effect *The Boss* seemed to have on anybody he encountered. It was almost a special talent.

'Err... different. It's the instinctive moments that are the most challenging, when I'm not one hundred per cent concentrating on the task in hand that prove the most interesting.' A broad, almost warm smile lit up the big man's face. The flash of what seemed like empathy soon faded as his attention turned to the willowy figure of Dr Gmitrowicz.

'So what have we done so far today?' No question was ever asked out of pure courtesy. The tension in the room went back to where it had been before the interruption.

'Sharing some personal observations on *the Process* I think.' *The Boss* rose swiftly from the chair he'd spent all of thirty seconds occupying.

'Well, enough words I think maybe now it's time to let action take over today. I've cleared my diary. I wish to oversee the exercises this morning. No time like the present, hey?' At last, enough theory it was time for the practical!

The heavy mist of midwinter morning hung lazily in the various dips within the wide-open expanse of land that made up the training facility. It was a shade above freezing, a full degree centigrade at best. Jane headed instinctively towards the portacabin, which acted as the makeshift centre of operations on this hastily assembled training ground. Steve could clearly make out the tell-tale freshly cut tractor tracks even at this distance in the still pitch black early morning, which proved that this facility was constructed recently and in haste. In fact, he could make out a heck of a lot of detail, including a small fox approximately five hundred metres away at the edge of a small spinney, transfixed as if in fear. Did it sense his stare, or did it sense that he was

different to the other people around him, did it somehow feel his altered biology? Steve glanced to his right at the large framed silhouette of *the Boss*. He seemed momentarily transfixed also, staring into what must have been black void to him, but spookily happened to be roughly the location of the animal. *The Boss* broke his thoughtful gaze to face Steve.
'Right then.' Removing his gloved, shovel like hands from his trench-coat pockets to rub them together with mock glee. 'Let's see what you can do in practice then!' The big man heavily patted Steve on the back as he finished the statement. It still felt like a jolt even to Steve's *en*hanced anatomy. With that, *the Boss* stepped back into the shadows, but remained outside to watch.

Along the left hand side of the training ground was a clear, long, single running track of loose gravel. As described in the briefings, it had a timer start button at one end, and a stop button at the other. The exercise? Simply switch on the timer and aim to get as quick a time as possible by pressing the stop button at the other end. "Speed is nothing without control" was the Doctors mantra on this test, otherwise simply having a police speed radar gun would have sufficed. Steve looked down at his feet. They felt normal, nothing wrong with them. Not even cold. He'd been so busy taking it all in that only now did he notice that. He could feel that the morning was cold, just did not feel that cold within his personal space. A hushed comment caught his attention.
'Pardon, sir?' he enquired as he turned.
'Err, I didn't say anything Fletcher, please carry on.' Steve was convinced he had heard someone whisper *get on with it*. Maybe he needed more sleep than he'd realised. Two deep breaths, then bang. Within just over ten seconds he'd reached the stop button. 'Whoa. That is crazy.' Almost stumbling over himself as he turned around to survey the distance he'd just covered.
<crack> 'And a little slower than we expected, that was the equivalent of Eighty Seconds for a normal man.' Gmitrowicz was not one to be easily impressed, to say the least. The noise the device had made as she opened the communication channel adding an urgent quality to her immediate feedback.
'I've been a civilian for over a year now, going to take a little while to get peak fitness back…'
Tapping the back of the intercom unit in an annoyed fashion, and forgetting that he was now roughly at least eight times stronger than before, the small black speaker and mike unit bounced in "Dam-buster" fashion out across the field. Steve frowned with the scowl of a naughty school boy who'd just broken a window

playing football in the garden, and then immediately did something else that would annoy his mother even further.

Time to try the next event in this personal mini Olympics. Lined up in a staggered diagonal, but all running in parallel, a series of ten disused train carriages reached out back over the distance he'd just sprinted. This exercise was about "using his strength to gain entry to a hostile, locked down environment". Ostensibly, it was practising break in and entry for the good guys. The key to this was allegedly control, the analogy being that anyone can blow up a house, but using just enough explosives to blast the front door off is the art.

'OK Steve, which scenario are you going to try first?' The Intercom behind the first carriage now being used to communicate with him, fortunate that he now had *en*hanced hearing or else it would not have been audible.

'The battering ram…' he stated, in a low monotone growl as he psyched himself up.

'Sorry Steve, you need to speak louder for the microphone to be able to properly pick it ….' The request was too late as he'd started the sprint and was already making his impact on the external entry door of what was, by the looks of it, a nineteen fifties reconditioned British Rail carriage. One that he soon discovered had many separate compartments within in it. Moments later, he spurted out of the other side and skimmed two or three times off the wet, freezing cold grass, coming to halt about sixty metres away.

'Ah, the battering ram was it? Well just to highlight the lesson here, in our computer simulation it has calculated that you've just killed or seriously injured about thirty per cent of the occupants of that carriage. Judging by how far you ricocheted out of the far end, you'd also have done some fatal damage in the next carriage in a real-life situation.' Jane clicked off the mike and turned her attention to recording her audio notes. 'Power ratios are comparable to the previous recipient of *the Process*, at this stage anyway. Still slightly behind where the original expected benchmark was set for that measure. Speed, considering subject age, is better than expected. Given that Fletcher has room for improvement fitness wise, this is encouraging as a first pass.'

The Doctor returned her focus to the monitor in front of her and could observe Steve's slow, staggering approach to the exit point he'd just blasted in the carriage structure. She didn't need to see his face to read the body language of disbelief. 'Suggest you try the alternative approach on the next carriage. And maybe slowly

ramp up the effort to rip the door off this time, and not go hell for leather at the outset?'
Meantime Steve was left speechless, staring wide eyed at the rough man-shaped outlines left through the various dividing walls in the carriage. It looked like a scene straight from a children's cartoon.
'Just what I would have done...' he pivoted in an instant, *The Boss's* thinking out loud as clear as if he'd stood next to him. Steve smiled.
'If it had been a real situation, I would have done the lower risk option first.' He replied out loud, forgetting for a moment that although *The Boss* was out of ear shot, the good doctor was not, courtesy of the wonders of technology.
'Sure, action men are generally renowned for their thoughtful and tactful approach.' That produced a chuckle. 'OK,' thinking to himself this time, 'Let's try the gentle touch.' The *sil-adrenalin* rush of the first attempt had subsided and now a more logical, quizzical approach ensued. Slowly, firmly but in a controlled manner Steve carefully climbed up the outside of the carriage and gripped the external handle. Then, changing tack, he swapped hands and slowly but effortlessly wedged his fingers into the gap between door and frame on the hinged side of the door before seeming to gently toss it to the side, accompanied by the wrenching and shearing of metal hinges and the shattering of glass. Shards and fragments of window and door bounced off his face as if they were made of sponge or light rubber. Not a blemish or a scratch caused by their bombardment. The door landed with a gentle thud twenty feet away, coming to ground like a giant metal autumn leaf. 'How was that? Better?' he enquired mockingly.

By the seventh train unit, Steve had perfected just about every option he could think of as a practical entry strategy. Punching through the roof, ripping out a window and finally banging down the door without over shooting. None had the comedy or drama of his first attempt however.
'Time to try out the next exercise now.' Even through the tininess of the intercom speaker there was a clear authoritative tone to Gmitrowicz's voice.
'And the next event in the *en*hanced decathlon is...' the high jump. Or to be more specific, a sheer hundred or so foot tall edifice, with a platform atop. 'You have got to be kidding me, right?' standing at its base it seemed to extend endlessly upwards.

'Remember Steve, *the Process* leaves you improved somewhere around eight times greater than your previous capabilities as a minimum, think laterally. Adrenaline is also affected similarly.' Eight times eight maximum, was that how it worked? Did this mean that his range of speed and strength was so vast as to be hard to control and predict? He certainly felt his heart beating powerfully in his chest. A good heart inherited from his father now somewhat altered further.

'Think I'll need a run up for this one, definitely.' As he paced out his approach, he quickly assessed the rudimentary plan for scaling the wall. With an angle of launch at around ten degrees from the vertical, he was estimating on landing somewhere around half way up the mock cliff face. From there, he'd simply utilise a combination of sheer strength to create hand/foot holes and climbing skills to make it the rest of the way. A burst of energy and in a split second he was soaring up passed the platform, taking a chunk off it and overshooting by at least the same distance again as its overall height. Then a brief moment of inertia accompanied by an almost weightless feeling momentarily before gravity finally caught a grip and began to return Steve hurtling back down to earth. With a literally sickening thud contact with the ground was made and he disappeared from sight. Three seconds later he stood up in the four-foot-deep crater he'd just created.

'It's going to be a long day...' commented Jane over the loud speaker.

The street lamps in London now gave out an eerie, grey almost smoggy glow. The Mayor had astounded and surprised everyone by announcing the ground-breaking switch to OLED (Organic Light Emitting Diode) lighting, London wide in early Twenty Seventeen. No-one would have appreciated that one side effect of this "greener" lighting would be an almost cinema-graphic, atmospheric effect, making certain parts of the capital appear almost like scenes straight from a Dickensian novel. No one had done analysis on whether crime had increased due to its influence but it would not have surprised Hayes if it was one day analysed and subsequently, retrospectively proven true. The events of roughly the past thirty-six hours had proven even more intriguing and in a positive way, in particular as the potential opportunity for forensic evidence had increased exponentially. The suspects had strayed from their standard modus operandi, it seemed by necessity rather than by choice. They'd left behind a bloody trail of victims and crucially their contraband merchandise. The artefact was now safely Queen's evidence. That alone had caused the team enough further headaches, finding somewhere appropriate to store it after the not too indelicate matter of gathering evidence from the priceless object from antiquity. He'd won the battle with his chain of command to retain leadership of the investigation at the expense of conceding to continued close liaison and co-operation with the murder squad, this investigation being concurrent to the unfortunate river victim case. "I'm really backing you on this one Philip. *Don't* let me down." More added pressure from Jenkins, just to increase the balance he carried around with him already. The activity and aftermath of last night meant an early morning briefing, therefore an early start for his newly expanded investigating team. This was all good as far as Hayes was concerned. It was great to have the operations centre so full at seven a.m.

'Morning Team, glad we all managed to make it in on time. First, for those that haven't already met them let me introduce Detective Inspector McCarthy and team who will be providing support and expertise around the apparent step change into violent crime and murder that our targets now appear to have taken.' The stout, half balding, man raised himself up and forward in his chair to signal his salutations.

'Notwithstanding that the loss of any life is tragic, the good news for our investigation is this should yield a comparative cornucopia of evidence for us forensically, that has previously been sadly lacking. Combined with our only surviving eyewitness, or should I also say suspect, hopefully regaining consciousness at some point soon, we may actually start piecing this jigsaw together.' Holding out a grey hand to signal that D.S. Killen should take over the proceedings from here. She took up his position in front of the ubiquitous interactive investigation whiteboard, looking like she'd hardly had an hour's sleep, which wasn't that far from the truth of the matter.

'Thanks sir. I'm sure we can all recall what has happened over the past fourteen or so hours,' pointing to the latest freshly drawn time line. 'I'll keep the summary of new evidence brief. We have nine dead suspects, who from our forensics initial assessment all appear to have suffered bullet wounds inflicted by the weapons left at the scene. All of which were either still in their grasp or lying on the ground nearby, as if being dropped as they fell immediately after being shot.' A member of the team seized the chance to interrupt with a question. 'You say suspects rather than victims?' Killen's green eyes glared almost as eerily as the lamp light outside. 'At this stage we should at minimum assume that all those found dead and our single survivor were at least implicated in the theft, in some way shape or form. They probably at minimum possessed illegal firearms which it doesn't take a world class detective to figure out means they were not there for legitimate purposes.' Pausing to regather the train of the briefing she had practiced previously. 'In keeping with the tradition of puzzling evidence encountered so far in the on-going investigative effort around the robberies, there are some immediate items to note.

a) We have fibres that seem to match the sweatshirt fibres previously found at a number of the robbery scenes.
b) Some of the fibres have been located around and WITHIN the bullet wounds of our yet to be identified bodies.
c) The bullets show an extremely odd pattern of deformation…' She could see this point had caused many quizzically raised eyebrows and murmurs that indicated further elaboration was required. 'To be a little more precise, they appear to demonstrate impact and explosion damage from more than one direction… as if some had been fired twice.
d) In addition it is worth noting that two of the men most probably died from slightly larger than bullet sized projectiles through the head. The forensic team are still searching the area surrounding the crime scene to find further evidence, especially the objects themselves. Whatever caused the wounds has travelled cleanly through their heads.
e) Finally, we have both the Sarcophagus and the van in our possession meaning at minimum we must be able to trace the recent history and journey by working backwards through local CCTV footage.'

Killen continued with the general briefing, assigning tasks and duties already agreed with the Detective Inspector prior to the briefing. Meanwhile, Hayes was digesting, in greater detail, the latest evidence factually stated in the report. One set of footprints headed away from the scene across a field to the west. Spaced impossibly but regularly apart, "as if each step was a record breaking, one footed long jump" to quote the old forensic verbatim. What exactly did that mean? The report made it clear that there did not appear to be missing prints or a misinterpretation, as the spacing was too regular and the conditions of the field meant there were no areas where prints could not be discerned. Roughly twenty-four foot strides. Size eleven feet. One man impossibly escaping the carnage, or one man who'd inflicted it? And what did the double impacted bullets mean? The forensic team was far from finished and he sincerely hoped that further work would draw out some more tangible and, importantly, understandable evidence. For all the bravado of his opening scene setting and the fact they did indeed have truckloads more evidence, Philip was quietly far from convinced any of it would lead substantively closer to identifying and capturing their targets.

'That's the priority Killen. We need to trace the route the van took and any sightings of something unusual here.'

Pointing with the laser at the boundary of the field by the M25.

'Witnesses or CCTV nearby there. We need to use this chance to track down some further geographical pointers here. Either an origin or a destination for the two journeys.' Hayes fell silent once more, obsessively engrossed in his own thoughts. The weapons were a hodgepodge, a mix and match of pistols, semi-automatics, and so on. If their probably middle-eastern victims had brought these in themselves from offshore, he would have expected standard issue and probably something ex-Russian. This array pointed to local sourcing, and very few in the London Market would be able to lay their hands on so many at short notice. He couldn't rule out a slowly cultivated stockpile but could feel the familiar tingle of another hunch developing. Time to call on the proverbial "Old Boy's Networks".

'Mr Bahajoub, it is a surprise to speak with you this morning.' It was either tiredness, not being fully awake or a morbid fascination that had compelled Grimes to answer the specific Pay As You Go mobile assigned for the King Tut project. The anonymity of the mobile number gave him a sense of security. In this high technology age he prayed it was not a false one.

'My client is also surprised... and a little lost for words on last night's events. Believe me this is not usual.' The polished Oxbridge accent gave only the merest inflexional clues to anything other than a British higher class's background.

'I bet he was and he was not alone in that. It appears that neither party particularly gained from this situation.' Quite where he was going with this, Grimes himself wasn't sure. But the inner business man (as he always put it) could not help but try to probe a little further. After all, he'd called him, right? And this time the call displayed a number (probably PAYG mobile again though). Suggested a spur of the moment gut reaction rather than a fully thought out, calculated move. It suggested a potential moment of weakness. Smelt like an opportunity. 'You obviously realise that

the police now have the, merchandise, so why have you rung?'
There was a long, almost tangible moment of contemplation. The whirring of brain cells, the formation of thought.
'My... client's interests and ventures take in a very wide portfolio of activities,' No doubt including extortion, murder and what else Grimes could only barely imagine. 'Your team has caught his attention somewhat. They were some of his best men in Britain last night.' Indeed they may well have been, but dealing with Dyer was, as he now knew, an altogether different proposition than anything they'd experienced previously.
'I'm sure your client would have many interesting opportunities to discuss but, how shall I put it? There is a tiny issue regarding trust between my associates and that particular, potential business partner.' If bullets had failed at a double cross attempt then what next? Bombs? And there was the small matter that it was only Dyer who had the apparent invulnerability to firearms. He had no desire to get caught in any future ensuing crossfire.
'In my experience, nothing breaks down barriers like a face to face... and upfront payment in full before any task is undertaken.' The final phrase temporarily cut through any fear, uncertainty and doubt he felt. Cash up front was always worth considering. It was enough to cause an involuntary raising of eyebrows and a smile at the thought.
'I will need to discuss this further with my associates. Shall I contact you once that is done on this number?' The salesperson in him looking to close out the deal and define the next steps.
'With pleasure. We'd like to instigate this meeting urgently so can I ask that you call me before midday?'
'We'll be in touch when we are ready.' Pressing the red handset button, instantly concluding the call before he could be questioned any further. It was only now Grimes remembered how long he and Dyer had spent out last night and the pounding of a hangover began its vicious onslaught. A long shower and breakfast were needed before he would talk to Dyer about this latest twist. For many obvious reasons, he needed his buy in _and_ his back up.

Steve's second attempt at mounting the high platform, although not the most aesthetically pleasing effort, was much more of a success. He slightly under cooked the jump, leaving himself hanging momentarily before a quick flick of his wrists propelled him up and onto the deck. The conveniently placed intercom crackled with Gmitrowicz's hollow sounding congratulations. His ears were however soon focused elsewhere. The unmistakable

screech of tyres and the clanking thud of metal on metal. And in-between and amongst it all, the screams of a small child.
'Stuff these tests, time for something a little more realistic.'
'Pardon, Steve?' but Jane's question was already too late to receive a response. Fletcher had launched himself in the direction of the accident, the elevation of the platform adding further distance to his leap taking him instantly out of the training ground and deep into the wooded area. Within six seconds Steve had sprinted a zigzag course through the trees to the perimeter of the military facility where he could clearly hear the young girl still screaming for her mother, who was not making any conscious sounds as far as he could hear. A bad sign. About two hundred metres down the perimeter road he could see the two vehicles and worse, he could smell petrol and a faint whiff of burning. In what must have seemed an almost instantaneous movement, as if teleported the short distance, Steve was by the car which held both the mother and child. The training previously with the train carriages then came to the fore, as he both threw the car door deep into the wood and hurriedly (even for his *en*hanced anatomy) pulled on the standard issue black balaclava that had been left in his room with the rest of the training kit. Grabbing the young girl he leapt a hundred metres or so up the road, placed her gently down and whispered -

'Stay here, I'll just get Mummy, OK?' Raising a finger to where his lips lay under the crude disguise. In the distance he could hear the recognisable chug of a military diesel vehicle approaching. Steve felt sure that t*he Boss* would be furious on the outside but also a little pleased at the chance to see how he performed on the impromptu, unofficial field test. Back to the car, driver's door discarded. The woman was just phasing in and out of consciousness but otherwise he could see no physical evidence of significant injury or trauma. The airbag had deployed and she was not trapped. Steve could hear what to him seemed to be the slow crackle of a full blown fire beginning to ignite in the engine bay. Whoever had been driving the other car had run off. *Brave.* Carefully but swiftly he raised the mother out of the driver's seat and strode purposefully at what would be a fast run for a normal man, getting to the young girl just as a fireball engulfed the wreckage, perfectly timed as *the Boss's* vehicle approached over the brow of the hill.
'Get In!' he barked, visibly irate as predicted. Fletcher launched himself, gently, into the rear of what was a land-rover based truck that was suitably unmarked and painted a nondescript dark

metallic grey. 'What the hell were you doing?' turning to glare intensely at Steve.

'I've seen enough dead, innocent children in service to last a life time... not prepared to let it happen again if I can help it. Besides,' lightening the mood which could easily register as deeply oppressive at that point of time, 'nothing like a field exercise to fully test out the capabilities, don't you think?' The big man's face took a few moments to change its expression from a scowl but eventually a broad grin and hefty chuckle ensued.

'Is that ambulance on its way?' he shouted down the wireless handset in the front cab, then twirled once more to face Steve. 'Did that pretty quickly too, the balaclava's a nice touch.'

'Hopefully the mother is alright, she was semi-conscious as I placed her by the child. Bit of luck she'll think anything that she witnessed that seemed extraordinary would be due to the shock or adrenaline.'

'We'll keep an eye on them. The road is closed off until the ambulance gets there.'

'Might be worth checking out the other cars driver, ran off before I got there. I didn't get a sense that they were watching me but just in case.' Fletcher glanced back through the rear screen as they turned out of sight once more.

'Agreed, don't want too many witnesses mouthing off, though I doubt if they'd want to draw attention to themselves. Probably joy riders. Either way, we don't want too much media focus, right on our bloody doorstep.'

Samantha sat staring aimlessly into space on the last leg of her journey into the office. Her life, although a little unconventional with her little side venture, had been pretty predictable and nicely in control recently. The past few days had thrown all that into the air. The side-line had gone weird for a start, normally a short nervous wait for money to transact but this time it had gone wrong and not concluded. Only a hurried "it's off, talk tomorrow" conversation, in fact, more of a one-way transmission than a two-way communication. She'd guessed one would not go smoothly one day but all this proved just how removed from the nature of "the business" she was. There was nothing in the news that morning to indicate anything major to do with the *Houdini Gang*, no arrests or anything like that. Still, it was actually more of a worry to be out of the loop than she'd bargained for; previously figuring the less she was involved the better for both her safety and peace of mind. Then there was Steve. What the hell was happening there? He'd completely disappeared off the radar with a couple of stilted, almost machine-like conversations and very scant details of what was the real reason for his absence. He was due home tonight and Sam had no idea how to play it. In fact, she wondered if her best option was avoidance altogether (for the moment). To purposefully not get home until very late. Maybe both issues occurring at once constituted some kind of a sign. Maybe she should push to get more involved in her little side-line? Better hung for a sheep than a lamb? Yes, she'd call the arranger as soon as she got off the tube. An evening meeting that helped her avoid the home life problem. Two birds with one stone. That was efficient, multi-tasking at its very best.

'So, you are confident that you will enlist their services then?' The gnarled looking middle aged, middle-eastern gentleman questioned, whilst surrounded by the sumptuous wealth that furnished his penthouse apartment. Bahajoub, sitting suitably in a less luxuriously appointed chair a few steps down from the mezzanine level, sat with a suitably respectful posture, both attentive and unthreatening.
'Yes, I believe that, as they say, money talks. I also feel that once they have heard what your desired next target is, that the challenge it presents will be the tipping point if the fee is not enough in its own right to entice them.' The stoutly built gentleman leant slightly forward as he lit a significant cigar.
'This is a win-win situation as far as I am concerned. If they accept and succeed we will have our primary objective acquired, if they fail they will undoubtedly be killed by the British Security Forces. If they do not accept, I will have our very best men tailing them and destroying their lives, slowly, one painful piece at a time.' Bahajoub shrugged his shoulders and nodded showing an almost reverend respect for a seemingly all-encompassing plan simply presented.
'The police have one of your men now?' the question visibly agitated the otherwise serene yet power-exuding man.
'I hope they have as little intelligence on our team as I believe. If they think this is mere "criminal" activity then they will not employ any, extreme, methods to gain information from him. Not before we deal with him at least.' The menace in his final words was enough to send a shiver down the back of the most hardened individual, let alone the gentile businessman.

If there was one thing you would be hard pressed to complain about within *the Organisation*, it would be the availability of data and the tools to manipulate it. You could have, it seemed, an almost limitless supply of instrumentation to collect and collate it and computational power to process and present such data into whatever informing format you could care to imagine. It was one of the big benefits, from an intellectual point of view. Jane revelled in it. Bearing in mind the earlier diversion in the training field, she was very glad that her imagination had stretched to equipping Fletcher with portable, Nano-computing monitors and data caches. The results and information gathered by them from his little excursion augmented the planned sessions to great effect. Now, she needed the quiet of her office to study and soak in their meaning.

Reaction times were of interest, particularly around the preceding moments to Steve's burst to the perimeter of the facility, through to being picked up by *The Boss*. The neuron activity demonstrated patterns and convergences she had not previously witnessed nor had they been computer simulated in any form. What this meant, she had no firm view of at this stage. Without further data mapping it was unclear but... She thought back to the data gathered during his time undergoing *the Process*. The indications and traces of possible Tachyon activity, which were higher than expected and conversely also higher than during Dyer's own exposure to *the Process*. Was this data indicating some kind of parallel thought processing? Reacting at the same time as or even marginally *before* receiving stimuli, rather than split seconds after? There could be some alternative tests and reports to run, to either corroborate this was potentially happening or identify alternative scenarios. It may simply be that Steve possessed a more anticipative style of reacting, much like an elite athlete reacting on where they think the ball will be, rather than where it is now. Jane became aware that she was twiddling with her crucifix necklace. "*More to heaven and earth...*" she thought to herself, pondering the possibilities. But science should be able to provide some further clarity yet. In addition, a somewhat unscientific hunch around possible Tachyon evidence seemed the most plausible possibility to her, if she (liberally) applied the principle of Occam's razor (the principle that when multiple explanations exist for a given outcome or phenomenon, usually the simplest answer is most likely the appropriate one) - assuming that the traces she had been analysing did indeed result from the hypothetical tachyon particles themselves.

'Look up research on Quantum Effects on reflex and response times'. <click> Leaving herself a note on the tiny dicta-phone, standard *Organisation* office issue. It was presumably linked wirelessly to the secure network, as within moments a clever piece of software will have converted it and logged it in her tasks list. 'Delegate.' And if she commanded it to, the networked resources would carry out the task for her where practical. It was like having her own team of magic helpers to do the grunt work. Yes, there were a lot of upsides to being a part of this *Organisation*.

'General report in.' Jane jumped, she still found the artificial PA voice announcing "important" e-mails a tad off-putting when engrossed in thought. She started to get up, ready for the final debriefing of the day with Steve before they "released" him back into the real world. But she decided just to have a quick glance at the science team's overall weekly report to her. It all seemed in order, apart from some abnormal electrical surges in section one in their other facility. The Storage Area. Or to be precise, the Secure Store. Her authority level meant only her, out of the whole of the team that administered *the Process*, knew exactly what was stored in there. She clicked on the text link to look at the graphically represented supporting data. Small, but noticeable and regular power surges immediately followed by small but noticeable dips. There was a minimum of three distinct instances in the last thirty six hours or so. One of which was certainly during *the Process* yesterday. Intriguing but they were almost certainly purely coincidental.

Without particularly thinking about anything, his mind began to wonder. The period of rest was scheduled as a part of the post *Process* recovery. The slow fog of semi consciousness drifted over him. His thoughts, though heightened in their speed, still noticeably began the process of jumbling and merging. With the absence of structure or cognitive control, an altered, dreamlike state began to take over.

Firstly, it was dark. Void, a complete and all enveloping nothingness. There was a sense of the almost primordial about its pervasive blankness. Slowly but surely, tiny yet immensely bright spots of light began to emerge from the gloomy background canvas. One, two, three, four. Three orbited the one, each connected to it and less so via the one to each other. The one at the centre seemed simultaneously both there and not at all. Of the remaining three one burned brightly like a bulb before it finally burned out. The second seemed both intense yet darker, as if made of a different material of sorts. The third seemed newer and somehow clearer, no almost purer than the others. Throughout a voice. In fact, more of an echo or facsimile of a thought repeated, a phrase, a concept. Nexus... Gradually more faint impressions of points of light filled the backdrop. As far and diverse as one's imagination could comprehend. Too numerous to contemplate a number that described the vastness and scale of these individual points, congregations and associations that they seemed to generate and communicate. Nexus.

The buzz of his room's doorbell stirred him from his slumber pretty swiftly. At the door was Dr Gmitrowicz.
'Are you coming to the final debrief for today?' she quizzed. The time was now thirteen ten, he was meant to meet her in the briefing room ten minutes ago.
'Ahh,,, yes… sorry, I'm feeling a little groggy.' She smiled in a quite genuinely forgiving manner.
'*The Process* will leave you feeling a little bit hung-over for a few days to come.' She commented sympathetically. Steve grabbed a quick glass of water and splashed a little on his face to try and shift the lethargic feeling.

The stats and facts about what changes had been occurring to his body over the past couple of days must have been fascinating for Jane, Fletcher surmised to himself. For him, however, well, he was living and feeling it. He grunted and nodded appropriately to resemble a state of involvement in the presentation, but at best was only half listening. The notepad in front of him was slowly but surely filling up with a doodle. The subconscious out pouring of his mind's inner most thoughts. Suddenly Steve became aware of the silence and the good doctor's presence straight in front of him.
'Oh, well Steve's art work has really come on this term.' She quipped, sarcastically. Back in a fully alert state of consciousness he could recognise what he had drawn. Or rather what it resembled. It was a detailed, almost stylised eye. But more like something… something artificial made in the likeness of an eye. Involuntarily he dropped the pencil and looked up.
'Does the word *Nexus* mean anything to you?'

Chapter Five

Despite the ever increasingly omnipresent, environmentally friendly, almost world dominating green movement's influence on global politics, as well as the years of improving water quality and pollution controls along its banks and surrounding area, the Thames still looked grey and dirty on a day like today. Like the filth, degradation and corruption of the capital itself stained it through some process other than mere chemical pollution. Like it took on the hue of the dark underbelly of London through some sort of morality osmosis. Dyer was sat on the riverside wall on the embankment, overlooking the London Eye and just a stone's throw from the Houses of Parliament. The past few months had been such a rollercoaster ride, one increasingly more exciting sil-adrenaline rush after another that he had seldom taken time to look back and think.

The very government that had sent him and hundreds like him on seemingly futile wars on the back of what he and millions of others now felt they knew were lies. And all for what? Greed? Oil? Being a good ally to the States? The fact that the government now was not the government previously was irrelevant. Whoever and whatever the political parties that got voted in, it was always the government that ran the country. That much was true it seemed, so much of the government machine was barely affected by who was at the helm. He could storm into the brown stoned building and tear the very heart out of it if he so wished. Before anyone could meaningfully react to it let alone try to prevent it. The power within in him could do that easily. But it would be too simple, and what would he do next? Take over the country? Hold it to ransom? What next after that? His irrational internal musings were interrupted by a familiar sound in the distance. Grimes had a distinctive gait that tip-tapped out his approach at a hundred paces. Luke turned to face east, the direction the sound was wafting from. His sense of personal injustice extended to far more recent and for now more intense indignations than those inflicted on him by the country's government and society at large.

'At least now I know why you never look as rough as I do the morning after a long session like that was.' Grimes joked as he extended a chubby hand in his direction. Dyer beamed a smile back as he gently but firmly accepted the outstretched palm.

'Yes, the effects are short and mercifully sweet,' his gaze returning out over the river to the south bank once more. 'I was intrigued by the news that our... investment of labour is maybe still recoverable.' The comment brought a small involuntary cough from the older man, maybe an involuntary nervous reaction perhaps?

'Yes, it was a rather surprising turn up for the books. However, it could be a lucrative one if..., a very big if... they are true to their words. When investing, this is what they mean by your rate of return is linked to your rate of risk exposure.' The broad smile made a fleeting return, followed by an awkward grimace. 'Are you sure you want to risk meeting them face to face?' Dyer once more turned to face his business partner.

'If you mean will I be on the lookout for you if it turns nasty... of course. How else will I get paid what I'm due?' His expression resembled a smile, but the eyes had the almost cold hypnotic stare of a predator, simply sizing his meal before seizing and devouring it. Almost the faintly psychotic stare of a vampire. Grimes could not tell if the look was for effect as a part of the joke or if it belied the humour to show how he actually felt. 'So where are we meeting our mysterious client?' the frosty coldness of the moment subsiding a little.

'Just up the road, in a coffee bar between Kings Cross and Covent Garden. The public setting was for my benefit, safety in numbers I felt.' With a little, low toned chuckle, Dyer turned to face westward once more and began a slow walk towards Embankment tube station.

'Well let's get going. Early bird catches the worm, hey?'

As they entered the café, their eyes were both immediately drawn to the tall, slim and instantly charismatic gentleman to the right of the seating area, who was calmly arranging his coat and bag on one of the four chairs circling the small beige table typical of this particular coffee bar chain. The weight of their stares took a few moments to attract his attention. Eventually he turned to face them, with the warm smile of a salesman he ushered them both to the two remaining chairs.

'Gentlemen, I took the liberty of ordering you both tea, I hope that is OK?' The accent and pleasantries seemed totally inappropriate bearing in mind both the setting and the circumstances. If it was meant to take out the tension in the situation, then it only worked for Grimes. Dyer visibly gave off the vibes of somebody who had severe trust issues, understandable if you were meeting somebody linked to the fact you had been shot at by about a dozen men in the past twenty-four hours.

'Thank you Mr Bahajoub, tea is fine for me at this time of day.' Mirroring the courteous behaviour as he sat down. His business partner remained silent, taking his seat more slowly and noticeably sizing up their host as he did so. Dyer pulled a small packet of white powder from his pocket, and began to stir it into his tea.
'Apologies, I should have got some sugar also.'
'That's OK, it's not sugar.'
'Ah, on a diet I presume. It is good to see another who is concerned so for their health.'
'Something like that.'
Dyer looked away out of the window with an expression of feigned mild disinterest. He was sure he'd seen the same two men walk past the window moments earlier and smiled an exaggerated greeting in their direction.
'I can see that you are indeed very professional. That is why my client would be very interested in your team's… services.' Bahajoub complimented him on his observation skills, noticing that his back up had been spotted a little too easily. The merest hint of nervousness flashed across the slender man's face momentarily. The café was pretty full and had the buzz one would expect of a location in the capital at lunch time. It made it very hard to discern one particular conversion out from the crowd, which was ideal.

'So,' Grimes decided to take the initiative, sensing that Luke's excessive testosterone could kick in at any minute, descending the discussion into at best a sabre rattling contest and at worst, well, who knew what. 'We have not got off to the best of starts for building a meaningful business partnership, have we? I guess we need to draw a line underneath the events of yesterday to move forward and I believe that your proposal of an upfront payment could go some way in doing that.' Pausing to gauge any reaction, of which there was none other than the return of the salesman's smile. 'So maybe we need to understand exactly what you, sorry your client, is proposing?' Bahajoub raised an eyebrow then a perceptible moment later leant over to his right and pulled out a folder from his bag in a swift, effortless motion.
'I have taken the rather risky step of documenting the proposal and target in this short paper. I hope that the fact my client is prepared to risk this, albeit high level plan, falling into undesirable hands goes someway to diffusing the understandable lack of trust you are feeling right now.' His intense stare fixated on Dyer's expressionless, borderline robotic gaze back. Grimes removed the two page document, scanned it in stunned silence

then, still struggling to fully take in the contents passed it to Luke. The target surpassed anything they had done before. It was an entirely different ball game let alone league. From that angle if what the client was trying to do was pander to Dyers ego and taste for a challenge it was right up there. It was the potential requirements behind the target, the use that they may have had in mind, the ramifications of it that shocked Grimes the most. Luke's facade of indifference faded as he got to the appropriate part of the paper.

'Are you serious?' he looked once more into the smiling eyes of their host. 'This is the challenge?' A slowly nodded acknowledgement of the question was the answer. A mischievous expression took over Dyer's face in return. 'A job like this is worth twice the fee described here, upfront...' waiting for signs or otherwise of a shocked response. Only the mask of contentment remained. Only Grimes reacted, jaw dropping incredulously lower at his partners still relatively cool demeanour. 'And for this fee, your team will take on the task as described?' A broad grin flashed across his face as he answered.
'We'll even gift wrap it for your client, for Christmas.' The irony of the response was not lost on Bahajoub, who chuckled somewhat affectedly.
'Then we have a deal.' Proceeding to half stand and leaning forward to offer a customary, sealing handshake. Luke cautiously accepted, half tempted to apply a little too much pressure in the grip as a thank you for the previous night's events. He thought better of it.
'Yes, it's an acceptable challenge.' Quickly, almost noticeably more so than normally possible, relinquishing his grip and returning his hand to by his side. Bahajoub stood up properly, raising his gaze and hand to Grimes as he did so. 'I expect you will contact me this evening with details of the account to which the fee should be paid?' the pair shook hands for a more respectable length of time. 'Indeed, I will be contacting our banker presently.' The gruffness of his normal accent tinged with a vain attempt to sound more polished than he did normally, more like his "tea partner". With that the meeting was over and their host made a discrete but swift exit, followed closely down the street by his two "baby sitters".

Silence fell on the table for an uncomfortably long couple of moments. Finally, Grimes broke the sound vacuum. 'This is way bigger than I thought... I cannot believe what has just happened. How can you be so calm? We should be walking away not embracing this. The stakes are too high!' Dyer gave a dismissive shrug, and held up his palms in a motion that echoed his words. 'Calm down, you really think walking away was an option? Look at it this way. We have more money than we could have possibly thought about acquiring lined up to hit our accounts, and I have bought me... bought us some time to figure out the next step. The, project, does have its attractions to me. Not least a way to get back at my old employer and a way to get closer to those who would have easily killed me last night but for my... gifts. It is the only logical choice we really have right now.' The big man's business brain kicked in once more.

'You are right, on this occasion I have to say emotions are hard to suppress, especially fear, but you are right in what you say.' Staring as if he had x-ray vision into a space six foot beyond the far end wall of the café. Deep in thought, contemplating further Dyer's words. 'I will get the banker on the phone and arrange the necessary details. She had expressed a desire to meet with some of the team she has worked with for so long without actually knowing…when I took the liberty of preparing her and lining up her services for this earlier today.' Luke smiled, it was good to see that despite living in morbid fear of death over the past eighteen hours or so the old fella's focus on the money had not diminished. It was one of the things he loved about him. No, to be precise it was *the* thing he loved about him.

'Well, let's do it. She should know a little more about our partnership, not too much mind. The more skin in the game she has, the more use she may well be…' The ominous undertone sent a slight chill down Grimes' back. Thank god he was a crucial member of this team, as it felt like Samantha would become merely a more closely managed pawn in the proceedings moving forward.

'I have a car waiting for you at the drop off point to get you home.' Yelled *the Boss* over the roar of the helicopter's rotor blades. 'I have a meeting with our *Civil Servant* friend tonight on our progress.' Steve nodded half listening, half remembering the last time he found himself in a wingless bird. The flashback's since *the Process* had been fewer again and considerably milder, replaced in some part by the strange dreams he'd been experiencing. Jane had blankly stared back at him after his question on *Nexus*. The first thing he would do when he got home, after dealing with what was now his mess of a home life, was look up what the hell the word meant to see if that shed any further light on the subject.

'I will meet with you at the City location in the morning, unless you hear anything different on the comms link.' a presumably modified version of his existing mobile phone, it now undoubtedly boasted an extremely *en*hanced security encryption capability as well as a secure hotline back to *HQ*. 'Then we can begin in earnest to hunt for our rogue element.' The large playing field where they would touch down was now directly below them. 'You have your diet supplements for the next month? Remember, they will be poisonous to anyone else so be carefully how you ingest them and where you store them.' The Doctor had come along for the ride, her professional pride driving her to oversee Fletcher's release "back into the wild" as it were.
'Yes, I will keep my special "milkshake" safe and secure.' Jane noticed that Steve was becoming progressively more pensive as the journey continued, a natural reaction to having to face what, despite the *Organisations* best efforts, would undoubtedly be an awkward home coming. The chopper touched down with a firm although muted thud and Steve disembarked, swiftly transferring to the standard issue silver-grey executive saloon car that as promised was awaiting his arrival.

Despite trying several times to insist that the car drop him a short walk from the flat, it's driver merely restated that his orders were to deliver him safely to the front door. Carrying out orders to the letter was something he'd strangely enough not missed in the past year or so. Steve hoped that he would still have an element of greater freedom in his new role. To an extent, the changes he'd gone through must have almost guaranteed such flexibility. Certainly, he'd considered simply jumping out of the car when it stopped. No door lock or even screeching of tyres would be much of a deterrent to him now that was for sure. However, it was probably simpler to be compliant and allow the car to deliver him home. It was six thirty in the evening and still a little earlier than Samantha would normally be home, so Steve was both surprised and a little unprepared for the sight of Sam coming down the stairs as he, slowly for him, began to climb. Both stopped momentarily, she was just as surprised it seemed to have bumped into him too.
'Hi, err.' They both uttered simultaneously. 'I'm…just going out to meet some colleagues… a bit of customer hospitality…' Sam was strangely awkward in a way that almost seemed like she'd been the one away for several days unannounced. 'I wasn't sure you'd be back…. this early.'
Steve flashed a tentative smile. 'Yeah, I'm, I'm sorry about the last few days… this contract is really important but…. I know it

wasn't planned but, well, the client is a demanding one… it could well happen again that I get called off on short notice err, I'll try to…' Why was he already positioning the fact that he'd be away more often? He'd only just got home…
'I guess it's like old times for you, hey…' Sam was either amazingly intuitive, or simply stating a view that echoed a little too close to the truth of the matter. Her smile in return was visibly one with the mouth and not the eyes. 'I'll be quite late, so don't wait up.' Were her parting words, delivered in a purposefully laisse-faire manner, as she resumed her descent down the stairs. Steve recognised an order when he heard one. In turn, he resumed the climb to their front door.
'Well, that went well…' he sarcastically quipped to himself turning the key in the door as he did so.

Whilst travelling back into town Sam felt a strange pang of woman's intuition in her stomach. The feeling that something should have been said that wasn't. A feeling that she should be at home saying those things right now, rather than being at the impromptu meeting with her decidedly unofficial business partners. Before the past couple of days she'd not really considered much the impact of what she was doing, arranging the transfer of monies for Grimes. The impact of it becoming something more than her secret second income may have on her and those around her. Steve being away got her suspecting him of all sorts, but how much of that was a projection of her own guilt? He looked genuinely like he'd missed her company, and disappointed (and a little relieved also) that she was going out. The clatter of entering a tunnel snapped her out of her internal world momentarily and back to focussing on the meeting in hand. The area of town they were meeting up in was not one she'd normally frequent, which was both a good and bad thing. Pretty unlikely she'd bump into anyone from work, but not the kind of place she'd like to be left alone in for too long either. A taxi home would be the most sensible plan, and she could certainly afford that.

'Ahh, good to see you again,' an anaemic, slightly clammy palm extended towards *the Boss* as he approached the bar, 'Can I get you a drink?' the big man shook the extended hand, the individual who had proffered it still not making full eye contact with him.
'I'll have an orange juice please, Mr Desmond, got to take care of the old heart a bit more nowadays…' Abstinence was clearly not the norm for the civil servant, who bore the tell-tale reddened

nose of an established, regular drinker. Desmond nodded to the attentive serving staff permanently hovering nearby. It was a private members club, all leather backed chairs and stuffy calmness, with an atmosphere that resembled a strange mixture of hotel bar and university library. *The Boss* slowly lowered himself into the chair opposite his evening "date". An officious expression fell upon the face of the already seated Mr Desmond.

'So, how is your latest project progressing?'
'Well, very well indeed. An excellent candidate who is as, of oh six hundred tomorrow, fully operational. I am convinced he will prove to be a valuable asset to *the Organisation* and our governmental partners alike.' Freshly squeezed blood red orange juice duly presented. 'We will have him focused on rectifying our...past recruitment errors... with immediate effect.' Desmond leant forward, sliding a small USB stick over the table at the same time.
'This may prove of use. Our network contact in Scotland Yard has delivered an interesting map of thefts that seem to fit a pattern attributable to your previous project subject. With Dr Gmitrowicz's talents for data sifting you may have a little more success at finding a discernible pattern than the boys in blue. That and the benefit of knowing a little more inside track than they on who to look for.'
'So, they are also making a connection on these... incidents?'
'An individual surmising on a hunch more than anything else it seems. Just make sure you keep the tracks covered, no loose ends as they say. It's bad enough that a previous failure is grabbing headlines all over the media like some, some modern day Kray Twins. We will intervene to suppress any hint at the true nature of *the Houdini gang* as best we can but.... The media world is global and virtual these days, and our ability to "influence" less so. Everyone is a reporter and camera man now.'
It rankled *the Boss* that his and his department's credibility had been tainted so that he could not simply answer flippantly and confidently that they would succeed. He needed Steve to prove to be the right candidate as all past successes had been cancelled out with Dyer. The glass of half consumed juice in his right hand fractured into numerous shards as he involuntarily felt the anger well inside. What did the anger management course tell him to do? Ahh, yes, breathe deep and focus on slowing down his heart-rate by thinking of what made him calm. Like all self-help, that was far easier said than practically achieved.
'We will try our best, Mr Desmond, our very best.' Desmond could not resist the chance of a cheap joke at his expense.

'Ensure you do, we don't want to end up with any more of a mess on our hands…'

Samantha took a moment to compose herself. She'd made it to the door of the Pub where they would finally meet, face to face. The "Broker", Mr Grimes and, as Grimes himself had put it, *the Houdini Gang,* Luke Dyer. Presumably he was the leader, the main force in the gang, the reason it existed. It seemed a bit of a pretentious way of addressing someone in her opinion. The guy obviously had a massive ego. Guessing that anyone who'd pulled off the sort of crimes he'd done over the past few months would be a little overly self-assured. She straightened her jacket then entered the less than salubrious surroundings. The rotund, grey suited gentleman at the far end of the bar she instantly figured out had to be Grimes. He also, unsurprisingly figured out who she was. Samantha looked the most out of place person there, being almost exclusively male clientele, most of whom looked as if they had not done a day's honest work in quite some time. A pained, falsely smiling expression covered her face as she tried nonchalantly to stroll over to their meeting. What the hell was she doing here?

'Samantha? Good to meet you face to face at last.' The pair shook hands, the sort of formal politeness anyone in business would recognise. 'Let me introduce you to Luke.' The two shook hands, and Sam remained silent still, although now due to the rather more pleasant surprise of finally meeting Dyer.

'Pleased to meet you.' Luke was noticeably more polite than Grimes had witnessed for some time. 'Let's get you a drink and then we can sit over in that booth to have a little more privacy whilst we discuss our latest project.'

After ten minutes of mildly flirtatious conversation, Samantha finally started to steer the conversation towards something resembling business.

'So, I think we need to talk a little more about some, well, longer term planning. From a finance point of view.' Dyer's countenance altered slightly, shifting perceptibly from convivial host to a colder, more focused concentration.

'In what way do you mean my dear?' queried Grimes, still somewhat handicapped with the occasional turn of phrase that was meant to be considerate but could easily be mistaken for condescending.

'Well, the base issue I guess we need to consider is that of traceability. We are slowly but surely running out of options to construct routes for the monies to securely and unnoticeably find their way through the systems of my banking suppliers globally. If we continue to transact for maybe hmmm, four or more projects, then. Well. It's a challenge and we are at a greater risk of detection as we start to retrace old ground.' Luke leant forward, mildly clearing his throat as he did so.

'Then I guess it is just as well that this latest objective affords a sum that between us will mean we can change the way we operate moving forward.' Slipping to her less than discreetly a scrap of paper with a very large number written on it.

'Woh, this surely means there is no need to ever do this again.' Her inner wish to eventually no longer be a part of this business inadvertently becoming "public".

'I am not sure that completely retiring is necessarily an option here... you're a part of the core team now,' the unwavering stare firmly fixated on her, 'but we could certainly change the way we operate, and maybe our base of operations. Though it would be a good idea to maybe take some time off immediately after this project. I think we have to face the fact that this is a longer term business we are in – our success so far should give us all confidence in that. But I think we are all well past the point of return now.' Grimes stared noticeably and uncharacteristically hard at him. The razor sharp clarity of his words shocking both for their accuracy and the fact that his compatriot had spoken them, and not he.

'He is right, I think we have to wake up and realise this is not a hobby, and our old lives are no longer relevant. We need to plan both how we do this, and how we live our lives from this point.' The ice cool realism of the big man's words caused Samantha to instantly down the remainder of the large white wine in front of her.

'Best we have another, there's a lot to talk about.' She remarked, a little excited and frightened in equal measure.

'...and finally, is it a bird, is it a plane? One little girl in Suffolk and her mother are safe in their beds tonight thanks to the help of a mystery hero this morning. The unknown passer by pulled little Sarah, five, and her mother from the wreckage of their car after another driver had run them off the road. Police were amused by the young lady's description of a man leaping to her rescue and ripping the car door off, throwing it away like a Frisbee. "She was probably a bit dazed from the crash and the rescuer must have appeared to be like a superhero to her, in her hour of need." A police spokeswoman stated. Suffolk police would like the unknown man to come forward as he may have seen what happened, they are also interested in tracing the driver of a

stolen red ford focus, which was abandoned at the scene <click>.'
Well, he'd made the news. Nice touch, the facts as told by the little girl not suppressed, not covered up. Just simply explained away as "an overactive imagination". Brilliant. No mention of the balaclava either, that could have had suspicions rising potentially. Funny. When he was at *The Organisations* facility he'd felt a little hemmed in, almost as if he were in a prison cell. Here, alone in... his flat? In the field? Either way he felt the same. It suddenly seems like just another four walls, closing in, restricting him. God knows where Sam had gone, or when she'd return. Sleep was something he never needed much of but right now he felt more alert than ever.
'Don't draw attention to yourself unnecessarily.' He recalled out loud. It was ten thirty at night in a great British winter. Cover of darkness could get no darker than this in London. Maybe a quick run out with his black tracksuit was just what the doctor ordered?

Chapter Six

Twenty Two forty five hours. It had taken Steve fifteen minutes to drag on his tracksuit (complete with balaclava) and cover roughly ten miles over roof tops, rear gardens and open, unlit, urban spaces. Despite the late hour London was alive and loud to his *en*hanced senses. Perched in a tree, set back some way from the road near the top of a hill in the vicinity of Harrow, he could hear a lot. Half a mile away a couple rowed vehemently, spitting their words like venom at each other, wielding phrases like machetes. How he and Sam maybe should have done a few hours ago, though the subject was about a drunken kiss at an office party rather than having seemingly gone AWOL for a few days. A general hum of drunken, good hearted joviality bubbled over from Watford town centre. Christmas was drawing near. It wasn't his hearing though that drew his attention to a side street about a mile to his left. No, it was more his instincts, his inner voice. Steve sensed some trouble, or the feeling of somebody's own mind being intent on making some.
'Maybe it's time for another field test...' he thought to himself as he leapt from his vantage point, sprinting in controlled bursts to where he could now hear what sounded like the start of a confrontation.

The woman was visibly terrified. She knew now that she should never have risked the short walk home alone but, Dutch courage, foolishness, who knows exactly what had tainted her judgement. Now she was ever so slightly quickening her pace, aware that she was not alone on the street now.
'Oi love, wait up.' The words filled her with dread. Wait for what?
'Oi, don't ignore me.'
The voice, male of course, now tinged with menace, frustration and anger. Flight or fight instincts began to kick in. She was damned if she was going to simply crumble and give in to this stranger. No! She would turn and confront him! As she did, the stranger drew closer, close enough for her to see his eyes. Black with menace visible even in the street lamp's half-light. And in his hand a flash of metal, silver, a blade? She involuntarily tried to let out a scream, but could not muster a sound. The stranger chuckled, a low grumble of a chuckle accompanied by his grinning, perverted, lust filled expression.
'This won't hurt... for too long...' Lunging forward, as if about to start a short sprint towards her.
The rest of what happened was a bit of a blur. All she could remember was seeing, well half seeing a black shadowy figure

leaping from over her, her right shoulder? She thought, maybe, could not completely sure. With a sort of whooshing noise the stranger had been knocked to the ground, disarmed and visibly dazed. Moments later her saviour had tied up the would be assailant to the lamppost nearby using some garden park fence chain (she had no idea where that had come from) and was standing in front of her, hands gently placed on her elbows almost holding her up.

'Are you Okay? He didn't manage to touch you did he?' the man asked.

All she could do was shake her head and splutter 'I'm Okay.'

'You may want to call the police.' Was the only other thing he had said before he was gone as quickly as he appeared, though he might have punched the attacker unconscious once more, as when she looked down he was more slouched and definitely out of it.

'Do you remember anything distinctive?' The police constable enquired, trying to establish some further facts.

'Err, not really. He was wearing a black…err or grey… ski mask… and… no, nothing else. He seemed to appear out of the shadows then simply join them again. Almost as if he'd never been there. Like some alien spaceship had beamed him up.' A nervous laugh accompanied the last remark.

The Organisation's City Office was pretty central. On the forty third floor of the Shard it had a fantastic panoramic view of most of the sprawling capital to the west, north and south. *The Boss* surveyed the horizon, which resembled a gigantic Christmas light display at oh seven hundred hours.

'Dyer could be somewhere right in front of me, right now.' He thought to himself, the voice in his head doing so in a frustrated manner. His silent contemplation interrupted by Jane entering the conference room.

'Do you ever sleep?' she enquired light heartedly.

'I find it harder to do so whilst our *wayward child* runs free…' a small flicker of a smile accompanied the genuine response. 'Besides, you need less sleep when you are older. You will find that out one day.' Jane smiled back. *The Boss* seemed uncharacteristically warm this morning. It was a pleasant change. The meeting room door swung open once more as Fletcher entered the room.

'Ahh, if it is not our infamous colleague.' *The Boss* stretched out a big, open and warmly welcoming hand. This was as good humoured as Jane had seen him in a long while. Steve however seemed a little pensive in reaction to the remark. As if it had put him a little bit on the back foot. 'Get yourselves a coffee then we can get started. I took the liberty of getting some made specifically for you, Steve.' Pointing to the flask marked "*En*hanced".

'Thanks very much.' Steve noticed that it only felt about half full as he poured himself a cup. 'Even secret government agencies had to watch the pennies these days...' he thought to himself. The trio, steaming cups in hand, sat around the mid-sized conference room table, each taking their own side. A built-in projector took up the fourth position and flickered instantly to life as *The Boss* picked up the remote control.

'It is time to get you fully operational Steve, your initial objective is a potential threat to the security of our country and possibly... probably our allies and enemies alike.' What appeared to be a recent, high quality surveillance photo blipped onto the screen. 'This was taken about three months ago. In the vicinity of Hyde Park in London. Unfortunately our representative on the ground was... discovered shortly afterwards by Dyer. Luckily the technology had already sent the photo and its co-ordinates back to base before he was neutralised.' Steve had not missed the dispassionate language sometimes used to describe the fortunes of war, but could tell that the language did not hide the fact that the big man was upset at the loss of a life.

'Why didn't, hasn't Dyer simple come after *The Organisation* and, well, neutralised it?' The question brought a small pause before Jane chipped in with her answer.

'Because you and he are *en*hanced not invincible. This is not a superhero comic!'

'It would make one hell of a graphic novel though.' Fletcher thought to himself.

'We know how to take him down...' The pause remained briefly, before *the Boss* added. 'That and we have changed all of our compromised and less secure locations immediately after he went "free-lance".' Then turning specifically to Jane. 'Speaking of locations, these files might help us track with a little more success where Dyer is now located or what his next target may be,' handing Desmond's little gift across the table. 'Somebody with your talent for analysis may be able to glean a pattern lesser mortals have failed to see.' The faintly warm smile once again flickered across the older man's face. Jane twirled the memory stick between her fingers.

'Well, we love a good puzzle don't we...'

Sam's head was a fuzzy, aching mess. Slowly, painfully she opened her left eye to survey the vicinity. She didn't recognise it at all. Through the pounding sensation and fluctuation of her vision she could see the silhouette of a man. A man who was obviously not Steve. Luke turned around from the window, seeming to sense Sam's sudden rebirth into consciousness. 'Good Morning.' Warmth and a hint of, what was it, almost gratitude in his voice. 'Mor..<cough>... morning?' the questioning inflection in part due to her genuinely being unsure what day, let alone what time it was. And why was he showing no visible effects of last night's excesses? Dyer sat, gently almost tentatively, on the edge of the bed. 'Coffee?' Sam nodded her approval and for a few moments lost the feeling of guilt and enjoyed the softly delivered attention.

Dyer supervised the coffee machine as it burbled out a normal and a "special" macchiato. Best not get them mixed up. For the first time in a long time he was bothered enough to not want any harm done to the woman who lay in his bed. And it was not merely due to her being "the banker" however important that may have been. Never mix business and pleasure, so they say. "They" also said crime doesn't pay, right? 'Just do what feels right.' he thought to himself. That mantra had worked so far. He carefully took the mugs of coffee into the bedroom, being sure not to hand the almost certainly fatally poisonous one to Sam. 'Here this ought to help steady you constitution.' She smiled, coming away from the floor to ceiling window that offered a fantastic view of the Thames.
'I better head off soon, don't want to get the sack before we complete this latest project... though we'd best consider another route for banking after this one...<sip> we will have ridden our luck probably as far as we can by then.' A girl after his own heart! It's all about the money.

The Boss looked blankly at Fletcher for about five seconds before he realised that the room had fallen silent.
'Are we boring you this morning?' Steve was shamed back into fully participating in the meeting.
'Ah...sorry...my mind just wandered for a second.' It was amazing what he could now doodle in a few moments. Something that looked like a map of a star constellation, or a global network of some description, dots and lines converging, splitting and linking in a very precise manner. Once again the word *Nexus* was involved, written in Italics. Steve thought he heard Gmitrowicz mumble something. 'Sorry Doctor, what was

that you just said?' Both of his companions in the meeting now looked at him blankly.
'Err, nothing? Didn't say a word.'
His brow crumpled with a look of confusion.
'Oh, I thought I heard you say something... Sauce? Source... the Source. Must have been my imagination.'
A very slight, almost imperceptibly slight, flicker of amazement mixed with shock seemed to momentarily dance across her face. And a sideways glance at the *Boss* for a moment too. *Nexus*, The Source, three bright lights nearer than all others, one connecting them all. The jumbled cacophony of thoughts was almost like a cryptic crossword clue or a riddle half written in English. It made no sense but seemed also to make perfect sense at the same time. Something fundamental was being kept from him, something he felt was important for him to know and he would need to be patient and seize the right time to find out what it was, and what it all meant.

The quiet calm of his flat was just what Luke needed right now. Samantha had gone, and the double glazing was doing its bit in keeping most of the rush hour traffic noise out, even with his *en*hanced hearing. There was no time like the present to plan exactly how he would enact his great challenge and extract the rewarding but difficult and dangerous prize. It would take a little time and due to the "owners" of this objective he felt sure that the risks of being detected before and being compromised during the project would be considerably higher. And this particular victim may just have a way to stop him, unlike any of the objectives before, or indeed the police force who he felt sure had no idea still as to how the crimes had been executed. He turned away from the window and sat down at the table, tablet computer at the ready. What he needed was a diversion, something that would distract any prying eyes in to looking elsewhere and hopefully missing any research activity and thinking he'd been focussing purely on something else. He put the tablet down and picked up a notepad and pen. Old tech was best for this plan, the internet would need to be accessed in a way that it could not link back to his pseudo identity or anywhere he may be regularly seen. As for the diversion, it could also prove a nice little earner too. He'd given himself two dates, sixteenth and seventeenth of December. Diversion and main event. The chaos of a fast-approaching Christmas would also help provide a little cover and make reacting that bit more difficult on the diversion front, and hopefully lead to a few lapses of concentration on the behalf of any potential pursuers. He wrote down three words. Tower of

London. The diversion would also cause embarrassment in the establishment he so loathed. A wry smile crossed his face.
'They'll never see these ones coming…'

'Where are we?'
'You do not have an accepted name for here, as your people only half know of its existence. It is the world between worlds, the space between spaces. It is both nowhere and everywhere, a paradox in itself. Anachronistic yet timeless.'
'Who are we?'
'Different yet the same, the beginning and the end of the line. Part of the same cycle. One and yet separate, where things connect. You do not have a name for us.'
'Why are we?'
'Because we are needed, because we are necessary, because we are. Because.'

'Damn! Damn!' Hayes slammed the phone down, his frustration making him forget his manners for once. Killen looked up, startled astonishment splashed across her face. Hayes caught the look, and obliged with an explanation. 'Our witness is dead. Flat lined.'
'Thought he would make a recovery?' Hayes frowned at the remark.
'Hmmm, McCarthy's lot are checking the CCTV just in case but no immediate, obvious signs of further foul play. Damn it!' This was the best chance so far of getting some kind of clue to *The Houdini Gang*, a physical description, accents, height, anything. The spurious shoe print and sweat shirt fibres were too vague and general. Too much of an enigma in themselves let alone when combined with the "double headed" bullets. 'Did we get the forensic update report overnight?' a swift shake of the head then a moment's hesitation before she elaborated.
'Think this one has them intrigued, it's the fibres on the bullets that have 'em really stumped.' The icy cold fire glinted momentarily in Hayes' eyes.
'Get your coat Killen, think we need to give our colleagues a bit more motivation.' Chucking the car keys in her direction.' 'You're driving.'

The unmarked car Hayes had matched perfectly with his wardrobe, gunpowder metallic grey hidden under a layer of almost fossilised city grime.
'About time this had a wash, guv?' he gave a deep throated chortle in response.

'When I have time to worry about that,' as they settled into the car, 'you can buy me my retirement present.' They made the short drive over to the forensic department's state of the art facility just off the south bank of the River Thames. One of the legacies to the Olympics was the previously secret drug testing facilities, built with private and public money. The Mayor had managed to conveniently commandeer the facility for the force and make it a national beacon for the scientific side of police investigations.

'How comes we still work in a sixties throw back when these guys get this...' Hayes smiled back at Killen's indignation.

'You'd miss the old world charm really, who needs clean marble floors and fancy lighting when you have lukewarm vending machine tea and the faint smell of dead vermin in the briefing room?'

The forensic looked up as they entered the testing area. Hayes thought to himself how much like the Easter Island statues he was in his unwavering, permanently expressionless gaze. What went on behind those glasses, what kept him up at night?

'Detective Inspector, how pleasantly unexpected.' Delivered with such a dead pan tone as to contradict the words uttered. Was it sarcasm? Nonchalance? Or an almost borderline autistic spectrum equivalent lack of appreciation of the need for social skills?

'I thought we'd double check that you guys hadn't taken a surprise trip to Paris or something without telling us? Been a bit quiet over the past day, hate to think you were having fun without us.' A mere flick of the left eyebrow was the only perceptible response.

'Time off would be a nice thought... but for some reason you keep bringing me these interesting crime scenes with ludicrous and spurious facets.'

'That's easy for you to say... talking of these fibres again? Are we sure they aren't a contamination from this makeshift facility?' A flash of something registered across his face and finally he stopped focussing on what he was looking at on his tablet and looked directly at the DI.

'No, we have something a little more puzzling than that,' swiping the screen of the small device to shift an image to the large wall come projection screen at the far end of the room. 'Recognise this Hayes? Killen?' The graphs filled the top and bottom of the screen.

'Looks like DNA, two sets wildly different?' Killen guessed, head quizzically slanted to one side.

'Yes, wildly different indeed...' The forensics speech being somewhat stilted, giving away his own feelings of confusion on the matter. 'Puzzling...'

Hayes decided to cut to the chase 'Why?' he curtly enquired. 'Well, the bottom one is human, one of the victims, the top one... makes no sense all. See the gaps?' Both detectives nodded slowly, curious as to where this was going. 'That's what they are, gaps. That is there is no recognisable DNA in a form our machines could measure and read. We have very little of the evidence to use but I have already run it three times, from two different crime scene sources. The partial DNA that is registering appears to correlate as being human, white male probably but the gaps are filled with something else... we need to run more tests but what they should be I do not know, I am at a loss as to how to proceed.' Hayes frowned disapprovingly.
'Surely it's just contaminated or something?'
The forensic peered over his glasses with an almost schoolteacher like distain.
'The gaps are identical on the two separate sources, from bullets found in two separate victims. I am waiting results on a third to ensure that contamination is highly unlikely. DNA doesn't corrupt that easily or consistently in twenty four hours.' It was at that moment a new mail trumpeted its arrival on the forensics laptop. 'Ah, now this might be pertinent.' Swiftly opening the mail with what must have been what passed for latent anticipation for him. The increasingly familiar flush of confusion blipped across his face once more.
'What is it?' Hayes patience was not exactly one of his well-known attributes.
'Silicon. The samples thus far have Silicon present in the gaps...It could be why the DNA tests originally showed gaps.'
'So... what does that mean?' quizzed Killen, with the merest hint of frustration in her voice. Hayes appeared to have drifted off in thought momentarily. The forensic stared expressionless at the DS.
'I don't know.'

'Get Steve in here ASAP!' *The Boss* yelled out of his office door after putting the phone down, it was easier and quicker than using the phone again to get his PA to summon him. Urgency and a hint of excitement tinged his voice. Steve suddenly appeared at the doorway, sensing something a little more pressing and interesting than a PowerPoint presentation was in the offing. 'We've got a situation that you can help with, a plane has been taken under siege at Stansted, with a number of passengers being held captive. Fancy a rescue mission?' The two men grinned in unison at the prospect. 'It's a shame you haven't had time to learn how to use the X2C. It would be ideal to get you there swiftly whilst not getting noticed.' *The Boss's* grin seemed to grow impossibly wider still.

The unmarked and anonymous black van sped out of *the Organisation's* car park in the basement of the Shard. Presently, it was almost instantly joined by two police cars, with their blues and twos flashing and blaring. Inside the van Dr Gmitrowicz sat beside Steve, talking him through the layout of the plane, where it was in the airport complex and the best route for him to take once they dropped him off at the edge of Epping Forest, which would provide cover for him to get there at his own speed rather than the comparatively rather pedestrian progress they'd make in the van. The day had turned into a generally damp, grey but mild one for the time of year. The overall poor light was a benefit for Steve to help pass through the countryside unnoticed, especially whilst wearing his *Organisation* standard issue outfit. Essentially a matt black boiler suit with reinforced black footwear and gloves. He held in his hands an integrated ski-mask balaclava which comprised built in mirrored one way lenses with a microscopic, encrypted voice and video communication system.
'We can see and hear what you do, it helps us to give advice and info if you need it. You can communicate with us likewise. We will liaise with the onsite emergency services and have already ensured that there is a media exclusion zone. The team have also ensured that all civilian mobile networks are down to stop any "live" video being shared, as a precaution.' She paused to take a sip of coffee. 'We will filter out any stored media that may be taken after you have secured the plane. Are you up to speed and ready to go alone from here?' Steve flashed a smile at Jane as he pulled his mask on.
'Got you at the end of the hotline if not.' He joked, tapping his right ear. The side door was flung open and he leapt clear of the van deep into the thick of Epping Forest, glancing at the GPS enabled map projected inside the left lens of his mask as he did so.

Running through the pre-planned wooded route was far trickier than he'd imagined it would be. Grip was the main issue, the human equivalent of wheel spinning in the mulch and mud that covered most of the initial part of the journey. He soon arrived at more open countryside comprising mostly of fields where he could at least find some grassy stretches to leap and sprint along, although the focus of concern now shifted to remaining unseen as he progressed. Then, a few minutes in he came upon the main stumbling blocks, the M11 motorway and outlying buildings surrounding the airport, which were both more open and heavily utilised than the few small roads he'd had to leap across to get this far. The simplest route was to use a small section of road-bridge to cross the motor way then dart behind the trees and shrubs that lined the main dual carriage way into the airport, but this could mean almost certainly that someone would see him. Whether they would recognise that the fast-moving object was human shaped would be a matter of pot luck. Maybe it would be better if he were to leap the Motorway just south of the Bridge, take the underpass (which he could time his run through so as not to be observed) and then dart into the foliage. Steve decided that would be better, and more of a challenge too!

'Second Son, please advise your location?' Jane was impatient to hear if he'd arrived, and figured that Steve should be there or thereabouts by now.

'I have just reached the perimeter fence, Mother Duck.' not the appropriate codename but it brought a mildly exasperated smiled to the Doctor's face.

'Ok, can you see the party from there?' Great turn of phrase, he was about to become the most unpopular gate crasher imaginable, Steve thought to himself. 'Yes, planning my grand entrance now, am I clear?'

'Proceed as briefed and good luck.' They were about to find out if he was the right man for the job for real now. The moment of truth indeed.

The tarmac was damp and a little slippery under foot. Fletcher had to tow a fine line between approaching swiftly and unnoticed versus losing his footing. He slid almost horizontally under the nose of the aircraft. In the meantime, a live feed of the cockpit's microphones had been switched to his earpiece. The stress in the cabin crew's voices clearly audible as they responded to their captor's barked requests. The briefing had identified the cabin as the best entry point for Steve, but an alternative to it could be via the luggage compartment to the rear. It depended on where the majority of the four armed terrorists were, which he had to try and ascertain using the scanning tech in what he'd just decided to call his "mask for all occasions". He switched on what was effectively x-ray vision via the small control that he wore like a conventional wristwatch. Two individuals stood at the rear of the plane with what looked like guns, two in the front cabin. Everyone else was seated. Great, which ever end he entered, only half the problem could be resolved effectively and immediately.

It was Hobson's choice essentially. At least if he neutralised the two at the rear, then any human shields taken by the remaining two would in all likelihood be cabin crew, who at least will have received some training on situations such as these. That would make the next two a slightly less difficult proposition than they may otherwise have been and hopefully reduce the risk to members of the general public, even if only marginally. Steve scrambled to the rear of the plane, to where the luggage compartment doors were still open as the cabin crew had only just begun the process of loading suitcases prior to the siege. 'Fortunately they will not be expecting a surprise entry through the floor.' He thought to himself, crawling into the tight cavity in an almost feline fashion, being mindful not to cause any perceptible shudder or noise as he did so. He could feel his *en*hanced heart pounding at a tremendous rate as he psyched himself up for the next step. He turned to face the direction of the two terrorists, then launched himself like a heavy-duty mechanical centre-punch through the floor of the passenger compartment of the plane. Hysterical screams filled the air, passengers and stewards alike startled at the unexpected turn of events. The terrorists themselves stared dumbstruck at the mangled pieces of plane and debris, then with burgeoning amazement at the black figure, looking like a cross between a displaced car mechanic and a Ninja, balancing on the edge of the freshly formed hole in the floor. Steve swiftly, almost invisible to the human eye, lunged at the armed assailants.

One of them reacted by launching a short burst of about half a dozen bullets rapid fire from his K11 assault rifle. The shells all hit Steve squarely in the abdomen as he pulled the firearm from his attackers grasp. The sharp, snapping thwacks of the exchange prompted further short sharp screams from the passengers, then silence. First he made sure that the weapons were now inoperable, by crushing the barrels in his grasp, then he made sure the terrorists were also inoperable, by knocking them clean out with the rear ends of the confiscated guns. He could feel that the bullets had lodged between his stomach muscles, nestled awkwardly in the soft flesh surrounding them. He momentarily relaxed and they fell to the floor, five flattened metal studs in all. Meanwhile, the cabin door swung open as the burst of gunfire and general commotion had alerted the other two

terrorists to his presence. Steve clocked a young man staring at the bullet holes roughly where his appendix would be. The single terrorist stood in the doorway, pilot or co-pilot conveniently held in front of him like his own personal shield.
'I hate it when I'm right.' He mumbled to himself out loud and edged slowly forward (not just a considered pace for him, but for anyone). His adversary pulled his "bodyguard" a little closer to the weapon pointed strategically towards his temple.
'*Stay where you are Steve, don't-*' <click> He couldn't think with the good Doctor in his ear, fortunately he'd taken time to figure out how to switch off the headphone feed.
'Stay where you are!' barked the gunman like a telepathic echo.
'That's Original.' He quipped, the joke obviously lost on everyone else present, stalling a little while he thought and calculated what to do next. In his right hand he twirled out of sight the sixth bullet that had hit him moments earlier. In a burst of unimaginable speed he flicked his hand out in front of him, the recycled projectile knocking the gun out of his opponents hand and also wounding his left shoulder in the process. His grip loosened on the aircrew member allowing him to wriggle free. Fletcher seized the chance, in a blur knocking out the third hijacker with probably a little too much force, causing one of the exit doors to blast open with his target shooting out slumped on the door like some kind of sleep surfer, scooting across the tarmac towards the armed response Police unit that had been assembled at a strategic point about two hundred metres away.

At that instant, something from deep within him made him instinctively, almost involuntarily spin around with his arms raised as the final target swung a large knife, a machete, down towards his rib cage. The crude blade was sharp enough to cut into the sleeves of his suit but then rested harmlessly on his forearms. The look of alarm from the last terrorist standing made Steve audibly laugh. The assailant dropped the weapon and slowly, warily raised his hands in submission. Steve wasted no time in in using the cable ties he'd been provided to bind the terrorists hands. Finally he was aware again of Jane screaming at him.
'What the hell is happening Steve?' Frantic to understand if the situation had been effectively dealt with.
'Everything is clear now.' No response. Suddenly a cold chill shivered its way down the back of his neck. The comms device was still switched off. He turned it on to hear the commotion that was "command central". 'All...all clear here. Will now exit and allow the boys in blue to do their work. No civilian casualties all assailants incapacitated and disarmed.' The final hostage taker

pulled a face that expressed his surprise at that comment, just as Steve used his elbow to render him unconscious and then exited the way he entered, leaving the passengers and crew in stunned silence as the armed response unit descended on the plane from all angles moments after.

Second Son and Mother Duck sat silently for a moment as Steve removed his head gear. Dr Gmitrowicz wore an expression that could sour milk. It softened once she could see the strange expression the man opposite her had on his face. He looked oddly spooked, not an expression she expected to see at all given the successful outcome of the mission.
'What the hell happened Steve?' She noticed the mild expression of apprehension flash a little stronger momentarily. A perceptible long pause preceded Steve's reply.
'I looked up the meaning of the word *Nexus* last night. It seemed to make some kind of sense to me for some reason. Since *the Process*. I feel something... a connection to a few and then many.' He could see Jane was a little perplexed by his inane rambling, but he continued. 'I have always gone with my gut feel. It has guided me in times of trouble. It now seems to have a clearer voice, and it seems to be... connected somehow. To something.' Steve could almost feel the concern radiating from Jane, and what else? A little relief? He'd never noticed the cross she wore before. 'Your faith is important to you, isn't it?' Jane smiled and nodded in reply, instinctively reaching for a moment the small crucifix. He sensed there was something more that she knew, something to do with whatever this *Nexus* was, but maybe she only guessed at it rather than definitely knew it. He leant a little closer. 'Did Dyer ever say he felt this...this change? This feeling?' Scanning her face for the meaning behind the words of any answer she gave.
'No. No but... he never had the level of empathy your psychoanalysis results showed. He was extremely self-contained, self-referenced.'
Both sat back a little, the tension of the assignment diminishing with the diversion of this conversation. Jane glanced a little nervously at the screen. There was something she was keeping from him, Fletcher was pretty sure of it.
'The fact is, Steve as you know there are things about the process we are not sure of, things...' She'd stopped herself through duty, fear, unsure of sharing information he was not cleared to know? The little voice whispered inside his head once more. He knew the questions he had to ask. It was the thought

she'd stifled from becoming her next spoken word. Steve fixed her with an intense stare and quizzed.

'What exactly is *The Source*?' Jane audibly sucked in her breathe a little at his direct and extremely intuitive question. Then the scientist in her took over. She was intrigued to understand. Why did he know that this was an appropriate question to ask? From the previous day he'd already used the phrase, but how did he know it was a phrase to be used? What was this *Nexus* he kept referring to? And why hadn't this, apparently strong and clear, intuition manifested itself on previous subjects. The Doctor spoke to the driver via the intercom.

'Change of plan, can we head to the facility in Rendlesham please, not the London Operation Centre.' Then facing Steve once more. 'I am hoping this will become clearer to the both of us very soon…' turning her attention to the keyboard and screen to file the operational report, and ensure that all news agencies would be contacted with a plausible explanation for any "leaks" that may get through the net from witness reports, most likely using disturbed sensory perception brought on by stress and trauma as a cause of any "bizarre" claims.

Chapter Seven

Silicon. It had been bugging him the entire journey back to the office. Why Silicon? Why did it seem to ring a bell to him? Hayes was unable to take his mind from that thought. Killen was used to the silent treatment but could not help but notice that Hayes was in a tight and insular world of his own deep thought. They made the short walk from the car to his office in complete silence. Killen broke it with her usual question.

'Coffee?' The light bulb flicked on, the question triggering a memory.

'That's it! That's what I was trying to remember!' The young Detective Sergeant looked blankly, puzzled by the sudden burst into communication mode once more. The grey man spurted into a flurry of activity, shifting what appeared to be randomly dispersed piles of files and paper on his desk until he finally settled on a new configuration of stacks. Bizarrely to his eyes this seemed perfect and brought a smile of accomplishment to his craggy countenance. 'There we have it.' Looking up at Killen. 'Silicon!'

'I'm sorry guv, not sure I am following you?' His enthusiasm undiminished by her lack of insight.

'Look-' pointing at the three piles of paper at the centre of the mess. 'These crimes are all linked. I can sense it. No evidence that helps identify the criminal, a seemingly improbably set of thefts of some bizarre products or aggregates that make no sense to specifically target in the first place, why would anyone want them? They all are either pure or contain high levels of one thing. Silicon. Why would anyone need to steal Silicon? What could they be using it for? Stealing it means two things, lack of money or a desire to have no audit trail of acquisition at minimum.' His excited state intrigued the DS, and she found herself slowly walking over to look at what had got him so agitated.

'But... what is the significance of the Silicon itself?' Once a detective... looking for the answers to the gaps of their knowledge was the first thing any good investigator would do instinctively. The simplicity of her question seemed to momentarily irritate Hayes; it was after all still an anomalous finding by the forensic.

'It has corrupted their DNA somehow so it must be pretty crucial to their Modus Operandi. Killen, let's look into the applications for Silicon, particularly with the military or in heavy machinery. It

must be the key as to how these crimes occur in such a spectacularly fantastic fashion.' The logic appeared somewhat sound, she had to admit, and nodded her agreement.
'And maybe I should also get the team looking at the previous crime scene reports, was there any Silicon present there?' Hayes half-heartedly shrugged his approval, thinking that it was not likely to have been noted if they did not see it as relevant or significant.
'Maybe get the forensics to have a look at those previous fibres for traces too. Don't know what we are looking for but it's a new angle. Who knows where it may lead us...'

The journey to the facility at Rendlesham had taken about an hour and a half. For most of the way Jane had been focussing on orchestrating the news reports and press statements being released post the successful neutralisation of the "believed" terrorists. Aside from the terrorists themselves, whose witness statements would not be reported on, for obvious reasons, and therefore time could be taken in ensuring they would not enter the mainstream consciousness, only two witnesses had made any comment on the unusual nature of the rescue. Most, it seemed, had assumed they had heard an explosion just before Steve burst through the aircraft floor, or that he was wearing body armour which explained how he was left unharmed from the gunfire. Even those witnesses whose comments could have been unusual seemed to self-rationalise that the "blur" of movement and "unnaturally fast reactions" were probably more their perception of how it happened. Still, subtle references to how stress can make you perceive things vastly differently from how they occurred would be mentioned in a few daily papers and on a couple of the news channels, just for good measure. It should at least provide a point of reference in the event of any more witnesses later becoming more vocal about the rescue mission. But for today, the SAS were getting the plaudits. Good PR for the UK Armed Forces and no civilian casualties. All in all, a marvellous result given what could have been. *The Boss* would be pleased, which was just as well as Dr Gmitrowicz knew he would not be so happy once he found out what else they were about to do that day. Fletcher sat silent for most of the journey, his thoughts wandering between reliving the Stansted rescue, thinking of Sam and becoming increasingly aware of his subconscious being on overdrive and becoming more tangible. As they got nearer to their destination, he began to slowly drift into a state of semi-conscious stupor, like the sleep of an early morning commuter on a tube train, vaguely aware of the stops but also drifting occasionally into another state of consciousness. It was as the doctor had predicted, his body was still adjusting fully to its new equilibrium.

Smoke and noise occupied every inch of space immediately around him. And dust, thick in the air like a gluey soup. The strange sensation of pain and numbness ebbed and flowed in competing claw strokes at his midriff for a few seconds, and then swiftly faded. He braced himself for the violent jolt of an explosion, which hit him suddenly and ferociously. He was pushed back a matter of inches but stood firm in the face of its onslaught. Then, through the dust and debris he could see comrades, trapped and injured by the bombs aftermath. He rushed to their aide, tossing rubble aside like used paper towels. They were saved if not safe and his attention turned to the direction of the enemy...

'Steve? Steve we are almost there now.' Dr Gmitrowicz seemed to try and awaken him with the gentle attention of a young mother tending to her first born. He opened his eyes and smiled just as they turned into the *Facility*. It was another military establishment, though this one appeared to have very little in the way of visible security bar the gate and small building, actually more of a hut than a building, where the sole army officer sat in splendid solitude. He didn't even look up, simply opened the gate and carried on doing what he was doing, which appeared to be reading a book.
'They already know we are cleared...' Jane stated, almost as if she had read *his* mind. Steve's smile merged into a wry smirk. They drove deeper into the site, taking about three minutes to arrive at a small white brick building with old metal framed windows. It was rather innocuous looking to say the least.
'Is this it?' enquired Steve, Dr Gmitrowicz nodded her response.
'You take me to the nicest places.'
Inside the building was empty, to the point of abandonment. In the centre a small rectangular brick structure with wooden double doors stood out as being odd for its mere existence and positioning there. Jane held her pass card up to the flaking painted wall at the right of the doors. They immediately slid away into the surrounding walls revealing far more aesthetically appealing shiny sheer brushed metal doors, which then opened to reveal a large lift fitted out with the same metal finish inside.
'These must be hard to keep clean.' Steve remarked out loud to himself through a quizzical expression.

'This lift would still be standing if a direct hit from a nuclear missile occurred, and we'd be perfectly safe inside too.' Steve curled his bottom lip in respectful admiration of that fact.
'Impressive. Be a bit small to spend the next ten thousand years in though.' Jane smiled and fixed her gaze directly at him.
'It's not the only part that would withstand that blast.' Her timing impeccable, as the doors opened to reveal another vast underground facility. 'In fact, nothing can get in or out of this facility without the right security clearance. Not even you.'

The floor they had arrived at had further lifts besides the one which they had exited, presumably for access to other levels though for what purpose it was not immediately obvious, the decor generally being dull, mundane with no signage visible anywhere. Somewhat unsurprisingly, considering it was a secret facility. They walked out across the cavernous space in front of them towards another metallic "door", which simply looked like a small flush shiny square set to one end of the dull wall about 200 metres from the lift-shaft. It was also rather overshadowed by the immense expanse of metal that occupied the wall to the left of it, two doors literally hundreds of metres square. Although Steve barely noticed them, his mind becoming aware of something behind the small door that they were headed for. He instinctively slowed a little as they drew nearer, surprising Jane a little with the look of instinctive caution on his face.
'What's wrong?' she enquired, stopping just in front of him and laying a hand gently on his shoulder.
'The *Source*, it is here isn't it? Beyond that door. I can feel it.' Then shifting his gaze to the Doctor rather than the door.
'We are connected somehow, aren't we?' Dr Gmitrowicz once again looked a little surprised, drew a subtle but sharp intake of breath and thought carefully about her response.
'In a way, yes I suppose you could say that…' They continued their progress in silence. Once inside the entrance, the more familiar sterile bright interior was present.
'It feels like a Prison Hospital in here.' Steve's voice tone not appearing to have any particular inflection to indicate whether he was simply making a statement or asking a question. Jane began to show Steve the way forward, only for him to walk ahead of her to stand in front of what looked like a mirrored glass door. He turned once again as if to say "OK, open the door then". Dr Gmitrowicz held her card to the locking device and then punched in a short command. Instead of opening however the mirrored effect faded to render the incredibly thick glass door transparent, and allow Steve to see inside.

The steam rose off the textured takeaway coffee cup in his hand as he looked out over the river. The medieval ramparts glowed softly in the artificial light and the bright lights on the other side of the Thames seemed to slightly twinkle in reply. Luke took a large glug of tepid beige liquid as he turned back around to look at the Tower of London itself. As a symbol of a bygone era, of Royal power, it was about as evocative as you could get in Britain. The perfect target to send a "coded" message back to his former employers in Her Majesty's Armed Forces, as well as hit the headlines. In the furore that would ensue afterwards no one would expect him to attempt to obtain the next target on his list, not least because it would be about as far away as you could get in mainland Britain from the Tower. It was also a very different bounty to the Crown Jewels, though both would probably be damaging to the powers that be, albeit for very differing reasons. He downed the remaining coffee with silicon additive and threw the empty receptacle into the nearest bin, got out his note pad once more and gently circled the entrance through which he planned to exit, to the East of the Waterloo Barracks.
'Been a fair while since Thomas Blood tried to do it.' He mused out loud, drawing a worried look from a Japanese tourist. 'It is 'bought time a professional had a go.'
And he would, on Monday sixteenth December at about fifteen hundred hours to be precise. And if he took his time for once, Luke was sure that the police response would provide him with some support if the resident security services weren't enough to ease his appetite for a good workout. "Get some rest this w'nd G, next week's gonna b bizi" he texted, then crushed the handset and dropped the jagged fragments into the same bin he'd just targeted from ten feet away. Very busy indeed. He returned his gaze to the opposite page of the pad, "Faslane" and tapped the tickets to Clyde Station in his pocket. It may take all day to get there, but the seventeenth promised to be even more of a thrill ride than the Tower. This weekend he'd be doing reconnaissance and planning for the main event, then travelling back to start the action on Monday afternoon. He felt the buzz of excitement and anticipation for the events to come.

The flat was empty, which was no surprise as she had come home quite a bit earlier than normal. Needed time to have a think about what her priorities in life were now as well as how she envisaged their next conversation going. Things had certainly changed in the last few days! Up until now she felt content, happy with everything as it was but now she was beginning to realise that it was never going to be possible to continue that way forever. Steve being away, Luke, the escalation of the *"Houdini Gang"* situation, there was a heck of a lot of sorting out to be done. All starting with her home life. Thanks to Steve's text letting her know he'd be late back she knew there was just enough time to have a bath with a glass of wine to help ease the stress she was feeling. Or rather ease the pressure that she'd put herself under. If nothing else, the liaison with Luke had helped to put one thing into a perspective of sorts. If Steve had been unfaithful, then they were even. Sam couldn't help but feel though that maybe, only she had that guilt to bear.

'Where are we?'
'In the space that binds us all together, the time only we can experience in this way. I thought it the best place for us to commune, we will not be interrupted here.'
'Who are those shadows over there?'
'The other ones, like us. They though cannot feel this space. To them the Nexus doesn't exist. They are blind to it. And we can only half see them through it.'
'So, who are you?'
'I am the one Jane calls "The Source".'
'And what do you call yourself?'
'Ruedrav'tor. My name is Ruedrav'tor. I am the closest to you from the space I originated in. I am also enhanced to be what I am. My purpose has always been to protect, though I did not know that it was so at first.'
'So we are the same... the same type?'
'In a way, I understand what you try to mean. We are the same but in different spaces. In different nows. You and your... brethren?... are not at the same distance in their journey as mine. So this is more difficult for me to explain in a way you will easily understand.'
'You... you are from another world?'
'Another everything. Both close yet to all intents and purposes impossibly far away. Only we can pass safely through the schism of the Nexus and stay in each other's realm unharmed for any great length of time. It is a side effect of our Enhancement. Before I came we could only send our machines to explore your universe in depth. There is such vastness of nothing in your realm, as in many.'
'Why have you come?'
'Because it was necessary, it had to be done, we have much to do together. But first you must stop one of the others... The one called Dyer. He should never have received our gift. His...soul?

He is not either brave warrior or protector. He will continue to think and act only for himself until all is destroyed. Fortunately his greed blinds him to much that you already know of what can be seen...'

'You mean this don't you? And hearing other things that haven't been spoken? Some form of extra sensory perception. Telepathy?'

'Space and time bend even though you cannot see it. "All this" and all you say are how we can get a sneak glimpse of that, seeing, feeling or hearing more than one instant at once. Dyer is blind to the possibilities, blind to the fact. Make no mistake though. His lack of empathy makes him dangerous in a different way altogether.'

Steve became aware again of Jane placing her hand on his shoulder.

'So how long has he been here?' Breaking the silence that had accompanied his long hard stare at *The Source*.

'Classified.' Was Jane's abrupt response, 'Longer than I have worked for *The Organisation*.' She added, essentially admitting that she ostensibly didn't precisely know either.

'Why is he sleeping?' Jane spun round to face Steve. The question seemed to catch her a little by surprise.

'*The Source* has been in an induced coma ever since we found it apparently.' Steve turned to face her, gazing with the quizzical intensity of somebody trying to second guess what had previously happened.

'You think he is an Extra-terrestrial, an Alien, don't you? From another world?'

'Well, probably. What other explanations are there? A genetically engineered agent of one of our world's superpowers?' Eyebrow's raised to emphasise the rhetorical challenge. Steve smiled the kind of smile that a child would have if they knew something you did not.

'You'd be surprised... He is the opposite of me, isn't he?' Jane shrugged to signal that the question seemed to her to be out of context, nonsensical.

'In what way do you mean?'

'Mostly Silicon based, a little bit of Carbon *en*hanced.' the doctor turned back to face *the Source*.

'We believe *The Source* comes from a world where Silicon and Carbon combined early in the evolutionary process. Certain functions are Carbon based, defensive/offensive processes we believe, though we are not clear why that would be the case from an evolutionary benefit perspective. Core processes are mostly carried out on Silicon based physiology, as is the external organ, the skin. The ufo-logists would probably classify it as a Reptilian, due to the appearance of the skin but that is where the similarity ends. What really fascinated us was how the different components interact, the fact that the Silicon compounds somehow get around the problem of the lack of symmetry typically inherent in silicon and ultimately that led us down the path to *the Process*.' Fletcher smiled once more and decided to keep his own council and not share the experience he'd just had. It was clear to him that in Ruedrav'tor's world Carbon and Silicon were themselves mirror images of our universe's basic laws. Hence why it would be advantageous to augment their physiology with Carbon in the first place. Jane continued. 'The one thing I have always wondered was why it was alone?' she asked almost as if she expected Steve to have the answer. 'Why its people have not come to rescue it?'

'Maybe he took a one-way ticket?' It was his turn to face his colleague 'Is it right to hold another being like this?'

'You know what you are capable of. It was deemed too much of a threat to our security to have an agent of an unknown power in a state that could pose a risk to our people or worse…' He could sense the words did not completely chime with her own world view, as Jane subconsciously reached for her crucifix.

The Boss had been kept up to date on the "rescue" mission at Stansted and latterly on the subsequent diversion home. He was glad that the mission had been successfully completed with seemingly little acknowledgement to the extraordinary methods employed. In a way, Steve's interest in *the Source* was also welcome. Thankfully it was something Dyer had shown no inclining of wanting to understand, no hint of an interest in where they had discovered the route to *the Process*. In both understanding some of the origin of his abilities Steve would also, implicitly, understand that he was genuinely not invulnerable too. Having a comparable being pragmatically shown as incarcerated would probably be enough to help ensure he did not develop some kind of "god" complex himself. Even if the way in which he'd guessed at *The Source's* very existence seemed somewhat otherworldly, almost supernatural.

'Sir? I have Mr Desmond on the phone, shall I put him through?' *The Boss* nodded his approval.

'Ahh, Mr Desmond. Good to hear from you so soon after our last meeting. I trust you have seen the latest on our little test operation?'

'Yes I have. Thought I would call to say congratulations. Somehow you seem to have pulled off a very public display without raising undue suspicion. Expertly done. It should go quite some way to allaying fears of creating another loose cannon.'
'Indeed. With reference to our "problem child", Dr Gmitrowicz thanked your sources for the data. Nothing conclusive as yet but it seems to certainly support a central, south eastern location as being a base of operations although there are several potential incidents of Silicon acquisition in the East Midlands area that the Met boys have not picked up on.'
'That is the other reason for the call… the Detectives I highlighted to you have been very diligent. A credit to the force it must be said. Well, in fairness, the forensic team has played no small part, mind you given the investment in their facilities it should be no surprise really. Anyhow, they have discovered something they do not know the significance of yet. Dyer's DNA. Thankfully we deleted his original DNA from the Armed Forces database as you suggested but they have worked out that the samples they have obtained from the recent shooting have been "corrupted" with Silicon. So the sooner our problem child is eradicated the better.'
In other words, Desmond was making the point that not enough had been done to warrant any easing up on *The Organisation's* half.
'I thought you were going to get the cases moved on?' That was certainly the impression that the *Civil Servant* had left him with yesterday evening.
'We have applied the necessary pressure subtly. Unfortunately this particular DI is well regarded so has been given some wiggle room by his superiors. I do not want to apply any greater force unless I really have to, that kind of influence has to be used sparingly. Too much noise, too often and someone somewhere might hear precisely what is going on…' *The Boss* knew exactly what Desmond was getting at and had to reluctantly agree.
'I am not in the business of destroying the career of someone who has been a good servant to our country. We will get to Dyer, Mr Desmond, I stake my life on it.' A moment's silence after the call was ended. *The Boss* found himself staring blankly at an old photo of his squad from the early eighties. He missed the camaraderie of being in the mainstream armed forces, even after all these years. The honest simplicity of giving and receiving orders. As the head of this *Organisation* he could often feel alone. Only as the years mounted this became something he was more and more aware of. 'You will be stopped, Dyer, make no mistake. I will not rest until I have undone what I have caused.' Running his fingers across the front of his hair line and

composing himself once more, this time conventionally pressing the comms link to his PA. 'Get me Gmitrowicz on the phone, please.'

Steve turned the key slowly in the front door, not expecting any sign of life in the flat. To his surprise, the lights were on and he could see a hurriedly and scruffily half packed suitcase on the bed.
'Sam?' It seemed a bit of a stupid thing to say in a questioning tone; obviously she was there unless a particularly targeted yet somewhat ham-fisted burglary was taking place. She emerged from behind a wardrobe door. 'What is going on?' continuing the well-constructed inquisition.
'I… I have been thinking over what has happened the last few days… and I think I need some time alone to figure out what it all means.' Steve didn't need his newly *en*hanced intuition to feel that this was about more than just his recent absence. But what?
'OK. I guess it has all turned a bit upside down lately…' He strangely did not feel as upset by this turn of events as he would've anticipated. 'Where are you going?' he enquired, almost casually.
'To stay with a friend. This isn't all about things you have done though. It's as much about how I am feeling as anything else, the last few days have just made me realise that.' She was holding back something, he could sense she daren't even think about it 'as she spoke. Which was unfortunate. He was sure though that to stay with a "friend" may not be actually where she was going.
'Pretty rubbish timing though.' Sam smiled her acknowledgement of that fact, throwing the last few garments she had selected into the case and zipping it shut tight. 'Let's talk after the weekend?' The words seemed genuine, but Steve could not help and think the sentiment was somewhat hollow and artificial.
'Okay.' Was his short response. Sam wrapped herself in her coat, and awkwardly kissed him on his cheek to say goodbye, then was gone. 'Great Friday night this is.' He sarcastically muttered to himself, and pulled out a small pack of silicon supplement, shaking it between his forefinger and thumb. 'Best order an Indian for one…'

'Desmond!' The civil servant answered his phone abruptly and with no small measure of arrogance. 'Ah minister, yes it has been a long week…' realising that it was one of his "unofficial seniors" his mode of communication instantly changed to sickening obsequiousness. The next ten minutes were spent explaining how he had personally overseen the successful liberation of the crew and passengers at Stansted and the subsequent, successful spin on how the rescue had taken place. The shameless self-promotion was somewhat wasted on its recipient however, who grew tired of the broadcast and finally cut to the chase of why she'd rung.

'Desmond, the reason for the late call is regarding our friends at the Metropolitan Police. You know they have stumbled on a possible link to Silicon and the "Houdini Gang"? Thankfully they have no reason as yet to suspect anything more than contamination as a reason for its presence but this character Hayes seems a surprisingly tenacious sort, given his length of service.'

'Yes indeed, he would appear to be a credit to his profession-'

'Which is precisely why we must tread carefully on how we steer him away from making any more accurate assessments as to what the silicon link means… Any suggestions?' Desmond visibly bristled at the blatant challenge for him to provide a quick solution. It was however something he had already thought long and hard about.

'Well, minister, I would suggest that we use some closer observation of this DI to ensure we are informed of as much of his thoughts and movements over the coming days, and perhaps we could find a way of restricting any budget that may possibly be used in fine tuning their understanding of the Silicon present in Dyer's DNA?' The minister was audibly proud of his swiftly delivered solutions.

'Seems you have thought long and hard about this. I'll authorise the tighter surveillance if you can get the papers on my home desk by Midnight and press the button on the "budget freeze" on further analysis of the DNA samples. I'd also suggest at some point we need to get some eyes and ears within their team without drawing too much attention to it. I'll let you figure out how and when we need to do that. We also need to find a plausible use for the Silicon that we can subtly introduce to the investigative team. Can you get some of the team on that?' The need to be able to think of one last thing was normally amusing to Desmond but felt like a cheap shot this late on a Friday.

'I am sure they have already thought of one…'

Chapter Eight

Sam awoke to that strange feeling of disorientation that you get when you are in an unfamiliar place. Not for the first time recently. However, today she was alone and the location was The Savoy, in a very expensive suite. What was the point of having a mini-existential crisis if you could not at least enjoy some of your ill-gotten gains? Clambering over the unceremoniously dumped travel bag in the middle of the floor, she arrived at the en-suite to inspect how she had faired that night. Looking tired, the rigours of a watershed week had left their mark. Grabbing her tooth brush she continued to stare thoughtfully into her own reflected eyes, looking absurdly for some kind of reaction. In the cold light of the morning one thing had managed to prove to be the right decision, not contacting Luke last night.

What she needed was space and time alone. It had enabled her to, at a minimum, understand her feelings for Steve a little better. And they were that he made Sam feel safe. That was, aside from anything physical or his sense of humour, the main thing he gave her. What she had now figured out was that mattered less than it had when they first got together. Time and life moved on. Safe could easily be bought now, somewhere sunnier and warmer and one hundred per cent on her terms. Excitement, uncertainty, variety. These things were what she really wanted, craved in fact. Luke could temporarily be a part of that. Things could change long term. It did not matter though; she would not need to rely on anybody else once the next *Houdini Gang* project had been fulfilled, in fact she had already reached that watershed some months ago, now being rich beyond her wildest dreams with the next pay day simply ensuring she'd never run out of money. She grabbed her phone.
'Hi Gel it is Sam here, how do you fancy a night on the town, on me...'

The sleeper train into Glasgow had been a mind numbingly boring experience for Dyer. Its seemingly endless, slow tedium seemed heightened by the low levels of *sil-adrenalin* that seemed to constantly course through his veins when he had an up and coming project to consider. He'd probably only slept a few hours and the reality was he would have been able to make the journey quicker under his own steam but that seemed a

somewhat extravagant waste of energy, energy he'd need in a couple of days' time. Now he stood silently on the shores of Loch Lomond, a matter of miles from the Naval Base at Faslane, merely a few moments of travel for him. He figured that this remote location, where naval nuclear warheads were kept, offered the best opportunity to get his hands on one and deliver it off-shore to Bahajoub's men. Nobody would expect him to be able to get the merchandise out into the sea without a pre-arranged and easily tracked power boat and certainly not that he would be able to get as far out as St Kilda under his own steam. In his opinion, it would be the most expedient and lowest risk option. Bahajoub had the task that weekend of getting a boat organised off the small Scottish Isle in the Atlantic, and had congratulated Dyer on his choice of handover location but had seemed too keen to understand how it could possibly be delivered there undetected and in such a small-time frame.
'It's how we do things here, the how is our intellectual property.' Was Luke's grandiose reply. 'If it was easy, everyone would be doing it...'

Dyer had his trusty pad and pen with him and sat on a nearby rock to draw out, in a blur, rough plans for extracting the target. From what he could see at the eastern perimeter of Faslane, there was approximately two to three miles between the outskirts of the facility and the complex of secure buildings and entrances set a little way back from the coast. The active warheads were stored underground in single entrance storage bunker. Bahajoub's team had provided him with excellent intelligence in that regard. One-way in, one way out. It was the simplest structure to defend with a heavily armed presence, allowing for all focus to be applied on letting no unauthorised personnel gain access to the devices, period. The sheer physicality of the location probably prevented even he from audaciously attempting to enter the secure chamber by any other route. Not that that mattered particularly, he was quite looking forward to a very visible and violent smash and grab raid. In his ruck sack, neatly rolled in military fashion were the camouflage overalls he'd worn whilst carrying out his reconnaissance mission, which he intended to wear for the full blown operation. They were tough but light and as there was no need to wear many layers (feeling cold was no longer an issue) there was no need to pile on restrictive padded clothing simply to avoid raising curious looks.

Jane sat alone in the control room at the Shard, sifting through the analytics that had been created overnight from the data handed over to her by *The Boss*. The Silicon related raids, when combined with the known and accepted *Houdini Gang* crimes provided a little insight as to the possible location from which Dyer was operating. Despite the odd location that seemed out of pattern, the majority of locations pointed to a central London base, probably Central to West London at first best guestimate. Still a staggeringly large area if considered from the statistical perspective how many homes were crammed into this densely populated part of Britain. In reality the data had only slightly reduced the size of haystack in which the needle they sought could be found. If any greater light was to be shed on this puzzle then some further cross correlating data would need to be applied to eke out the desired clarity. A far monitor suddenly caught her attention. A traffic camera monitoring a stretch of the A40 road. In the periphery of the picture, she could see the familiar square outline of a standard issue traffic control speed camera. How many of those things were there in and around London? Moreover, how often were they triggered off when no visible, or logical, reason was apparent? Maybe that data existed somewhere and possibly it would hold the key to narrowing down their search area. In the mean-time focussing *Organisation* operatives on "keeping an eye out" from London Bridge westwards was about all Dr Gmitrowicz could meaningfully advise.

At that moment, with his usual robustness, *The Boss* burst into the room for their meeting arranged late on Friday night. He perched precariously on the edge of a desk surface a few feet away from her.
'So, apart from taking unilateral decisions on divulging information classified way, way above DV level clearance what else have you managed to over achieve on since we last sat down together?' Scathing, pointed sarcasm. On the positive side, it was good to be able to understand precisely what mood the big man was in this morning.
'I don't know if this counts precisely but I can state some potentially interesting observations on our latest recruit and I would be interested from a professional perspective to understand your view on them.' *The Boss* grunted his interest and compliance to Jane's request. The scientist continued her tack of steering the conversation away from her recent unilateral decision making. 'You were part of the original team on *Project Enhance*? Do you know if there was any... any attempt at dialogue with *The Source*? Was there any form of communication had with it?'

'The creature was captured just outside our facility in Rendlesham, in what was best described as a near incapacitated state, just barely conscious from what could be seen by those present... yet...' His hesitation did not seem to be purely due to remembering facts from an event that happened in the previous century. 'Yet, the special force's team that secured *the Source* and brought it to the original secure location all independently reported during their debrief a sense of... a sense of being at ease with the creature. An odd sort of ease, they thought they instinctively knew they should be alarmed, on edge, or maybe in fear of it but felt as if... as if they had been personally assured it meant them no harm. One individual reported that despite orders he had made prolonged eye contact with the creature and described the feeling as being as safe and reassuring as looking into his parent's eyes.'

The Boss refocused his thoughts. 'What relevance does this have to Steve?' Gmitrowicz paused for thought, still unsure exactly how to frame her observations, aligned to her somewhat unscientific gut feel.
'Just that when he was in close proximity to *the Source* there was a few moments when Steve appeared to be, distant I guess. Day dreaming, unaware and unresponsive. Then shortly after when we spoke there was a strange guardedness to the conversation. Like he already knew some of the answers to questions he was asking.' She lingered for a moment, and then tapped the computer screen in front of her to bring up a chart. *The Boss* leant towards the screen for a better view, commenting 'You scientists love a graph...'
'And this one is showing a small but significant surge in power consumption at the same time as our visit to the facility. That is the blue line. The other lines are the key diagnostics we have been measuring for life support. The purple one we believe corresponds to brain wave activity. Probably equivalent to REM sleep associated Alpha Waves in humans.'
'Believe?' the big man interjected.
'Yes, we are dealing with a unique and previously unknown morphology here. And as the creature has been sedated for longer than the records go back, we have no firm benchmark on what conscious vital signs would look like. It is a pretty educated "Believe" though.'
'So why is this significant or related to Steve?'
'Well, it's the fact that this activity occurred whilst he was present. It's an unusual coincidence aligned to an observed subtle change in behaviour from Steve also. Might be just a pure coincidence.'

The Boss chewed over the information for a few moments.
'And this is a completely new set of measures.' Jane smiled at his inquisitive clarification.
'No, no there was a recent similar set of results recorded during *The Process*. Along with some other anomalous readings that may have been caused by the presence of Tachyons. In fact, looking through the records there were two other incidents of power surges noted, corresponding with less pronounced brain wave activity. I'll need to cross correlate with some additional data to see if there is any sort of pattern here.'
'So if it has happened pre Steve's *Process*, can I assume that they occurred during Dyer's?'
'That I have checked already and no dates match with anything that could tie into Dyer. One occurred before he was even selected for the original process. Many years ago in fact. I can't rule out previous occurrences before Nineteen Ninety Five either. We simply were not in a position to monitor anything meaningfully prior to that point.'
The Boss looked intensely at Jane.
'If this can point to anything that is an advantage over Dyer then we need to monopolise it. Our *Organisation* has already seen its reputation become in danger of going down the pan, yesterday has started to reverse that situation but we need to recover some more of our positive reputation soonest.' Gmitrowicz sat a little straighter in her chair, having a visible flash of clarity, an epiphany.
'Down the pan… do we still have those Micro-bots from the operation to find and destroy any terrorist packages hidden in obscure locations?' *The Boss* nodded, a little bemused at his colleagues complete change of tack. 'Excellent. With a little recalibration they may be able to help us track down our target…' then her focus returned to the readings.

The heavily crumpled brow on *The Boss's* face, even when in a relaxed state, summed up the man quite perfectly. It bore the tell-tale marks of ageing aligned to the internal and external strength he still possessed. It also acted as a very visual signal that he was in deep thought, contemplating what Gmitrowicz was implying, reading between the lines a little too.
'Being a part of *the Organisation* has brought our team many perks,' breaking the moments silence 'but it also has its limitations, Jane. We have quite remarkable levels of funding in one respect, but from a different point of view you could say that we have nowhere near enough support. This is a being from

another world. The greatest discovery and secret of our time, probably of all time. Yet we really have no concept of where or why it is here. For over thirty years that creature has lain in a state of artificial hibernation, yet there appear to be no perceptible visible signs of it growing old. Unlike me.' Chuckling heartily at his introspective thought. 'We understand little more about its origins then we did that day in December 1980. Who knows how that thing communicates? Frankly we can only guess, assume that it is in an induced coma in the first place. For all we know, it could be merely meditating or faking unconsciousness altogether.' Jane nodded in reflective partial agreement then interjected.

'So it is conceivable that this creature communicates in a way we do not understand. Something that resembles say telepathy, or some other process? And that those skills also could be transferred during *the Process*.' The Boss threw her a curious glance.

'What makes you jump to that conclusion?'

'A few things he has said and done. Steve feels a change in his, his equilibrium I guess. It could merely be a mix of his natural intuitive thoughts and processes coupled with his heightened senses making him feel more aware, or it being more accurate through greater stimuli reception. But…'

'But this is the real world, we are at the cutting edge of real science, this is not some weirdo experiment into parapsychology Doctor. We need to deal with facts. We can only manage what we know. You need to keep an eye on this and quantify objectively what is happening. If Steve is experiencing something that gives him an advantage we need to exploit it, if Dyer is capable of something similar he will be even more of a threat than we already think.'

Jenkins noticed that the main briefing room door was open and the familiar sound of soft, firm footsteps could also be heard gently padding around inside. She poked her head around the corner to see Philip slowly pacing back and forth in front of the white board. 'Hayes? What are you doing here this morning, do you not have a home to mope around in?'

'I'm trying to join the dots on this lot. You heard about the consistently contaminated DNA?' The Super nodded acknowledgement. 'Been looking at what Silicon is actually used for, other than as a waterproof bathroom sealant. Obviously it is also used in electronics, in various space technologies. It appears in certain ceramics and well, frankly in a lot more things than I had previously thought. It is not though used in any exotic explosive compounds or known for anything else that could remotely explain its presence at every crime scene suspect DNA sample that we can think of.'

'Could it not be a by-product of some kind of machine? A device they are using to gain access forcibly?'

'Possibly, but why would Silicon be present in such a pervasive way? And why also at the Murder scene we discussed the other day? What reason to kill that woman with such a brutal machine, risking a witness to what must be a pretty large piece of kit, bearing in mind what it would appear to be capable of?' By now Helen had fully entered the room and was sat in a swivel chair surveying the array of information scattered around. 'I was going to ask forensics if they could run some more detailed tests on the DNA samples and other evidence from the main thefts and the murder scene, to try and figure out how they got corrupted so completely by this element.'

'Unfortunately that may be a bit of an issue. I received this note from the Mayor's office this morning via e-mail.' Handing a printed copy to Hayes, who was very much a tactile paper-full rather than paper-less office kind of person. 'Budget freezes, a little earlier than I had expected this year but no surprise really.'

The flash of anger in the DI's eyes diminished almost as quickly as it arose. 'Maybe it is a case of cutting your cloth accordingly. Instead of trying to find out what the cause is I need to get the team to try and figure out how to find the root cause.' Jenkins momentarily crumpled her bottom lip to signify that she did not understand the slightly nuanced difference between the two approaches as he'd stated them. 'Refocus on the reasons for the crimes rather than the mechanics of the operation or trying to establish exactly how they are being carried out. Why are these items being taken? How are they profiting from these raids? Are they getting orders before they obtain the items or vice-versa?'

'The team should be looking at that anyway Hayes.' Chastising him like a head teacher would an errant pupil.

'They are, but not solely with focus… we only have so much money to spend on man power.' Smirking a little at his unsubtle dig at budgets. 'I also want to issue this photo-fit.' Sliding the open file across the desk to his superior. 'It's based on eye witness descriptions of the man last seen with our "unrelated" murder victim.'

'You want to alert the gang to our suspicions of their involvement in this murder? And the public too?'

'Why not? The media think we haven't a clue, so do the criminals themselves probably. Just because we know we haven't joined all the dots doesn't mean we shouldn't give the impression we know more than we do… put some pressure on them. A bit of fear makes you act and think a bit quicker and irrationally, and that brings the possibility of them making a mistake. Which may just give us the break we need.'

'The knock on effect of the public perception could play well here too.' Pausing to gather her thoughts. 'There is a sort of anti-hero fascination with this gang, a romanticised "Robin Hood" image with some members of the public. The murder of an innocent girl being linked to them could spur someone into coming forward. Great idea Philip, you have my backing.'

For a few moments more Hayes stood in silence in front of the whiteboard. Then, he burst into action, the first call being to his trusted DS. 'Killen? Did I wake you? Look, I want you to get out and about, tap up a few contacts. Someone somewhere must have a sniff of how this lot gets shifted or even better, what the next big job may be. We'll have more luck working in the criminal world we understand rather than trying to figure out the world of science fiction the forensic evidence is leading us down. Careful with the incentives though, the budgets are being squeezed again…'

It was in many respects surprisingly green, open and wild just a few miles north of the M25 motorway that encircled Greater London. Fletcher stood alone at the top of a small hillock surveying the fields, spinneys and thicker clumps of full blown forest that made up the Hertfordshire countryside. Sure there were towns and villages interspersed throughout the panorama in front and behind him but he was quite alone, unseen by any human eyes. It was the perfect place to practice a little further some of his newly acquired skills and abilities. Having already jogged at seventy miles per hour for about thirty miles or so, now was time to do some weight training as well as try to work out some of the frustration he was feeling at what was happening to him personally. The felled oak tree trunk was bulky enough to present a little bit of resistance for him though in all honesty it felt a little light to truly be a test. He knew he could have used the facilities at *the Organisation* but, well, he felt like feeling the wind in his face today. To be free to think, as much as anything else. Worst case he was wearing his "uniform" black track kit and had the balaclava ready just in case.

Chucking the tree to one side he sat down on an old stump and listened, with more than just his ears. He began to feel his own thoughts as if they were as tangible as the mulch on the floor below his feet. This crazy situation, the improbable changes that *the Process* had delivered, *the Organisation*, even Sam leaving, it all seemed to make some kind of weird sense. Almost like he'd waited half his life for this time to happen. It was amazing how much information you could take on when you can read at eight times the speed you previously could. Sat in front of his tablet scanning reams of virtual world pages on multiple dimensions, multiverses, quantum physics, theories of existence and what it means to be alive, contemplating the nature of reality itself. There were some real wackos on the net. Well, to be precise Steve would have thought them completely mad before but now some of the more outlandish theories seemed to make some sense, given what he had experienced in the past week.

As well as his own thoughts, the sounds of people, animals, machines near and far were all crystal clear to him. In addition, he was aware that *The Source* could be simultaneously next to him and a long way away. There if he wanted to communicate with it. Which he did not right now. This was pretty much as close to solitude as you could get south of Yorkshire, allowing some much-needed space. Steve skimmed a stone across the body of water approximately half a kilometre down the slope from where he sat. It pounded into the bank opposite, causing debris to be flung up in the air as if by an explosion. Why could he feel a creature from another now yet feel nothing of Sam, of where she was or how she felt? Or anything of Dyer, aside from a half-seen shadow in the back of a thought? 'The more you know, the more you are able to realise how much you don't understand.' He muttered to himself, rising to his feet. A swift jog back to the car was probably the best thing to do now. And maybe a visit to his Father's grave on Sunday. Maybe that would help him square off some of the madness that had recently happed to him, as well as that which had yet to come to pass.

Bahajoub was a picture of gentlemanly elegance, resplendent in the opulence of the hotel tea room where he felt most definitely at home. He'd organised the unit to collect the "package" from Dyer's team off the remote Scottish island, pausing only momentarily to wonder how or indeed if it was even plausible for them to get the merchandise there on time, without being pursued by the military. This was, however, the *Houdini Gang* after all, and their exploits were the stuff of modern legend, the talk of sitting rooms up and down the land, globally in fact. The

phone vibrated discreetly on the table top once more. It was his client.
'Ah sir, you have once again pre-empted the need for me to call you. We have a plan, a delivery date and we also have transportation to deliver the tool you wish to obtain safely into your hands. Our friends have asked if we could help off load some items from their diversion which may be of interest to you also. I am sending some information to you via our secure shared server. No, no I have a plan B which I will be getting one of my representatives to talk to me about a little later, as I know that this is the kind purchase only a few would be brave enough to consider taking on.' A long pause ensued, the mildly delusional rantings of an egotist mixed with almost unbridled machismo and self-referential rhetoric around the fact that nothing would be too bold for him, that is until he saw the objects to which Bahajoub was referring. Then a gentle but none the less swift dismount from his self-erected pedestal. Although adding a smaller item from the available shop front for his own, private, mementos collection was a possibility. Then a cursory congratulation getting the complex operation organised thus far and a sinister offering of "good luck" to finish, backed with an unspoken dose of menace. Placing his phone down next to the fine china tea cup with the careful dexterity of a wine merchant laying down a fine bottle of Chateau Lafite, Bahajoub's air of reserved control was completely unbroken. 'Excuse me, another tea please?' Self-assured in the fact that if anything were to go wrong it would be before he had any direct responsibility over the merchandise that was being acquired.

It was a fairly standard, retro-styled set of low level, recently built apartment blocks. As Killen pulled up outside the sheer ordinariness of the location struck her. It screamed nothing to see here. Move on. Except in flat Twenty-Two B lived a girl with her finger firmly on the pulse of the London high end black market. Want to buy a rare example of a model T Ford? She could find the "supply route" and arrange for the shipping too. Want to sell a somewhat "hot" piece of exclusive sculpture, a buyer would be found but for a price. And unfortunately "price" was also a consideration when it came to information. Luckily though price is derived from value, which is not always best measured in money. She pressed the intercom button for Twenty-Two B.
'It's Killen.' The buzzer triggered, no words spoken at the other end. When she got to the second floor flat the front door was already open ajar. Inside there was enough technology and computing power to run a small nation.

'So, you're after some help with your enquiries DS?' Her accent and precise pronunciation giving the air of a professional business meeting to discuss paper supplies for a major multi-national business. Killen pulled up a six-wheeled leather office chair and sat right by the smart but unassuming woman in her late thirties.
'Well, I naturally thought of you when I asked myself the question "who would know the latest gossip in the London underground market".' The dealer chuckled at the unintentional pun.
'Very good. Kind of giving away the secrets of the trade that one, don't you think?' The DS shrugged nonchalantly in reply.
'Sort of showing you the "Crown Jewels" of my unique value proposition, as it were.' And once again laughing at the comment and particularly the emphasis. Killen screwed up her face in puzzlement. 'I guess so…'
'What is in it for me this time? It's not exactly reputation enhancing to risk my various clients' confidentiality or their supply routes suddenly getting closed down in a way that points the finger of blame anywhere near my direction? Not to mention the personal costs of missing out on a lucrative deal commission.' Killen lent a little further forward.
'Bold move, getting yourself this flat in your own name. Makes you a little more visible to those who might be unaware of your arrangements with Her Majesty's Metropolitan police force. On both sides of the track…' allowing a little instant for the connotation implied within the statement to fully sink home.
'Would only take for one loose comment in the wrong environment and who knows what people might think? Or do?'
'I thought protection rackets were illegal?' remarked the dealer, slouching further back into her own leather clad chair and folding her arms instinctively to form a protective barrier between them.
'We're here to protect and serve…' If sarcasm were a liquid, that comment would have looked and felt like treacle.
'OK. Well there are a few rumbles on the grape vine. Not got much on the painting from the Gherkin but have heard about some pre-orders for a large job being sought. Sounds the sort of audacious target the objects of your desire would attempt. And you don't get many more high profile locations than where they reside…'

Chapter Nine

Monday had arrived. The big day. A day which would permanently affect so many destinies. The day before one that could change the political landscape of the world forever. Perhaps fittingly, everyone was up and "at work" early today. Hayes and Killen were briefing the team on the intelligence received and in part corroborated over the weekend. All information appeared to confirm the potential attempt to steal the Crown Jewels that evening. In fact, as far as Hayes was concerned, too many unconnected individuals seemed to have an inkling that the target was a possible goer. It smelt a little suspicious to his old nose, borderline publicised. But it was a pretty definitive, positive lead, something they could work with, which was a vast improvement on their position seventy-two hours earlier.

The consensus decision was that a small team of undercover police would be deployed, posing as beefeaters, at the Tower of London from ten hundred hours that morning, with the armed response unit to be installed on standby at the nearby Tower Bridge Police Station. The greater team was notified of their roles and responsibilities, with staffing resources set to peak around twenty-three hundred hours until oh two hundred hours that night, the most likely time window for the attempt to take place due to a number of factors, not least the fact that there would be fewer witnesses and less traffic to hinder the planned getaway. The command centre would be patched into a number of surrounding area CCTV units at strategically selected vantage points too, with monitoring for any unusual activity already taking place. Any recorded material from these locations over the past week was being reviewed to also identify any clues that could pre-warn the operation of any information that may help.
'Killen, anything worthwhile cropped up from the video playbacks?'
'Nothing as yet guv, it's a needle in a haystack search to say the least, and we don't know what that needle looks like. There are a hell of a lot of visitors to the Tower of London every day, even in winter.'
Hayes nodded his acknowledgement whilst picking up the phone to speak with the forensic. He knew the budgets had been squeezed but also knew that curiosity would have driven him to try and ascertain something more than he had previously. The

call went through to voicemail and he left a message anyway. The frustration of being potentially a lot nearer to capturing the criminals yet still having very little clue as to what to be prepared for ate at him, adding to his nervousness and apprehension. This was as close to stage fright as he had ever experienced.

The Boss, Gmitrowicz and Fletcher were all in the meeting room at *The Organisation's* offices located at The Shard for an early morning brief as well. Mr Desmond had handily passed on the intelligence gained from the Met's operation over to *The Boss* late on Sunday evening, with constant updates on the mobilisation of the forces throughout the day being patched straight to the "war-board" projected on to the meeting room presentation centre suite.
'How reliable are the sources being used by the boys in blue?' enquired Jane, trying as always to objectively assess what needed to be planned for and how likely the potential need to mobilise swiftly later that day would be.
'Well, dealing with a bunch of informants and individuals that operate in the black economy and criminal underworld has some inherent risks around the integrity of any information forthcoming but the old adage, no smoke without fire, would seem rather apt don't you think? Certainly our friends in law enforcement seem pretty convinced, they have a significant team of people involved in this operation so appear themselves to rate it as very likely to occur.'
'I guess we have a slight advantage in that we know the nature of the thief and the potential route he will take to gain access to the objective?' Fletcher surmised inquisitively eyeing the war-board.
'Possibly Steve, I believe that the logic they have used to build a view of the logistics around gaining access obviously assumes a vehicle is always required for getaway purposes. Dyer will still want to retain an air of mystery about how the crimes are committed so I would see access coming from somewhere around the Byward Tower towards the south west side of the complex. Though, to be frank, almost any direction is a possibility. I have, however, punched access into a number of cameras around the West London area we identified over the weekend as a possible base of operations for Dyer, just in case it gives us a few moments advantage in intercepting him before he gets there.'
'As luck would have it, we are somewhat ideally placed to observe and react from our location here. Steve, I suggest that you take in the briefing and training sessions on the X2C as

planned in the training centre and we will keep the intercom line open to patch through anything of note to you.'

'Do you think I will need to use this X2C against Dyer today?' *The Boss* momentarily wore a very school boy grin. 'Ahh, no. you will see why once you've had the brief. But having the capability to use it as soon as possible will be a benefit to your operational capabilities in the future. You never know when it may come in handy...'

'But you will definitely need this,' Dr Gmitrowicz carefully handed over a small package. 'Have you ever had to use an adrenalin pen before? This works on the same principle, except it is diamond tipped to ensure it can efficiently pierce *En*hanced skin and has enough bio-engineered sedative to send you to sleep for about twenty four hours. Should be just the trick for you to incapacitate Dyer.'

Grimes sat at his old imperious desk, staring into space. The next forty-eight hours would be massively eventful even in comparison to some of the times that had recently gone before. The practice would need to be shut down swiftly and without providing any clues or any trace as to where he personally had moved on to, or indeed who he'd become. It would also still need to appear completely unconnected with *The Houdini Gang*, to look like simply a middle-aged guy who'd had enough with the daily grind and jacked it all in to see the world. Fed up with the rat race. 'It's 'bought time I had a mid-life crisis anyhow.' He thought out loud, comfortable that nobody was within earshot. His subconscious was guiding his pen as he sat thinking. Splurging out his innermost thoughts in a seemingly random series of swirls, diamonds and lines. "Why?" was suddenly scrawled next to his attempt at surrealist art. The thought made him sit upright and alert in the leather-bound chair, attentive to his own minds subconscious machinations. Why indeed. Why wait for this extremely risky set of transactions to become complete? Could he not escape right now, flee before anyone was alerted to the fact that the objective of tomorrow's project would make the disappearance of the Crown Jewels appear to be somewhat trivial, irrelevant? The universe conspired to give him an answer to his musings of fleeing forthwith.

The mobile on his desk vibrated, the number displayed was unmistakeably another pay as you go handset utilised by Dyer. He doubted that the planet was big enough to offer somewhere safe from discovery by Luke and that made being caught by the

authorities seem like a seven star hotel in Dubai in comparison to whatever punishment he would exact.
'Bit slow on answering the phone this morning old boy? Too much pre-work relaxation last night was it?' Dyer was obviously high on adrenalin and anticipation already.
'No, no I was just a little bit away from the handset. Everything on track your end?'
'Yes, I have the timeline for instigation of our first shopping raid and will drop off the packages at our agreed destination en-route to shopping expedition two. The courier for further delivery has been organised I take it?'
'Yes, at the agreed meet point at Grantham services. Have you spoken to the banker?'
'Not yet, next call on my list.' Luke paused, thinking a moment on how he felt about that conversation. 'we are pretty much prepared and ready to roll. I will make contact with you tomorrow morning on the next set of phones.' And the call was ended, leaving Grimes to his private thoughts once more.

Luke destroyed the handset as he normally did, then produced a second phone and proceeded to ring Sam. They had not spoken any further that weekend and although Luke felt that was probably best, a little pang of something did momentarily come into existence as he rang the number. Sam meanwhile was already in the office doing her best to look like she was bothered with the day job. She felt the buzz of the phone on vibrate in her pocket.
'Hi, are we ready to receive our little extra gifts from tonight and the final instalment tomorrow?'
'Everything is set and ready to go…' The pregnant pause was long and awkward. Sam ended it.
'I guess we can meet after the project is completed to, well, talk about the next steps?'
'Sounds like a good idea. I will get back to my apartment in the afternoon. Let's meet at the coffee bar opposite, should be able to have shaken any tails I may have picked up by the time I have finished the journey.'
Dyer smiled to himself as he disposed of the second phone and checked his watch, wishing the hours away.

Jane was back in her office, both reviewing the data sift which had been further processed on *The Houdini Gang* and the other linked crimes information as well as keeping a half eye on the monitoring taking place as Fletcher went through his paces. There was nothing major to note in the data sift so she turned her attention once more to the diagnostic information on the mission at Stansted Airport and the aftermath at the installation where *The Source* was housed. So much of what they were doing here was at the edge, well way beyond the cutting edge of scientific understanding. She wouldn't have minded betting that if they could directly detect Tachyons then they would have been present.

Her focus shifted a little, bringing up the data file on *the Source* itself. The initial team of scientists involved with studying the being and ultimately developing *the Process* had taken an unsurprisingly clinical view of proceedings and of the subject. Very cold, factually based observations. But little in the file, little that she could access anyway, suggested more than a cursory discussion and analysis of where it originated from or why it appeared to be anthropomorphic. The main reasoning appeared to be an assumption of some form of Galactic Convergent Evolution, an acceptance that the basic humanoid shape was a "universal blueprint" for intelligent life. Why? They had no directly observable evidence as to whether this creature was or was not truly intelligent. They had not really considered the potential for it to be no more than some sort of artificial, biologically engineered robotic probe, something made to resemble the shape of the dominant, sentient creatures it would encounter on Earth. Essentially Jane posited that there was no such thing as truly objective truth and that the facts were probably interpreted to back up their own opinions and views at that time. It was, after all, decades ago, scientific thinking and knowledge had moved on at an unstoppably exponential pace since that point.

The power surges that had occurred on Friday when Steve was at the facility were not currently present as he trained on the X2C. Gmitrowicz had set up access to the real-time monitoring of *the Source* and associated measurements from the facility on her smartphone so she could observe significant changes as they happened.
'All we can do now is sit and wait.' She murmured to herself as she reclined gently in the chair, staring at the air conditioning ceiling vent just above her desk. 'Hi, can we ensure Steve is posted from noon in the operations van just outside the Tower? Network Engineers will be the cover story.'

The Tower was particularly packed that afternoon, given it was a Monday and still technically school time. Ordinarily three p.m. was probably the worst time you could pick to attempt an audacious theft of a set of high profile national treasures. Perfect. So many innocent bystanders would significantly inhibit the ability of the police and any onsite army personnel to respond swiftly with force, and the surrounding melee of weekday traffic would add to the difficulty for Her Majesty's constabulary to impede escape. Dyer had breezed in like any other tourist, paying cash on the door to be certain there were no easily identifiable traces that would give the boys in blue too many clues, though he figured that it would only be a matter of time before some link was made after this robbery by his former employers, and if not definitely the next one! The security had carried out a little bit more than a normal cursory inspection of the ruck sack but they essentially had no reason to suspect that the folds of material at the bottom were anything other than a pack-a-mac or similar, though the scan for explosives did make him raise a subtle eyebrow. There was nothing in there to raise any suspicion, no tools or weapons. This would be an event that would confuse, excite and amaze the authorities and the general public at large. The anticipation he felt was almost unbearable.

Ten past three. Dyer was now approaching the Jewel House. There were two Beefeaters guarding the entrance and a further couple situated at the exit. Despite the relatively meticulous planning hitherto of raids, Luke had not quite made his mind up on when to neutralise the guards in the vicinity of the objective, until now. Placing the ruck sack on his back, a cap and dark glasses on his head and cracking his knuckles, then swiftly in a blur almost too quickly for the human eye to see, he sprang from a standing start. In one smooth motion, he launched both of the guards thirty foot into the air in opposite directions, one of them being used as a living bowling ball to take out the guards manning the exit as he landed, solving two problems in one hit.

Eleven minutes past three. In *the Organisation's* mobile command centre the onset of the raid had been spotted and Fletcher despatched, leaping silently and unobserved over the north wall, headed straight for the Jewel House. In parallel, the ops room at the Tower Hill police station had received the garbled message of what was apparently an explosion taking out all of the undercover policemen guarding the Jewel Room. The CCTV appeared to show the after effects of the explosion but no flash or evidence of any resultant damage. It also appeared to show a single individual entering the room.
'Shit, how the hell did they get their equipment in there without us noticing? Scramble the armed response team NOW.' Hayes

swivelled on his chair and faced Killen, 'We should have them now, can't believe they have the arrogance to try this one in broad daylight!'

'Get the public evacuated now!' Ordered Killen over the radio link to the team on site. 'Bring up the CCTV feed from the objective on the main screen.'

Inside the room, Dyer unfurled the large sports bag into which he intended to load the spoils. Moments later, he stood before the main display cabinet to re-appraise himself of where the precise merchandise he had selected to resell sat. These were the items that would make a significant statement against the country, against the crown, as well as fetch the highest return for the investment of his effort. Then, before enacting the extraction, he threw two small coins, one at each of the CCTV cameras that were observing the interior of the jewel room, blasting them from their mountings and rendering them inoperable. The Queen's head used to disable the Queen's security cameras. What beautiful irony. Only now, assured that his methods would retain an air of mystery, Dyer smashed through the thickened safety glass and within a matter of mere seconds had loaded all of the items into his bag.

'The feeds have gone off line.' Stated one of the officers positioned in front of the monitors, in a rather matter of fact manner.

'What? How the hell?' Hayes reacted immediately and aggressively. Due to his heightened state of focus thoughts and spoken words were merged as one.

'They have literally just gone off line; here are the pictures just before they went off.'

Twelve minutes past. The sound of warning sirens rang out all around the grounds.

'Can everyone please move swiftly towards the exits? This is not a drill. Repeat, this is not a drill.'

The guards, police and Beefeaters were very suddenly everywhere, surrounding at a safe distance of about twenty five metres the Jewel Room. Fletcher stood somewhat unnoticed on a high wall directly overlooking the chaos, like a boiler suited, balaclava wearing gargoyle. He knew from his earpiece that Dyer was already inside and had disabled the cameras so there would be no chance of unauthorised hands capturing images of either of them inside, but that did not stop the fact that the CCTV outside the building was still functional.

'Big Brother is now off air.' Crackled the voice in his ear, prompting him to launch himself with pretty much spot on accuracy towards the same entrance via which Dyer had entered, landing squarely through the doorway and several feet into the building.

'Have we got our eyeball in place yet?' Hayes was incandescent with anger at being completely cut off from what was happening on the ground.
'Yes, all immediately available resources are in place, surrounding the scene at a safe distance. Patching through to the mobile head cam now.'
The pixelated image sprang to life on the main screen, showing nothing more than the entrance and exit to the building. All was reasonably calm given the circumstances.
'This is Hayes here, initiate contact with the suspect please, let them know we are there and armed.' Though only two armed officers were in attendance now, he figured only they knew that fact. The officer in command on site duly obliged.

Meanwhile, within the room, Dyer turned to face the dark silhouette of a stranger.
'Oh dear, what do we have here a "have a go" hero? Mate, you really do not want to try my patience.' The stranger stood motionless and silently. 'Seriously, the whole ninja thing might do it for your girlfriend but it is not working on me.' Under the material Fletcher smiled.
'Well Luke, I am not sure that Sceptre is really in your colour either. It's a bit ostentatious don't you think?' The arrogant and mocking expression on Dyer's face dropped into a mixture of shock and inquisitiveness, then in moments was replaced by the look of pure aggression as he took the said precious object and swung it rapidly at Steve's head only for it to be caught relatively simply, the knuckle side of his hand momentarily touching his left cheek. A partially pallid look of realisation now took over Luke's countenance.
'Fight fire with fire?' Then the more familiar faintly maniacal grin returned as Dyer pushed Steve back with immense force into the solid stone wall behind him and blurred out of the room in one continuous flowing movement.

Three Thirteen. First Dyer then Fletcher burst out of the Jewel Room to witness the cordon of armed and unarmed personnel.
'Friends of yours?' Quipped Luke before leaping effortlessly towards the river side of the Tower before the officer in charge could even start to bark orders for them both to stand still and put their hands up. The ensemble, still staring in motionless

amazement skyward in the direction Luke had travelled were then further dumfounded by the dark and featureless outline of Fletcher following on in hot pursuit. A couple of tourists who were still in the vicinity had managed to get out their mobile phones and capture the very tail end of the seemingly impossible escape made by the second of the two individuals that they would later presume to be members of the famous *Houdini Gang*. Dyer landed on the perimeter wall overlooking the river and turned to face his pursuer just as he slammed into him at waist height in a classic rugby style tackle. They fell to the concrete below, causing cracks to radiate out in concentric circles, as if a mini-earthquake had affected a twenty-foot square area of the City. With fantastic agility, Luke kicked Fletcher off him and high into the London air, his silhouette barely visible in the fading winter light. The shock and unexpected stress caused by this surprise turn of events fuelled the exact exciting thrill he'd been craving for some time now. Dyer launched himself at a trajectory intended to intercept Steve's arcing fall. The impact sending them both back into the Tower's grounds, deflecting off the perimeter wall as they travelled causing untold expensive damage to the ancient rampart as they did so.

The police team were rooted to the spot, transfixed by the spectacle of a cartoon battle made real.
'What the hell? Are you getting this back at base?' Killen and Hayes certainly were, and both were dumbstruck at the scenes they were witnessing. 'How shall we proceed, over?'
'They appear to be fighting, Guv.' The DS felt obliged to fill the void with an observation. Stating the exceedingly bloody obvious.
'Yes... Maybe they have had a disagreement over the spoils.' Then directing his next comment to the team on the ground.
'Issue them a warning that you will open fire, then if they do not cease, aim to immobilise them both.'

Three Fourteen.
'I am ordering you to put down your weapons and raise your hands in the air otherwise we will open fire. Do you understand?' The barked order caught both their attentions momentarily. Steve seized the moment of slight distraction and launched a thunderous right hook square on Dyer's chin, sending him ten foot to the left of where they had landed, smashing into a bench and removing it from its securely mounted position.
'Ah, just what I need.' remarked Luke as he swivelled on the spot and flung the mangled metalwork directly towards the armed police, just as the order to fire was about to be issued. With

sickening accuracy, it scythed several of the officers down. Fletcher witnessed the carnage in horror. The disgust turning quickly into anger. 'Well this has been fun but I really must try to get these goods to their buyers.' Turning towards the south once more and sprinting off. Luke's sarcasm and evident indifference at the pain inflicted further fuelled Steve's rage as he followed in hot pursuit.

Within moments they had leapt over the rampart once more and landed near to the crater they had recently created. Dyer turned to face Steve once more. Fletcher felt the modified *sil-adrenaline-pen* that would deliver the specifically designed sedative directly into the bloodstream in his jacket pocket. However, he did not take it out in readiness to administer it. Instead, intuition kicked in and he rapidly dived to his left in an attempt to avoid the spinning projectile Luke was in the process of unleashing. It struck with immense force, tearing through his right shoulder just above the chest and exited instantly just below the shoulder blade, causing him to momentarily black out through the searing pain whilst thudding into the pavement. In the moments of unconsciousness, Dyer seized his chance of escape, retrieving the Koh-I-Noor diamond, his improvised projectile of choice as he did so, heading straight for the Thames leaping fifty plus feet into the grey murky waters below. Steve came to, the blood had stopped and the healing process was already progressing. Looking around, still dazed and not knowing what had happened to his target he too took to the river to avoid further witnesses, though with much less speed and grace, tumbling in to it a matter of feet from the riverbank itself.

The carnage at the Tower was still visible on the main screen in the ops room. Hayes barked an order to stop the images being patched to the wall, causing the screen to flicker off and the images to only be visible on the small monitor by Philip and his Sergeant.
'What the bloody hell just happened here?' Killen thought out loud, momentarily forgetting her usual fastidious respectful phraseology in front of her superior officer.
'The Armed response unit are arriving now, sir.' Interjected one of the team.
'Damn it! Too late. We should have seen this coming. It's just like this lot to attempt something like this, doing the unthinkable and pulling this off in the middle of the day!' Slumping into his chair as he made the remark, turning to face Killen very close up. 'That was insane; we definitely both saw that didn't we?' She nodded

her reply. 'We need to look again at the video we have managed to receive as soon as we get that area secure – Get the chopper in the air and feeds from the surrounding CCTV cameras ASAP. We need to get a fix on how these two escaped and where they have gone.' They probably simply disappeared in a puff of smoke or got beamed up, Hayes thought to himself.

'At least we have the frames from inside the Jewel room before the cameras ceased functioning, sir. We should be able to get some level of ID for one of them. It might be our best lead yet.' Killen's optimism drawing out the merest hint of hope from the Inspector's eyes.

Confusion, chaos. Murky smoky clouds billowing this way and that. Floating almost weightlessly in the thick of it all. Stabbing, tormenting pain throughout his torso, slowly but surely subsiding but agonising none the less. The dull echo of a distant, violent explosion. People, in the shadows, familiar yet distant. Have to help them, must get to them.

'Steve. Steve you cannot help them now.'

'Why? I must, it's my duty, my job.'

'Indeed, it's your calling if you must. But you cannot help these echoes. Their time has gone, you cannot reach back to fix what has been. Only what will be-.'

<'Help me - Take...my...hand...Ste-.'>

'I… I remember that voice.'

'And you will always. But you cannot blame yourself for their fate. You were not able to help then as you can now. You were learning to be the protector you are meant to be. It is those who aggressed who are to blame. Your future will help you find peace with their memory.'

A deafening, sickening thud. The shadows were no longer in view though he could feel their presence still, suppressed and nagging. The swirling grey clouds threatened to envelop him forever. Then the Source called to him once more through the Nexus, shining a beacon to show him the route to escape.

'You will succeed, You must. Let the shadows of the past lie where they be.' *And he felt the strong guiding hand helping him clear of the gloom, towards freedom. One final glance at the dancing stars, three of them – two closer, one further, the third almost out of view. Then, escape.*

Back by the south bank of the Thames, Steve phased back firmly into reality, what was left of the entry and exit wounds rapidly becoming less scarred and the movement in his shoulder almost back to "normal". About a hundred yards up stream he could see the small unmarked *Organisation* boat and feeling his senses had properly returned, swam rapidly in torpedo like fashion towards it, leaping effortlessly onto the rear deck then disappearing inside the blacked-out cabin before he could be seen.

'Did you get the tracking device onto him?' barked Jane, who could see the obligatory questions about how he felt were not as relevant as they were thirty seconds prior.

'I got it somewhere as I fell, though it may have been on the bag. A bit of a split-second reaction.' Gmitrowicz looked at the small left hand monitor.

'We have a connection and it's moving. West, along the Thames. Already beyond Westminster bridge. Patch us into the CCTV network along the West London Thames area.'

There were crowds everywhere around the north bank of the Thames by Westminster Bridge and the less than perfect quality of some of the CCTV cameras available meant it was near impossible to make out one bag carrying approximately six-foot-tall male from another, especially when a number of the images were in black and white. The tracking device though appeared to be remaining motionless.

'Can we get a fix on the tracker device's precise co-ordinates?' asked Jane of one of her colleagues sharing the floating office with them. 'TBHP-224-MJH seems to be the best bet camera-wise Doctor Gmitrowicz, good vantage point with colour and zoom capability. We will try to get a clearer image immediately.'

Holding their breath in anticipation momentarily, the image was patched to the main screen as the instructions were fed into the remote eye. The picture grew clearer, the details of the spot where the signal was emanating from more visible. The fact that there was no one in the vicinity even remotely matching Dyer became obvious seconds before the detached device became visible, attached precariously to a vertical drain pipe on the wall by the pavement about four feet from the ground.

'Damn it! Uh!' uncharacteristically Jane let her temper get the better of her, not so much thumping the table as firmly letting it know how she felt. A plastic cup of water wobbled for a few small moments. 'He is either very lucky or rightly paranoid and found the device too quickly.'

'Shall we continue monitoring the CCTV in the area Doctor?' She frowned at the request for direction. They were back in the realm of searching for needles in haystacks once more.

'Yes for the next ten minutes or so, and take in key vantage points to the west for a bit longer. A long shot but he may be

going back to base first and that may bring us the lucky break *we* need.' Even with the tech at their disposal, the sheer number of people and the size of task involved in finding Luke in such a short window of opportunity was a challenge. Steve had already been thinking of a solution.
'Jane, could we not get the Met looking too, in the areas we suspect he may have headed into? Anonymously? We can monitor exactly what they are doing, right?' Gmitrowicz nodded her response, quizzical at where his thought pattern was going. 'Let's give them a hint, keep out an ear for anything positive and I try to get there before too much attention is drawn to the scene? Not like we could be much more exposed publicly than we already are with what has just happened, is it?' Fletcher remained steely faced, staring disconcertingly and unwaveringly. 'I need to run that pass *the Boss*, we've already pushed the boundaries a few times in the last week, haven't we?'

'I have the merchandise, am on route and will be on time.' Dyer then disposed of the phone in the obligatory manner, whilst disappearing down the subway to the tube station. The car he'd sourced for cash a few days earlier was parked at Brent Cross, from where he would head towards the A1 and north to the drop off point at Grantham Services. Luke banked on the police still not fully grasping his abilities and therefore not looking for him on the underground network so far away from the Tower, so soon after the robbery. He hadn't, however, considered that *the Organisation* would be in a position to engage him at the Tower or be alerted to his activity today. That made him nervous and a little excited. At last a foe worthy of the challenge. On the tube he drew nothing more than suppressed and stifled interest from his fellow passengers. Only on a London tube would a soaking wet man in December be so purposefully ignored. Many passengers fearing what reaction staring too intently at such a clearly deranged individual could bring. Dyer smirked quietly to himself, gripping firmly the ill-gotten gains of the past hours work as he left the Tube and nonchalantly strolled towards the public car park, placing, with the gentle care of a mother laying her newly born child down to sleep, the Crown Jewels into the foot well by the rear passenger side seat. Now for the two-hour journey to the drop off point, then the long trek back up to Faslane and the main course!

It didn't take long for the news of the latest *Houdini Gang* robbery to be trumpeted on every available channel and source. Social media almost completely crashed under the surge, especially when the footage of a somewhat pixelated shadow seemingly leaping through the air in the distance was posted then inexplicably removed only a matter of moments later. #HoaxHoudini trended as much as #WTFflyingthief and general chatter on the #Conspiracy line about the video being removed by the #Illuminati, #PrimeMinister or #Pope amongst numerous others. "Was it an imported and escaped Chubacupra?" became a contentious debating point within ten minutes of the raid, then someone who knew their London mythology hit on the theme that would stick.

"#SpringHeeledJack is obviously back from the dead, straight out of Victorian London!" the comment grabbed the mood and pretty soon London Radio stations had picked up on it and referenced it in their subsequent *Houdini Gang* bulletins. "Is Spring Heeled Jack the culprit behind all of the *Houdini Gang* crimes?" with a number of phone in radio stations getting equally vociferous callers bemoaning the censorship of the mobile phone clip by the powers that be with others bitterly complaining about the blatantly made up story of the two "eye witnesses" who now could conveniently no longer find the video clip file on their handsets either. "Does *Houdini Gang* have secret government weaponry?" was probably the most sensible, grounded sound bite to be heard in the immediate aftermath and furore of this latest incident, which, let's face it, would still be pretty ridiculous if it wasn't ironically quite accurate in this case. None of this, however, seemed to be pointing at anything particularly substantial, the Police were pretty tight lipped about the whole affair and, more importantly, no further witnesses had, as yet, come forward to state they had seen one or both men disappearing into the Thames, or emerging elsewhere. The speed of the incident hitting cyberspace had thankfully still lagged behind the reality of the two *en*hanced individuals escaping in that regard. This did not stop the perceptible rage burning off *The Boss* filling the room back at *The Organisation's* Headquarters.

'Dyer appears to have slipped through the CCTV net before we could get another fix on him. We have surveillance operating in the west London area so will have a fix on him when and if he heads back to where we believe he is based.' Jane avoided making direct eye contact with the big man much like one would avert their eyes when in the presence of a Silverback Gorilla, for fear of provoking an attack. It did not stop him from emitting a low groan reminiscent of a growl.

'How is Steve?' The barked tone of the question making all in the command room stiffen up a little.

'Appears fully recovered, he is being checked over in the Medical room, scanning for any internal damage that has not healed but,' glancing at her tablet 'all appears in order.' Looking at the device prompted her to note that the tell-tale signs of a suspected Tachyon spike and power surge at the facility where *the Source* was house had recently occurred, precisely around the time of the incident at the Tower. The icy atmosphere was abruptly cut in two by the shrill ring of *The Boss's* mobile. It was the *Civil Servant*, no doubt ringing to voice governmental displeasure at the whole situation. He threw the phone to one of the team present.

'Take that will you, and tell him I will call him back when I have a positive update to share.' Turning his incandescent glare back to Dr Gmitrowicz 'We need to get a fix on Dyer now, and Steve needs to be ready and prepared to take him down, no matter what it takes. Do I make myself clear?' Jane visibly gulped.

'I think we should be in a position to know at least one location where we will find him within the next two hours.'

'I sincerely hope so, Jane. I do not want to annoy my old Doctor by having to personally take the stress of resolving Dyer.' She had no idea quite what *the Boss* meant by the threat but she knew it was a line that really ought not to be crossed.

'We have teams looking for clues around the area where the tracking device became detached. We may find something useful that could help point to his next move.'

The immediate environment was dark, dank and toxic. The smell of methane and rotten detritus lay heavy in the air with vomit-inducing intensity. Although it seemed impossible, life thrived even in this rancid location, with slimy jelly-like mounds of bacteria rising like stalagmites at sporadic and random intervals. Through the dingy air it was possible to make out the sound of small, four-footed animals scurrying busily around, scratching out a meagre living. It is a little-known fact that the Greater London Area sewerage system predominantly uses gravity to help waste flow west to east, although, as the original Victorian infrastructure was expanded and augmented, pumping systems had been installed to provide a more artificial flushing of the system. One such system exists in Chelsea.

It presented a massive obstacle for two of the seven Micro-bots that had been deployed into the sewers at separate locations around West London. Fortunately they were all linked via an artificial intelligence system that acted very much like a "hive-mind", relaying the trail of evidence they had picked up on to their cohort elsewhere in the vast labyrinthine tunnel and pipe system. As they slowly began to converge on an ever increasingly smaller area, the unusually high levels of Silicate residue began to increase and point inexorably towards the source from where it entered the complex system. That point lied somewhere within a square mile area of the network and it would only be a matter of time before those Micro-bots, not inhibited by the Chelsea Pumping Station, would pinpoint it. Dr Gmitrowicz had truly thought outside the box for this unique piece of detective work and it was very, very close to bearing fruit.

In a somewhat narcissistic manner, Dyer listened intently to every news radio station he encountered as he travelled at a sensible pace along the A1, not wanting to delay himself further whilst carrying the "petty cash" merchandise en-route to delivery, by having to deal with the traffic police. Apart from anything else, there was a desire to conserve energy before the main event, and the drive was still a long one albeit not an overly taxing one for an *en*hanced individual. The Chupacabra theory in particular made him chuckle and appealed to his sense of being "an alien" stranger, an outsider in the normal world everybody else inhabited. Luke had never heard of Spring Heeled Jack and found himself listening intently to various wacky "experts" coming out of the woodwork, describing the odd mix of demonic and almost steampunk Victorian vision of futuristic technological gizmos attributed to his new alias. Either handle was infinitely more agreeable and accurate a description of him than that of *The Houdini Gang*, which now was only used to describe the fact that two of its members had been spotted using the same technical wizardry to both overpower and escape the long arms of the law. The Met Police spokesperson had very little to say, though speculation that they had been tipped off about the raid and had still failed in apprehending them was rife. Good, the more pillars of the establishment he could singlehandedly tarnish or even totally bring down by his actions the better.

Despite the decidedly pedestrian progress towards Grantham, the time passed swiftly and he arrived at the services, parked up and waited for the Blue van to arrive and give the prearranged three flashes of its headlights to signal arrival, which it duly did. Dyer had taken the precaution of changing into some dry clothes whilst he waited, taking virtually no time at all to do so even in the confines of the car. A final, now instinctive, glance around the vicinity, before heading towards the van to hand over the inconspicuous bag to the two occupants. They observed him with the fearful respect one might use when seeing a wild tiger entering the forest clearing you had been camping in. He relaxed a little; these were traders not fighters who evidently felt uncomfortably out of their depth in his company. Playfully he gave the Van a slight but perceptibly violent tap as he strolled away, drawing childlike squeals of fear from the men and causing him to laugh a little theatrically in reply. All in all a good days work, with the main event sure to be even more exciting. *The Organisation* had both failed to stop him neither would it be able to identify where he was now headed, this he was sure of. There would be no reason for them to even suspect he would try another operation tomorrow, let alone guess at the location or the target of his ambition. It was, after all, a complete departure from anything he'd targeted before so why should he change his pattern? Not even an *en*hanced operative could cover the ground from London to Faslane in sufficient time to interfere with his plan. That rematch would have to wait for another day and gave him something else to look forward to.

It was amazing that despite the constant pressure on budgets, the minute something smelt like a high profile, highly visible failure, there was seemingly no end to the staggering amount of expensive resources that would appear out of the woodwork to pick the bones of the failed carcass. If as many officers had been allocated to the Tower operation as were now engaged in dissecting its every orifice it would have almost undoubtedly have been an overwhelming success.
'Frankly ma'am, these are extraordinary, unprecedented circumstances here. We're dealing with criminals that go way beyond the level of professional. They presumably had the tech to jam the entire CCTV networks within a significant radius around the Tower, their mode of escape, whatever the hell the weapons were that they possess, left our team horribly exposed and under prepared-'
'But,' interjected Jenkins 'but irrespective of that, your operation fundamentally failed to consider the potential time they decided to execute, was slow to react-'
'And on what basis were we to reasonably be able to come to the conclusion that they'd seriously attempt such an operation in the middle of the afternoon?' Hayes' generally grey façade looking remarkably scarlet with genuine incredulity, tinged with an inward embarrassment at being subjected to such a dressing down. Jenkins broke her gaze to consult her notes.

'Just like this lot to try something like this – That's what you stated to Sergeant Killen was it not?' Philip sighed with the emotion of a naughty pupil being caught out by their teacher for lying about what they had done with their homework.
'With hindsight. That comment was made with the benefit of hindsight.' The silence filled the gap with all the cold comfort of frozen slush occupying the space between a foot and its sock within the confines of a boot.
'People are watching very closely now, Philip. You have no further margin for error, we need to see some significant progress within the next forty-eight hours or I will have to move this project on to someone else. It is too political now to accommodate your…your personal style and idiosyncrasies.'

Back in his office the rampant indignation he felt began to slowly ease. Through the glass in the door the scene of the internal inquisition that was taking place could be viewed in detached solitude. Killen broke that third eye serenity with a gentle tap requesting permission to enter, which was given begrudgingly.
'You will not like what I have to tell you, sir.' To which Hayes pulled an expression of resigned submission to the realisation that the universe was definitely against him. 'The CCTV files are corrupted.' Silence. The DI slowly raised himself out of the chair and floated over to the edge of the room.
'Corrupted?' Killen nodded her reply. 'Then we are pretty screwed. Is the IT bunch looking at the problem?'
'The specialists are the ones who have given us this news. We could look to see if the Cybercrime unit could spare some resource, just in case they have been purposely tampered with but…' Hayes interjected during the natural pause of her speech.
'But our stock is not so high right now? They're pretty unlikely to wish to be seen to be involved at the moment?' Another nod of agreement. 'How I hate inter-department politics.' Glancing down at his shoes. 'Nothing from the crime scene to help us so far?'
'No guv, nothing immediate. We can't find anything that indicates what explosives were used, what weapons they possess. The eyewitness statements make absolutely zero sense; you should have a preliminary report in your inbox by nineteen thirty tonight. It will not make pleasant bed-time reading though.' Hayes looked directly into the Sergeant's eyes.
'Thanks Killen. I will take it home with me and pray for some divine inspiration. Any progress on figuring out what the silicon has been used for?' Killen gave a look that summed up her answer perfectly. 'Looks like we both have some searching to do tonight.'

It had seemed an age since the events at the Tower. Patience was one of the virtues she had inherited from her mother but even Jane had been infected via some sort of emotional osmosis by the perceptible anxiousness that *The Boss* had whipped up around *the Organisation's* Headquarters. It was, therefore, with quite some relief that she received the two pieces of news that a phone had been recovered just a few hundred yards north of the detached tracking device as well as the Micro-bots converging at the main sewer entrance from a very exclusive block of apartments by the Thames. That was about as definitive as they could have hoped for. This gave them at least a location to observe and await the eventual return of Dyer, though there was still the potential of getting an even more precise location. It was also suitably close enough for them to deploy Fletcher from HQ, so he could remain available to be despatched and engage if their number one target was identified in another location in the meantime. The mobile phone was literally being delivered to the "on demand" science lab, which sat directly behind the command centre as she returned from the relative peace and quiet of her office. News that the Micro-bots had more or less located where Dyer lived had already filtered through to *The Boss*, tempering his mood.

'Doctor Gmitrowicz?' Her colleagues questioning tone aimed at getting her attention. 'This package has just arrived.' Handing over the hermetically sealed parcel. It was obvious without opening the pack that what lay inside was a fragmented device. 'Hmmm, John, can you see if we can get some forensic confirmation that this was indeed our targets phone, and try and get some data from it?' Jane's colleague gave a look of self-assured derision. 'And what is wrong?'
'It was a pretty basic handset Doctor, doubt there's much data to recover?' Gmitrowicz took the opportunity to give a glance of condescending smugness by return.
'Should be able to get some call details, or even just the telephone number? I can figure out the rest.' With which she continued to proceed towards where the big man stood. For a few moments they stood silently side by side, watching minutes of CCTV images whizz by in fast scan mode on the big screen.
'Steve had quite a good suggestion at little earlier. How we could get the Met Police helping us out. Got me thinking. With the details I can extract from that device there may be a contact they can look into that will help us get to Dyer sooner than simply waiting for him to return to where we think he is living. After all,

he might have homes all over the UK for all we know.' At that moment *The Boss* looked down at his mobile phone which buzzed in a frustrated manner, in keeping with the general mood. This time he took the call from the *Civil Servant*.
'Ahh, I'm glad you called. We might have a couple of breakthroughs in finding our target. We might also need you to get some information to the Met without giving away where it has come from.' Turning toward Gmitrowicz, a small smile as they glanced at each other momentarily. Adversity could be a fantastic team building experience, and they'd been through that a lot together in their time with *The Organisation*.

It was around eight thirty in the evening by the time Hayes eventually decided to leave the office and take the report back home to finish reading. So deep in thought as he left the building that before he realised it his progress home was stopped on the street corner by a stranger, a woman who was faintly familiar.
'Inspector Hayes? I'm Keeley Whitworth.' The outstretched hand was met with blank indifference. 'My readers wonder how you are feeling about the failed operation today?' Ahh, a reporter for The London News.
'Ms Whitworth, you should know better than to try this cheap seventies gutter press trick on me, really. You know I cannot comment on any ongoing investigation outside of designated press conferences. You have all the comment we can give at this stage.' Moving to leave as the reporter grabbed his arm. The moved stunned him a little, stopping him in his tracks.
'There must be a great deal of pressure on you to get a result here, Philip? All this talk of impossible escapes, Victorian monster myths reborn, crazy weapons. What is the real story here? Why the elaborate smoke screen, hiding the truth but what is that truth?' The questions drew no further visual response, though they had given him half a thought, a feeling of something to be looked into. Whitworth obviously thought there was a conspiracy of some sorts. That intrigued and raised his curiosity a little. With perfect timing a familiar car pulled up to the kerb beside them.
'I think this may be my ride, good evening and good luck with the research into Victorian super-villains back from the dead.' Smirking at the ludicrous notion whilst removing himself from her grip and jumping into the passenger seat.

'Thank you Ma'am.' He exclaimed gratefully whilst firmly ensuring the seat belt was engaged. Jenkins drove them away from the frustrated reporter.

'A little young for you Philip, don't you think.' They smiled at each other to both politely acknowledge the poor attempt at humour. Hayes carried the essence of the thought generated from his brief encounter.

'Why do I get the sense somebody somewhere wants me off this case?' Looking for some sort of reaction. A tell-tale involuntary, neuro-linguistic, subconscious signal from his superior. No such responses were forthcoming.

'I don't think there is anything personal Philip, just a lot of unhealthy political poking in of noses where they normally wouldn't be. These crimes are being treated like some kind of parliamentary football at the moment. I hate to say it but almost any result, regardless of whether it is the main one, would help the cause immensely. Very short sighted, though I would not admit to saying that outside this car.' Smiling much more warmly than in their earlier encounter. 'I rather hoped I would catch you before you entered the underground, we have just had this delivered for your attention.' Pulling out a large brown padded envelope. Hayes felt it but was none the wiser.

'What is it?' He enquired as he slowly peeled it open at one end.

'Call records from a recently destroyed mobile phone. Well, details of a single call. Not long after our friends decided to make a mess of the Tower this afternoon. As I said, any result that is a quick one couldn't be any timelier. If not our gang then the buyers network might help satiate some of the baying for blood from our friends in Westminster. Get your team looking into it ASAP Philip, I don't like having to carry out orders I feel are wrong just as much as you.' Pulling up outside the next station along from his usual one.

'No, I know you don't.' Getting out of the car as he acknowledged her candour. 'But you have learned to hide your feelings a lot better than me on that score.'

The sun rose slowly on what was a crisp, clear December morning. It was the type of day that could easily fool you into thinking spring was on its way, not that is wasn't even past the winter solstice yet. The mist against the hills played out as a seemingly smoky backdrop to the overall vista. Dyer had hardly slept, the buzz of the past few days and his *en*hanced morphology combining to negate the need for much rest. A mile or so, over the hills opposite where he stood, lay Faslane. This was it. The type of day he'd wanted to be involved in ever since he went AWOL. Looking down into his outstretched right palm where he cradled the Saint Christopher his father had given him, he reflected. The charm was there to protect him, apparently. To remind him of the regular beatings he'd taken in the name of discipline, for exhibiting bad behaviour, a symbol of paternal dominance more like. The red mist in his soul boiled over and he launched the potent symbol at the distant horizon. Despite all he'd achieved, his strength, his revenge, the emotions of what had happened still haunted him. Now, with that last act of petulant rage, Luke felt completely and fully released. Freed. And the rush from it was almost overwhelming, causing him to violently shake with sil-adrenaline. This vibration was so rapid as to create the effect of having a fuzzy glow at the edges to the normal human eye.

The Organisation's Tech team had been working through the night trying to piece together as much information out of the fragments of data they'd scrambled together from the call records, the smashed device, the video feeds and the ever-decreasing range of the sewers the micro-bots had been scouring for the source of abnormal levels of silicon in the system. They had located the building, and in fact one device had managed to get up and into the building's internal drainage systems itself. To be able to precisely identify where that was they would need to gain entry to the building itself. The sewer theme gave an obvious cover for the team they sent in at oh eight hundred hours to finally enter the apartment. There were two obvious candidate rooms, with both leaseholders having suspected fake (though excellent quality) identities. One of these apartments turned out to be a fairly famous film star's secret London pad. However, they now knew that the micro-bot had stopped just short of the toilet bowl itself in the other apartment, the residence that had to be Dyer's. Somewhat surreptitiously they gained entry, essentially illegally but needs must.
'Message for *Big Man*, we have found our *Wayward Child's* den. He might want to see this.' Instantly sending a digital image of a note pad left out on the glass top table.' The screen in the control room filled with a couple of scrawled words. "FASLANE TUESDAY".
'Get Gmitrowicz and Steve in here – now!' a moment's pause, 'And get Desmond on the line ASAP.'

It was so long ago as to seem more of a dream than a memory. War had raged for so long that the three worlds were as vast empty shells, harbouring large open wastelands where Mother Nature had begun to slowly reclaim what was always by rights hers. The last great battle had ended almost a generation ago. Only a handful of warriors remained in service and although the truce was a fragile one, the memory of two centuries of conflict was strong enough to marshal and control any hints of re-igniting the flames of aggression. For ten years now he had overseen this peace as well as negotiating, with sensitivity, small steps between all the remaining peoples to become as they once were, various, different but united. For millennia his world had relied on the seers for guidance. Originally they came from all the races of their people but over time the parentage of offspring became controlled to pre select the next generation, making succession an easier process. Over time they had slowly begun to split off into a closely related but nonetheless separate species. Gifted cousins aloof but connected by the family bond. All but three were killed in the wars, their gift of foresight seeming only to ensure they knew how and when their demise could occur, not enabling anyone to prevent what now was known to be the inevitable slaughter.

Ruedrav'tor therefore knew that if the Oracle was calling for him, something significant must have been foreseen. To his culture, the seers were so revered as to be almost godlike, even as his people themselves were more or less as powerful as the gods of their archaic religious belief (the popularity of which had resurged as a beacon of hope during the wasted years of war). Entering the calm, dimly lit sanctum that was the Oracle's residence, the great warrior bowed down on one knee, mindful not to use the full speed and force he possessed lest it damage the delicate silicate floor mosaic that stretched wall to wall.
'Please, rise mighty one. You of all people should be comfortable to stand eye to eye with me.' Rue stood up, still slightly bowed, his immense frame after all significantly dwarfed his companion's.
'I fear that fate has lent me a frame too tall to achieve that comfortably, wise one.' The statement of fact drawing a hearty chuckle.
'Then sit we must, I do not want to have your discomfort on my conscious at this time.' Pointing to two onyx black stones that presented the closest thing to chairs in the room. 'You are aware that our ancestors discovered the true nature of the multiverse many eons ago?' A nodded response sufficed. 'And that in a moment of galactic time we understood that one could not traverse from one plane to another, as the natural laws are different in every other now that is?' A further silent acknowledgement of this known fact, then a spoken response. 'It is why we can only send machines, briefly, to explore those spaces just next to our own.'

'Well, I have had a vision, an epiphany if you will. Some can leave our space-time and enter that of another, but only a special few. Those who possess something, unique.'

The old sage paused, a discernible look of anxiety on his face. It was disconcerting for Ruedrav'tor to witness. He'd never seen one such as he visibly express this emotion before. The Oracle began to elucidate further, 'And it is a vision based on a secret my predecessors have held for as long as our knowledge of the multi-verse, though the full truth has only really been aware to us through the wars we have seen so recently. The true nature of our enemy has filled in the blanks and opened up new questions unanswered.' The focused energy in his gaze returned once more, 'I know I can trust your judgement when I say this must only be spoken of to those as true as you are, Ruedrav'tor. There is a controlling force, malevolent, benevolent and ambivalent in its nature – not caring for the fate of those they control or use for their sole purpose. They operate from beyond our world, beyond all worlds. In the space between spaces, influencing and coercing the weak and power hungry to do their bidding blind of their final objective. One we cannot know or understand as we cannot enter their realm as we cannot enter those other realms of reality.'

Pausing to take a sip of water and then continuing. 'They are the Nemesis, they are the reasons our ancient ancestors believed in Demons and Angels, for in many ways that is what they are. They exist in a way that is separate yet aligned to our existence. They control and influence the thoughts of others, people in our world and beyond, causing conflict and strife where it would otherwise not exist and sometimes providing hope and guidance where it is missing also. In some ways they treat the worlds of others like mere games, playgrounds to act out their will with no determinable outcome or gain.' He stopped abruptly. Silence was the normal state within The Oracle's dominion but this one seemed cutting and electric. The Old Sage intensely concentrating on the Old Warriors expression.

Rue knew that when he spoke, it was often what was not said that was as important as what was. He closed his eyes briefly, and a flavour of a memory from the War flickered momentarily. 'I guess that explains how perfectly the conflict came to be, at a time when our ancestors all believed we had evolved beyond such seemingly primitive occupations as war. For these, these Nemesis willed it to be so… but why they did so, even you do not know.'

'Nor will I ever. It is as the tides or day and night. I know how they come to be, I know what they are. But I do not know why they are, they just are – you see?' Ruedrav'tor nodded agreement somewhat unconvincingly. 'But interfere they do, in many realms other than our own too. And that is why I should bring you into my confidence. I am afraid, noble one, that your services are needed once more. The fate of more than our universe hangs on your selflessness in defence of what is right. And the science that has made you as mighty in this realm means only your kind could survive the mission I have envisaged. And only you of your kind is worthy enough to be willing to sacrifice oneself and accept travelling through the Nexus, the place between places to fulfil it.' Rue visibly edged backwards.
'The Nexus is how you consort with those who have passed on? I do not understand.' He'd never really believed in a literal Nexus, preferring to think of it as merely a metaphor for the legacy all people passed on through their family line. An "inherited" immortality of the genes if you will, a connectedness with the past and the future.
'You are right and wrong mighty one. I have much to share with you of the true nature of the multi-verse. It will be reassuring and disturbing in equal measure, I am sure. And you must only share this knowledge with the ones who demonstrate they are as you are. Lest the Nemesis gain access to our plans through those more susceptible than you or I to their ways.'

The machinery of the country's combined defence forces, both secret and the more conventional and publically visible, can move with amazing speed if the threat level is appropriately high enough. The threat that Luke Dyer now appeared to immediately present was as high as you can get – critical. This terrorism threat level is defined as being "an attack is expected imminently" and nobody could argue that that statement didn't best sum up the current situation. Post his call with Mr Desmond *The Boss* had full clearance to co-ordinate the efforts and forces that would be involved in defending the nuclear armoury housed at Faslane, which was the undoubted probable target they believed their *Wayward Child,* as Dyer would be officially referred to hereon in, was aiming to seize. The purpose of such an acquisition could only be guessed at; it was a left of field move in terms of the previous targets. And that was simply one more disturbing aspect of this new development. Within two minutes of the call, various heads of service and several civil servants, the secretary for Defence, the Prime Minister and the rest of COBRA were all patched into a video conference with *The Organisations* main control centre.

'Good morning all.' *The Boss* addressed the ensemble with remarkable calm as well as his usual authoritarian gravitas. 'Hello, I take it that voice is … *The Boss*. Forgive me for interjecting but there seems to be a problem with your video link.' The Prime Minister speaking out and, as to be expected, looking to stamp a little authority on the somewhat alien situation, especially having to refer to another as *The Boss*.
'Apologies Prime Minister, but the nature of my team's work somewhat dictates an air of secrecy, even from those on this panel. I am sorry also that I have what is a rather unfortunate code name given your respective positions but please, let me get everyone up to speed on the situation. By now you should have the brief on the terrorist group codenamed "*Wayward Child*"?' Nods and grumbles constituted their responses. 'Our sources cannot be described as one hundred percent accurate but given the gravity of the situation I am sure you all agree that we must act swiftly to avert a potential major catastrophe on many, many levels.'
'Can I ask why you feel your, *Organisation*, should be leading our response to this threat?' The Chief of General Staff set out his stall rather predictably, it was massively unprecedented to have his authority discounted so swiftly and comprehensively.
'Because we are the only people with the right security clearance and inside knowledge to deal with it effectively in such short timescales. Any dilution of our specialist knowledge or extension of the circle of individuals with the total picture would put our entire nation at severe risk and indeed many of our international partners.' In the background, Steve smirked at the exchange. A few short weeks ago he'd have never imagined he'd have direct knowledge of facts that The Chief was not allowed to even guess at. Gmitrowicz handed the small package over to Steve and silently mouthed 'Good Luck.'
'We are now dispatching our small response team to the location. It should be on the ground in around ten minutes.'
'That is very fortunate, that your team happen to be located closely to the anticipated event.' Remarked the Prime Minister. 'Is it the case that this threat should have been highlighted a lot sooner?'
The Boss grinned. 'It is fortunate that our team are relatively nearby, the threat was only identified fully fifteen minutes ago.' Meanwhile, Steve had left the room dressed in the obligatory black uniform augmented with integrated goggles and full face

mask. It was time to put the training on the X2C to full use. 'Can I ask that you clear a communications channel for me through to the commanding officer at Faslane immediately? I will then hand over to my colleague, who will perform the role of head of operations for the next few minutes until we neutralise the threat.'

At the top of the Shard a concealed entrance opened just enough to allow something to exit at very high speed. As fast in fact as to appear to be a mere trick of the light. This was accompanied by the rather unfamiliar sound of a sonic boom, which was also easily confused with a rogue clap of thunder above the general noise of the capital in the midst of full, Tuesday, business as usual activity. The X2C at first glance resembled a small relative of the US Stealth fighter, much smaller, possessing a barely ten-foot-wide wingspan and approximately six foot in length. If you could focus on it long enough you would be able to discern that in fact it was barely more than a wing, a tiny RAM jet engine and the fuselage was in fact a man. If you could see below the mask you would also note a grin about as wide as you could possess as Steve experienced for real the rush that the training had promised piloting the X2C would deliver. The outskirts of London were dispatched fairly swiftly as the compact "pocket rocket" continued to accelerate towards its maximum velocity and Faslane.

'Shoulders Back, eyes Front!' The barked familiar phrase brought his thoughts back to the task in hand and caused a small chuckle to be emitted as Luke nonchalantly strode towards the heavily guarded entrance to Faslane. The noticeably extremely heavily guarded entrance, in fact. The palpable alert responsiveness of the troops merely added to his sense of hungry anticipation for what was about to occur. Drawing closer, the pace of his strutting slowed until he stood staring, seemingly calmly, at the nearest armed guard. A few metres back he could easily overhear another of the assembled troops whisper discretely into her radio 'I think we have a potential eyeball on one of our expected threats, sir.' What the hell? Was the base really expecting his arrival or was this a mere coincidence, after all, the country never seemed to be in anything other than a heightened terrorist threat level over the past few decades. Or was Bahajoub part of some sort of elaborate sting operation? No, that made no sense whatsoever and anyway, they'd have tried to engage with him earlier, surely? Maybe that was why he'd been met with such a warm welcoming committee at the sarcophagus hand over? Luke

took in a large lung full of air and refocused on the task in hand, his *sil-drenaline* well and truly flowing now.
'Hello boys, it's good to be back amongst friends and colleagues.' The faintly reptilian smile flashed once more across his face, then he made his first move, tearing the horizontal road barrier from its base whilst the sound of small automatic weapons fire rang out across the open water which the Faslane facility bordered on to.

'We have confirmation that our people on the ground have engaged with a single white male at the entrance, he should be effectively dealt with as we speak.' *The Boss* gave a wry smile at the Chief of General Staff's comment. It was after all an understandable underestimation of the situation in which they found themselves. Automatically he glanced towards Gmitrowicz.
'He should be at the objective within approximately sixty seconds.' Stated Jane, without breaking her gaze from the control screen directly in front of where she sat, the faint sound of Steve's boyish half giggles being the main sound that her single earpiece was relaying to her.
'If you can, captain, order your teams to not get within 50 feet of the attacker... best let us handle him from here.' The Captain on the ground could see exactly why *the Boss* had given such advice and ordered his troops to adopt a managed retreat whilst slowly attempting to contain him. 'If you could also ensure he is kept away from the nuclear warheads that would be a plus.'
'Steve, Dyer has begun his attack, several personnel have already encountered him with presumed severe casualties sustained, preventing further casualties is desired but the main objective is to protect the assets, do you understand.'
<click> 'Yes – understood.' The information having the intended effect of bringing him back to the severity of the situation instantly. The amount of G-force being encountered as the X2C rapidly slowed for landing would have killed you or I, crushing internal organs like jelly between two bricks. For Steve, there was the merest sensation of feeling travel sick momentarily. Then an elongated skidding-thud as his feet made contact with the ground, performing the function of landing skids on a plane touching down at an artic runway, where wheels would be redundant. The spectacle went unwitnessed as the melee within the secure facility continued to escalate.

Fletcher hit the quick release mechanism and in a blur rested the wings down by a sturdy pine tree, the needles gently rained down from the force of his hand on the trunk.

'Our *wayward child* appears to be enjoying himself a little too much.' Catching one poor soldier who'd been tossed, like an old unwanted action figure, over Dyer's shoulder as he progressed steadily towards the entrance of the storage facility. 'I presume emergency services have been alerted?'
'They have been told to keep a safe distance until I give the all-clear signal.'
'Best I get a move on then,' Steve paused 'looks like he's a little more anxious and alert than yesterday, he's scanning all around as he cuts his way through.' At that moment, Dyer stopped and turned to face him, picking out his voice over the chaos that reigned all around. Steve seized the opportunity, throwing a small smoke grenade then, milliseconds after its foggy impact, launched himself towards his target. Meanwhile, Gmitrowicz glanced at the activity monitor feed once more. No tell-tale spike indicating Tachyon activity, only readings consistent with a heightened state of readiness for battle. Through the artificial mist, Fletcher emerged like a human battering ram sending Dyer high into the air over the entrance to the highly secure storage centre for the UK's trident missile system's warheads.
'Let our "team" handle it from here Captain, get your troops to form a four hundred metre perimeter and hold.' *The Boss* knew full well that utilising the armed troops would be like fighting a battleship with a rubber dingy and catapult but they may well prove useful as a distraction nonetheless. The team would have their hands full with cleaning up and satisfying eye witness perceptions on this one. Glancing at Jane momentarily, he noticed she was twirling her crucifix in her fingers once more. If there was a God, they could do with a little divine intervention right now.

To those surrounding them, their movements at times seemed a smudged, confused amalgam of shapes and positions. To each other, those same eye witnesses seemed as statues, single instants frozen in time. Luke sprung back to his feet almost instantaneously and in a split second ran at full pelt towards the unassumingly dull, heavily secured and built doors. They moved back barely quarter of an inch on impact. The heavily armoured Land Rover parked nearby caught his eye, just as Steve reappeared in front of him.
'Twice in as many days, this is becoming a habit.' A moment's pause to reflect. 'Hadn't bargained on you having superfast wings I must admit.' Fletcher was in no mood for small talk, pulling out the heavy-duty adrenalin pen in readiness as he lunged once more. Dyer on the other hand was using his

normally underutilised *en*hanced thinking muscle, deciding that avoiding hand to hand combat on this occasion was the smart move, leaping over his would-be assailant, kicking out at his head as he passed, causing Steve to slam with even greater force into the security doors. This made a perceptible gap appear of around half a foot. Steve steadied himself once more, with just enough time spare to brace himself for the impact of the rapidly approaching armoured vehicle Luke had hurled towards him. Man and Machine met and travelled together at pace through the now breeched entrance. Seizing his chance with vigour Dyer sped past the wreckage to locate and seize the prize within.

Ten seconds passed. Slowly a hand reached out from behind the mangled Land-rover, gripped at the furthest point it could reach, digging finger tips deep into the metal. Then, with an almighty shunt the wreckage was flung outwards by about thirty feet. It was situations like these that the comms-link built into his suit was encased in Kevlar for. Not so well protected was his obligatory black outfit which was now looking the worse for wear. Shaking the loose dust from his head, Steve regained focus just in time to witness Dyer rush past with a very large waterproof bag which evidently contained at least one warhead extracted from the breached facility within. Momentarily, he let the screams of those within distract him. The orders were clear but he was damned if he'd leave without checking on the hapless victims. Jane glanced at the readings once more. They were off the chart. Biometrics, potential Tachyon measures, electrical discharges for muscle activity, brainwaves all measures seemed locked in on the highest possible readings available on their respective scales. Through the "on-board" camera she could see mostly dusty mist and debris being jettisoned in all directions.
'What's happening?' there were a few moments that passed before a response.
'Sorry, just had to open up the collapsed entrance to the warhead warehouse. Tell the emergency services to get in here quick, five injured two seriously.'
'You were told to-'
'I know. I have not lost our *wayward child*. I know exactly where he is headed and I have the one thing he doesn't,' pausing to catch a deep breath 'wings.'

The death by briefing he'd experienced after undergoing *The Process* had highlighted that he would undergo a complete change in equilibrium but nothing would have prepared him for this. From the bird's eye vantage point the X2C gave him,

everything was crystal clear despite the wintry weather conditions. He could also "feel" where Dyer was headed. Out, towards the open waters beyond the Isle of Arran. Like an Eagle hunting a rodent, he could clearly make out the wake of a small boat that Dyer was frantically self-propelling out across the rolling grey expanse, headed straight for the expensive looking power yacht which looked suspiciously out of place in its surroundings.
'Target spotted, and his rendezvous by the looks of it too. I will engage him once the target destination is confirmed.' Fletcher could almost smell an odd mix of fear and excitement in the air, that was what it made him think of anyway. He was sure that the source was Dyer. The *sil-adrenaline* must have been thick in his blood. It certainly meant he was hitting an impressive rate of knots across the sea, resembling a skimming stone loosely hugging the surface of the water. As anticipated, Dyer drew up with a splash of spray that resembled a water-skier violently changing direction alongside the Yacht.
'Dropping down to re-engage.'
'Remember the main focus is the warheads first, Dyer is a secondary concern at this moment on time.'
'Understood.'

Luke hauled himself aboard the luxury yacht where Bahajoub's men awaited their "package". The customary small automatic weapons' barrels greeted him.
'Now, now boys, is that any way to treat Santa?' placing carefully on the deck the bag containing the two warheads he'd managed to procure in his short visit. The stout machine gun-wielding individual gently, tentatively drew back the waterproof opening of the covers to reveal the potent, deadly cargo within.
'Don't worry chaps. It won't blow unless you connect one of these detonators.' Luke flippantly advised, waiting for the men in the background to look up directly at him before tossing one of the devices playfully in his direction. The stench of panic was almost visible as he let loose his grip from his own firearm to desperately catch the incoming object. Dyer very audibly laughed in a patronising tone before he too turned to see what else had now taken the half dozen crew members' attention away from his witty repartee. The stout man mumbled
'It's a demon...' just as the X2C came close to the stern of the vessel.

Steve hit the release switch in time to allow him to fall to the rear deck and hold the jet pack in his left hand as its thruster swiftly ceased to burn in the grey environment that surrounded them.

Predictably, small automatic arms fire suddenly crackled through the turbulent air, causing enough of a distraction for Luke to dive under the waves once more, almost unnoticed. Steve slowly moved towards the man now clutching the warheads as the firestorm stopped as suddenly as it had started. The men shouted anxiously in fear, all now thoroughly convinced that indeed, a demon was upon them. The taller man who had caught the detonator held it aloft in the vain and irrational hope that it would cause the black figure of Fletcher to back down. Instead, it merely served to attract his attention momentarily, just long enough to allow him to throw out a hand and wrench the device from the man's grasp. In panic two of the other crew members leapt into the gnarly sea surrounding them, the timing almost perfectly disguising Dyer's re-emergence on deck by the X2C, taking a moment to evaluate whether to try and fly the thing or stick to his original plan, which he decided so to do by throwing it out into the sea then swiftly following it and recommencing his self-propelled hydrofoil back to the main land.

Meanwhile, the stout man gently relinquished his hold of the warheads, placing them between himself and Fletcher whilst backing away as if laying a juicy steak down to distract a hungry Lion from deciding to make him his latest meal. Steve assessed his options. He'd noticed Dyer's extravagant get away and disposal of his best means of catching him up. He had also noticed the life raft dangling from an expensive looking crane mechanism at the rear of the Yacht. The priority was the warheads, he had those now.

'I have the devices in my possession. Our *wayward child* has left the scene and disabled my wings on his exit. Shall I continue to pursue him?' *The Boss* responded instantaneously

'No, we have your location keep the devices secure, a chinook will be with you in five minutes to bring you and your guests back to Faslane. We will deal with our ongoing problem when he returns to London. We have our ears open to track down his associates as well as surveillance on his base of operations.' A few moments silence. 'Well done, *lone star.*'

The strange term took Steve back a little, it wasn't any agreed code name. Perhaps the Old Boy was improvising for the collective audience back at HQ?

'*Wayward child* is definitely headed south, I will await our lift back to base as instructed, we have two overboard so hypothermia will probably need to be treated to ensure they stay fit to face judgement.'

'Well, *Boss* <ahem> your team seems to have averted a pretty embarrassing and more to the point massively dangerous security threat at pretty short notice…' The Prime Minister paused whilst one of his aides whispered something in his ear. 'I will look forward to a full debrief through the same channel as your alert was received, if that is appropriate? I will leave you all to it from here.' And with that the video link cut out. *The Boss* glanced at Gmitrowicz who mouthed 'Desmond?' to which he smiled his acknowledgement.

'Gentlemen, I'd prefer your full co-operation in keeping the lid on this. We will handle the external communications but if you could keep all personnel silent on the matter until our back up team is on location to do a full debrief we'd really appreciate it.' And with that, the assembled COBRA meeting was ended before any further questions could be posed.

'I'll get our team up their ASAP, Sir.' Jane committed, whilst she simultaneously set the electronic wheels in motion.

'Good job, get our friends in the navy looking for the X2C too please, I don't have a limitless budget…' *The Boss* then took a swig of coffee, immediately spitting it back out again. 'Can somebody get me a cup of coffee from my office? I need it rather than this muck.'

Chapter Ten

Bahajoub had expected to have had confirmation that the "package" had been safely delivered in the past half an hour. The lack of communication could only mean something had not gone to plan though what that meant was anyone's guess. The boat crew had strict instructions not to communicate in the event of an issue, ensuring a level of difficulty in tracing a trail back to him, protecting the majority at the expense of the minority. The innocuous black phone on his desk abruptly began to ring.
'Ahh, an unexpected pleasure to hear from you. I must say your timing is somewhat uncanny… yes, I think I could meet you this afternoon. At the alternative location? Excellent, see you there.'
His slender hand placing down both the traditional old phone's handset and cancelling the entered digits on the mobile on which he'd just begun to dial the pre-agreed number to call Grimes, once receipt of the warheads had been confirmed. Best to not waste a call to him right now, Bahajoub had a feeling that he'd be better served waiting until his unplanned meeting had concluded. Certainly he'd be better informed, of that he felt sure.

The mobile phone record that had been somewhat irregularly handed to his team via Jenkins turned out to be most illuminating. Considering how incredibly difficult getting any sort of lead had proven thus far, it almost seemed too good to be true. The number dialled belonged to a known suspected handler of stolen goods, mostly high end jewellery, based in the East Midlands in a small town just north of Peterborough. Judging by the call activity on the number in question, the team had taken the proactive step of accessing that information first thing, something pretty major must have been occurring in the last twenty-four hours. Normally Hayes would have passed this one on but, given his unofficial one to one last night, there was the opportunity for some sort of quick result to alleviate the pressure building on his combined *Houdini Gang* team. As such, he'd taken the executive decision that both he and Killen would personally oversee the arrest of the suspect once they'd been located, liaising with the appropriate team in the local constabulary to ensure all was done to his satisfaction. An action that did not win him any particular friends in that police force, but such things did not concern him at the best of times.

Thanks to being a well-known person of interest in the area, the suspect's whereabouts were soon confirmed and the pair left for the town of Stamford to rendezvous with the small party of local police that would carry out the arrest. An hour and a half in the car would give them both plenty of time to review the extraordinary events of the past day.

'So, where are we on trying to retrieve any relevant images from CCTV cameras not affected by the convenient black out around The Tower?' Watching the people they passed by from the comfort of his usual passenger seat position. There was something about riding in a car that appealed to Hayes. It afforded him the environment to not appear rude by ignoring any attempt at eye contact, allowing him the chance to fully focus his thoughts, unencumbered by etiquette.

'Nothing meaningful, sir. Our suspects could easily have been there all day or even the night before, for all we know. Our investigation into our main culprits is still pretty much in the dark at the present time.' The DS paused, expecting her DI to interject or even reprimand her pragmatic negativity. No such chiding comment was forthcoming. The awkward silence held for a few moments more before Philip spoke once more.

'Let's just say you have found a way to pull off some incredible crimes. A way in which to achieve the improbable, seemingly impossible, in the course of your modus operandi. A technology perhaps, mixed with applied skill. That capability could afford you some pretty powerful friends, could it not?' Killen nodded in agreement.

'If you knew how to get in front of the right people, who knows where your notoriety could take you.' Her green eyes glancing briefly in Hayes' direction. He gave out a loud moan of agreement.

It was at that moment Hayes stopped looking out of the passenger window, suddenly turning sharply to face the road ahead.

'Alternatively, what if you were in a position of some power or maybe of significant influence? Someone deep in the establishment. And during your time you were privileged enough to come upon a tool or capability that was unique, quirky, outlandish. Say the idea of that technology sparked a thought. What if I could use that for my own gain, what could I use that for? If you were self-concerned enough, single minded in your desire to gain more riches, power, control, freedom, whatever you craved. The temptation, aligned to your personal desire, greed, it might be too great to resist...' It was Killen's turn to murmur her approval, though she did so with far less vocal certainty. 'What if your influence extended enough that you could protect a third party, one that carried out the sharp end whilst you manipulated the background environment? You'd have to be extremely clever and or extremely connected, but you could possibly hide your tracks and those of anyone who might expose you and there'd never be enough evidence to make you even half a suspect.'

'You sound like a conspiracy theorist, guv.' Joked Killen, Hayes turned to face his fellow traveller.

'It's just I get the distinct impression we have been thrown an obvious bone some way away from the trail of the fox we are chasing. Being treated like dumb blood hounds, thrown off the scent and being conditioned to gratefully grab the obvious diversion. And I don't like being played.'

'Ah, actually there is something else to mention,' Killen pulled out a folded piece of paper from her jacket pocket. 'when we traced where and when the mobile had been bought, which was about eighteen months ago, apparently, we discovered that it was paid for by what turns out to be a credit card registered to a fake I.D. A very professionally created fake I.D. at that, which leads to a dead end *but* it was not the only phone purchased. Fifty-Four in total, bought in various stores over a period of a few days. Five of which have so far never been used. Most of these devices have been used solely for the purpose of contacting another device that was purchased at the same time.'

The corners of his tight lips curled into a hearty grin. 'We may have our first advantage in this hunt then... soon as they use one of those as yet unused phones, we will have a fix on where they are calling from and who they are calling, too.'

'And, we have the numbers called from the previous forty-eight call records to go at as well, those that were not part of this bulk purchase of pay as you go mobiles. Intended bone or not, indirectly it may have given use a goldmine of leads to follow up on.'

The familiar surroundings of the coffee bar helped Bahajoub relax, in an almost cathartic way at times. The process of meeting someone here, the familiarity, it all seemed to help ensure any stresses or concerns playing on his mind felt a little easier. In fact he could leave those concerns at the door, this was where the business was really done and that had always been a good thing as far as he was concerned. But he had never met with this contact here before. Mostly because their previous meetings were normally very late at night and in a somewhat more rarefied atmosphere of exclusivity. Pouring his tea he became aware of the presence of his guest.

'Please sit down, Mr Desmond.' As always, courteously indicating that he had left the most comfortable chair for his esteemed guest. It was still some way short of the opulence of *the Civil Servants* normal second office, an exclusive west end private club's expensively upholstered chair. 'I guess that this unexpected pleasure is not purely a social one, given its hasty arrangement?'

'Now, you know I always enjoy our chats.' Lowering himself into the chair whilst emanating a trademark insincere smile. 'But you are quite correct. I had not expected you to have been so, expert, in your recruitment of a team to extract the prize from Scotland.' The relative brazen bluntness of Desmond's statement brought a mild look of surprise.

'I take it you are in some way unsupportive of the choice.' Was the only quick witted response he could conjure up.

'Only in so much as there is an unfortunate consequence of getting such a high profile,' pausing as if to calculate the potential ramifications of what he was about to say. '*individual* to attempt the operation.' A moment of thought to build emphasis and gauge reaction. 'You have met with Dyer, Bahajoub?'

'An interesting, if understandably arrogant individual indeed, Mr Desmond. One of my contacts became aware of his unique talents quite by accident.' The mild sport of verbal jousting only momentarily distracting him from what he felt was the important thing in life. 'In fact, I am somewhat concerned at the lack of a progress update on his acquisition excursion. Nothing to do with you I take it?' His slender fingers wrapping themselves around each other as he sat a little further back in the chair.

'No it is not, quite the opposite. Had I been made aware of the proposed involvement a little earlier, I would maybe have been able to ensure a slightly easier passage through. Unfortunately I had to act as was appropriate of one in my professional capacity, in such an urgent circumstance.'

'From what I have heard, I find it hard to believe any would have stopped him. He is quite a force of nature you could say.' Desmond leant forward to reduce the need for volume in his answer.

'That I could agree with, unfortunately he is not one hundred percent unique. I take it you have not paid too much attention to the news or to that matter the darker corners of the web over the past twenty-four hours? Tall tales of two phantoms fighting it out at the Tower, of secret government experiments gone wrong and

all sorts of conspiracy theories? "London's Chupracabra"? As they say, no smoke without fire.' Slowly returning back to a more comfortable seating position. 'Our associates have many plans for Mr Dyer; he could be a valuable asset in our shared cause. They'd not, however, considered this situation as being one in which he should have been involved.' Bahajoub sipped his half full cup, then placed it precisely back on its saucer.
'I take it that there have been complications with the extraction of our prize.'
'That is of little concern to you. What is of concern to us all is that certain details that jeopardise the relative anonymity of Dyer sit with someone over whom I currently have only partial and tenuous influence. Concern as they could find a trail back to yourself and your… current paymasters. It is our ability to work in the shadows that will ultimately deliver our associates' vision. Your choice in tools to deliver the plan is the problem here.' Despite their overall appearance of being cool and calmly collected, both gentlemen bore the slightly tacky glow of mild perspiration on their foreheads, which betrayed the stress that they each currently felt under. 'I would be advising you to do the honourable thing if it were not a fact that you have yet more significant orders to undertake, Bahajoub. *They* have a definite plan for you.' Sliding over a new smartphone across the table. 'You will need to use this from now on as your old one may be compromised. You'll need to burn it completely and dispose of the remains carefully, separated out if need be. And I would suggest that no further contact be made with anybody connected to this sorry debacle.' Then Desmond announced in a slightly less hushed tone. 'Yes, a holiday might be the thing for you right now, get away from the rat race. Get the monkeys off your back. I think you'll find that they'll soon resolve themselves.' Bahajoub picked up the shiny new device, turning it left and right as if unfamiliar with its like. He then looked straight into the slippery old fox's eyes.
'I hear the Maldives are particularly pleasant at this time of year. The perfect place to get my life into some kind of *new order*.' Desmond nodded his agreement.
'Best make sure there are no loose ends though before you depart.'

The office seemed small. The boxes strewn across it rose like a miniature replica of any one of a number of American cities. The umpteen bags of shredded paper tied and stacked neatly in one corner. It had been a lot of work over the past day with little time for sleep but Grimes was almost there, nearly ready to throw

away his old life and begin a new one. A Nomadic one but nonetheless one that is rich and free from any ties. Free from any further chance of incarceration, more's to the point. Tony had been so involved in the shredding of evidence and the filing of his more legitimate business records that the time had eluded him. It was only now, with a faint pang of hunger, that he glanced up at the clock. The deed should have been well and truly done by now and the handover complete. Why hadn't Luke called through to alert him? Had he bypassed the old route altogether and contacted Sam directly? Grimes dialled the number for Sam.
'No movement here today, only yesterday's transaction showing.' Was her abrupt and to the point response. She was still, after all, in an environment where freedom of communication was limited due to colleagues being within earshot.
'Have you heard anything from our man?' There was a noticeable delay to her response.
'I haven't spoken with him for a while now...' Grimes knew that mixing business with pleasure was a no go area. He'd learnt that one the hard way many years ago. The tone in Samantha's voice merely confirmed that it was a lesson well learnt, even if the likelihood of such an opportunity presenting itself to him was now very slim, unlike his physique. Truth was that in his new life such petty concerns would be irrelevant; being openly stinking rich would undoubtedly attract every gold-digging potential trophy wife he could desire.
'OK, let me know if you do hear anything directly, we need to stay tight on this one.' Grimes could just about make out the faint "uh-huh" on the end of the line just before she hung off. Checking his phone for a text, knowing that it was highly unlikely Dyer would risk communicating anything meaningful that way.

The shrill of the desk top phone startled him. It could only be either Luke or Bahajoub breaking with the agreed method of communication. Grimes looked at the caller I.D. display and it was a private number / no number given. Huffing loudly to himself he picked up the handset. 'Grimes?' was the question, before he could even say his own name as a salutation.
'Yes, Luke, is that you?' There was a little bit of background noise and a poor sound quality to the line. Dyer was evidently calling from a payphone in a public area.
'The project has failed. We had some unforeseen interference with our handover team.'
'What the hell happened? Did they try to double cross you again? Surely they would not risk-'

'No, my old employer has at long last somehow managed to hire a replacement. I only found that out yesterday. I thought that our phase one would have thrown them off the scent but… shit!' the expletive communicating his very evident self-frustration. 'But I had no idea they could react as quickly as they have today. Best you get yourself out of sight, Tony. I'm sure our clients have figured out something is wrong and there is no guarantee that some kind of news story won't break in the next half hour that gives them all they need to know to exact some kind of action at us. Meet me at the coffee bar opposite my flat, I will give you the address but make sure you do not leave any trace of it in your office, right?'

'I'll take the pad and pen with me so not even an imprint.'

'Good, I will get back there as soon as I get myself some wheels …'

The journey back from Faslane took considerably longer than the one there. The helicopter had to stop to refuel and in total it was a little over three and a half hours before Steve was back in the capital, being ferried from the Docklands City Airport in a standard issue metallic grey car towards the Shard. The good news (both professionally and from a personal perspective) was that the Navy had recovered the X2C successfully. Being so close to one of the main bases for their submarines had proved a little fortuitous in that regard. Things had moved so fast in recent days it was easy to forget that Steve was still learning to live within his *enhanced* body, still acclimatising to its facets. This was currently demonstrated in becoming aware of how to control the greater range of his "inner voice", the manifestation of his intuition which had developed into something akin to an unpredictable six sense. In fact, it rather encompassed elements of precognition, telepathy and remote sensing where he could feel roughly where somebody was, if he thought long and hard enough about it. This awareness led him to believe that Luke was headed south, down the western side of the country. Unfortunately, he could not muster much more than a rough guide, a gut feel that could equally simply be a logical guess at his whereabouts. The clarity and certainty he'd felt on the boat had significantly diminished in direct correlation to the distance between them.

Both *The Boss* and Doctor Gmitrowicz were waiting for him as he entered the control room. They appeared to be studying a network map of some description, overlaid onto a map of West London. It was a map of all the CCTV cameras in the vicinity, with about 50% of them highlighted in blue. These were the ones that they could easily access and effectively monitor with *the Organisation's* face recognition programme.

'Well done on preventing an internationally embarrassing breach of national security, Fletcher.' *The Boss* maintained his scrutiny of the screen before him, treating the incident with an almost laissez-faire, business as usual, air.

'Not to mention preventing many millions of lives being needlessly sacrificed in the name of an ideology or in the name of terror.' Jane afforded him full attention and a smile as he sat down beside them.

'Presume we are expecting Dyer to return to his apartment?' His question was more like a statement in its tone. Steve knew the answer was yes.

'We've managed to get about a half of our usable network sampling in real-time HD, so we have an almost complete peripheral field of surveillance at about ten miles radius to alert us he is near.' The Doctor turned to face the screen once more. 'So best get some food and rest. You need to be one hundred percent operationally fit for the capture.'

The Boss frankly did not like being at anyone else's beck and call but unfortunately, we all work for somebody along the way, whether we like it or not. Desmond was that somebody, in this instance, and the timing of the meeting was a little irritating to say the least. But given the line of support, funding *and* the need to report back on *The Organisation* itself, ultimately he had to be respected and tolerated. It was also highly unusual for Mr Desmond to want to visit any operational location, so time was made to meet.

'Old friend,' reaching out a slightly cold and limp hand to shake his, 'it has been an eventful few days, has it not?' *The Boss* could not help but think to himself that *the Civil Servant* could at least make more of an effort to cover up his obvious lack of empathy or enjoyment of the false pleasantries that society enforced upon him. The temptation to squeeze his hand a little too hard subsided as quickly as it arose.

'Indeed it has. It has taken our most talented spooks and spin doctors to keep enough of a lid on the realities of the operation at the Tower so as not to fan the flames of public curiosity to a point of uncontrollability.' Indicating, as he spoke, that he should feel free to take a seat as he talked. 'Can I get you a coffee?'

'Yes, I see you have a jug on the go already.' *The Boss* glanced momentarily at his personal coffee machine.

'That will be no good for you now Mr Desmond, I'll get a fresh one made for you.' Nodding the order to his PA, who had just started to hover around the door awaiting such a requirement. 'I take it that there is something pressing and sensitive for you to have been able to visit our Bijou facility?' his turn to offer a sense of insincere platitudes.

'As much as your performance on the call to the PM this morning has already reached the status of an Urban Legend at Whitehall, you are right in your assumption. You know how much I support your operation and its work but such high-profile failures in such a short space of time are not really helping me in securing the future plans we have for *The Organisation.* I need you to understand that if you do not deal with Dyer with some degree of finality in the next twenty-four hours, I will be asked to take some drastic right-sizing activity.'

Desmond's words were, as always, calculated and on this occasion precise. *The Boss* drummed on his desk with such force that the room appeared to rumble and groan a little in response.

'I think that threatening to put me out to grass is not a threat that should be made lightly. I am this *Organisation.* It is me.' His breathing swiftly returning to normal after a brief spell of deep and rapid half-pants. 'But be assured, he will be dealt with before today is out. I personally guarantee that.'

'Good, good.' The Civil Servant sat back a little in his chair, glancing at one of the monitoring screens to the right of the big man's desk. 'Tell me, how is Dr Gmitrowicz getting on with her research projects? Having one of the brightest physicists on the planet as one of the team is definitely a bit of a coup for you isn't it.'

'She is progressing things slowly. Ultimately, she is as much operational here as the rest of us. Understanding how things work is important but getting results is how we are measured, as you have rightly reminded me.' Pausing for a moment's reflection. 'Maybe, when we have dealt with the issue at hand, I should arrange for her to present some of her findings over the past six months?'

As luck would have it, there was a very nice Neon Blue Porsche conveniently parked far enough away from the main entrance of the roadside services building to ensure that he was not obviously overlooked by those people milling around and walking by. There was a security camera but being recognised was not really a main concern for him. In the blink of an eye he'd opened the door, opened the bonnet and physically removed the immobiliser and alarm, meaning that the alarm had barely sounded at all, almost as if it had just bleeped to acknowledge that the remote central locking had been activated. Then after a few more moments he'd directly rewired the car to by-pass the security on the ignition system and hit the starter button to hear the glorious roar of the finely tuned engine. After-all, if you were going to steal a car to make a swift journey the length of the country then why not pick one with a bit of style?

Luke made good time down the west side of Britain. Okay, he'd be able to travel quicker under his own power but even with his *en*hanced physiology, running for four hundred odd miles would be somewhat tiring, especially after the exertions of that morning. Fixed and average speed cameras were ignored, where it was possible to break the speed limit given the traffic on the roads. Only where he spotted a police vehicle or caught a glimpse of a uniform in a plain police car, did Luke take more caution. It was when he'd just passed the slip road for Stoke that the sound of sirens accompanied by flashing blue lights erupted, despite having slowed down when he saw the familiar white, fluorescent yellow and blue markings ahead.
'That took long enough.' He muttered to himself as he thrust the accelerator pedal to the floor. 'At least it stops the journey becoming boring?' He glanced again in the mirror, allowing himself a little chuckle of amusement.

The chase ensued for ten minutes until the next junction, where Dyer made a last-minute decision to veer off the motorway and take the pursuit to the more challenging country roads and by lanes, causing one innocent motorist to lose control and slam sickeningly into the side of a Juggernaut just after the junction itself. The police driver tracking him was more skilled at avoiding such situations, managing to just about follow him up the slip road in one piece. The Porsche screeched around the roundabout, taking the third exit. Luke had always enjoyed driving fast despite no formal training, so his enhanced reflexes made up for his lack of ability and skill in comparison to his adversary. The police patrol car followed in quick succession behind the Porsche; in part, his route was made easier by the traffic being brought to a halt by Dyer's recklessness.

It took a further ten minutes until Luke spotted exactly what he was looking for. A hard-right handbrake turn followed by the full on locking of brakes, he brought his car to rest in a wooded, tree covered lay-by. The pursuing police could hardly believe their luck. Slamming to a halt, then reversing back up to block the entrance/exit.

'Has the suspect left the vehicle?' The officer in the passenger seat asked the helicopter support unit that had been providing aerial assistance as eyes in the sky for about the last seven minutes of the pursuit.

'The suspect is just standing by the vehicle, making no attempt to flee the scene. Suggest proceed with caution, he does not appear to be armed but not attempting to escape is an unusual response in this situation.' The two officers slowly stepped out of the car, hands rested on their batons in readiness.

'What kept you?' Dyer taunted them arrogantly as they approached him.

'We have reason to believe that this vehicle was stolen earlier today by a man who matches your description. Could you please step away from the vehicle sir?'

'Why of course officer. Will you be wanting to put handcuffs on me too?' The two officers glanced at each other raising their eyebrows briefly as Dyer proffered his wrists in readiness. 'Best to do these things properly, don't you think?' With deliberate caution, the second officer took out his handcuffs and placed them firmly onto his wrists, gently turning him around as he did so, to ensure that his hands were placed behind his back.

'Do you have any form of identification on you?' enquired the other officer as they led him to the rear driver side door of the Police vehicle.

'No. but my name is Luke Dyer.' Making every attempt to maintain eye contact whilst he stooped to get into the back of the car.

Dyer waited for about five minutes of the journey to be certain that the Helicopter was well and truly stood down. Out across the open farmland he could clearly see the motorway services station that he'd spotted minutes earlier whilst in the middle of the chase. This was the ideal spot to alight from his brief ride at her Majesty's pleasure.

'Well gentlemen, it has been a really enjoyable experience. Thank you for breaking up the monotony of the long trek home, but I do have a rather pressing engagement.' With that he snapped the handcuffs apart, threw a pound coin with enough vigour to disable the police radio and reached over to drag both seated officers violently back over their seats and out through the rear window. He then bounded into the driver's seat, bringing the car under control just in time to swerve and avoid a head-on collision. 'Time for a detour.' Luke took the police car off road through a barely secured gate and out across the fields towards the rear of the service station, eventually dumping the vehicle by a small spinney of trees to complete the remainder of the jaunt on foot. He hoped that there was a Maserati he could "borrow" this time, he'd always liked Maserati's.

Steve sat watching the Television news report, one analysing the merest glimpse of what he knew was his pursuit of Luke at the tower the day before, one of the few clips still remaining in the public domain. The high level of interest in the *Houdini Gang* alone would have afforded a few days of protracted reporting, analysis, views and opinions being offered on the robbery at the Tower. But the added furore of the almost seemingly doctored mobile phone clips and the garbled nature of the few eyewitnesses that were allowed to comment (there was no meaningful formal statement from the police) had given the news programme editors a rich vein of alternative theories and opinions to fill the endless minutes of scheduled news minutes available.

One theory was that the clips were actually part of an elaborate hoax, manufactured on a computer in a special effects studio. Several potential flaws in the recording were pointed to as evidence of this, whilst an alternative expert stated the same anomalies were actually evidence that the footage was genuine. A further segment was filled with potential "advanced super soldier" technology projects that were being touted as the potential solution as to how such a feat could be achieved. How and why "top secret" and exclusive military equipment would have been made available to the world's most famous thieves was the intriguing question left unanswered. The reporting finished with a quick montage of a number of "normal passers-by" at the Tower being asked what they thought of the recent incident, finishing with one woman pondering "was this the same person they've dubbed Spring Heeled Jack, who came to the rescue of that young woman a few days ago?" to which the news anchor woman pulled a rather dismissive expression before moving on to the next topic.

Not a single mention was being made of the events at Faslane. A firm lid on just how close the country had come to having a couple live nuclear warheads go AWOL. In some respects it worried Steve that he found himself thinking some things were better left out of the public gaze, no need for a widespread panic to be initiated. But then the recent past had opened his eyes, in a way he could never have imagined previously, to just how little of the world was truly transparent and openly visible. He took a large glug of a sip from his *sil*-shake as he turned off the TV. The concept of resting was somewhat different to that which had prevailed before *The Process*, with a minimal recovery time needed after extreme exertion. It was hard to explain but not doing anything was mildly uncomfortable for him after a short while, giving him a slightly irritable feeling in his muscles that would almost proactively encourage him to get up and do something. He grabbed his towel and decided a small work out was the best course of action to alleviate his twitchiness. After about ten minutes on the treadmill and bench press his solitude was ended abruptly by Jane bursting through the doors of the Gym.

'There you are! We've managed to track an incident in Staffordshire that undoubtedly involved our *Wayward Child*. Two police officers critically injured in unexplained circumstances whilst travelling back to base after they had apprehended a suspected car thief, who gave his name as Luke Dyer. We think he should be arriving at his apartment in approximately two hours, at the rate of travel he appears to be taking. Assuming he doesn't decide to go under his own steam instead, which would mean he could be arriving any time soon.' Fletcher stopped pumping the massively high resistance bench press.

'I better get ready to roll then?'

'We leave in ten minutes via the river – that way we will avoid having to stop the rush hour traffic and get there in about half an hour.'

'Excellent – I've missed that Thames these last twenty-four hours. So warm this time of year.'

Jane let out a hearty laugh. She paused for a moment, then decided now was as good a time as any to share with Steve what she'd began to hypothesise around the anomalous readings she'd been observing.

'I think I may have made a little progress in explaining your heightened gut feelings. Well, understanding it at least.' Steve nodded his interest. 'It's a little at the edge of science but, I guess that's where we start our day jobs. There are a number of theoretical particles in quantum physics. Indeed most of what we think the universe itself is made of is a guess, really. Dark Matter, Dark Energy, particles that have great mass but hardly interact at all with the particles and atoms we recognise as being the solid world we occupy. As scientists we have difficulty measuring what we cannot observe, so we have to look for the effects we can see. I think your *en*hanced sense, your gut feel and quick reactions are based on your altered anatomy being able to… to feel a particular type of theoretical particle. A Tachyon, that exists in our universe but cannot slow down to reach the speed of light, let alone travel slower than that barrier. That moves so fast it seems to us to travel backwards in time. I have measured activity that may be the consequence of Tachyons both around yourself and… and around *The Source*. I guess I am saying I believe you.' Steve looked at her a little puzzled.

'Err, thank you. I know that I am able to feel more than I could before and with more senses than I realised I had.' Pausing to gather his thoughts a little more, getting over the slight indignation that his integrity or indeed his sanity might have been questioned. He guessed you had to experience it to know it was real. 'That Rue would also be generating side effects makes perfect sense to me.' Catching Jane's quizzical glance. '*The Source. The Source* is called Ruedrav'tor. I haven't yet mastered how, let alone why or where, but I can communicate with him. It feels almost like a vivid, lucid dream. In a place referred to as "the space between spaces", if that helps at all.' Dr Gmitrowicz frowned a little, staring into space as she did so.

'Maybe… We will have to talk some more but,' glancing at her watch, 'now we need to get operationally ready.'

For Hayes and Killen this was as close to an easy day at work as they could experience. The local CID had arranged everything. Arrest plan, personnel, vehicles and timescales, everything they needed. All whilst they had travelled up from London.

'OK Philip, we are ready to proceed now, do you want to do the honours?' Hayes was looking forward to an old-fashioned arrest. It had been quite a while since he'd worn a standard issue stab proof vest. He nodded his approval to the local officer in charge of the operation. 'We are all clear to commence, let's be on our toes.'

Hayes turned to face Killen as they approached the front door and gave it the lightest of knocks.

'Police, can you please open the door?' smiling to his colleague at how uncharacteristically timid he sounded. 'I think that counts officially as no response, DS. Do you agree?' her green eyes flashed her amusement.

'Yes I think it does.' Signalling to the accompanying officer who was wielding the battering ram that his time had come. One swift swing was indeed all that was required as they gained access forcibly. Inside the small terraced house was a scene of basic squalor. For a criminal gang that had managed to acquire the crown jewels, this was really the complete opposite of what one may have expected. And it was clear that the two individuals in residence were evidently caught completely by surprise, one of them sat with a takeaway pizza box on his lap dressed only in his underwear, the other in mid battle on his video game console.

'Gentlemen, we have reason to believe you are Owen Saunders and Robert Macintyre, is that correct?' The suspects, still a little dazed at the abrupt entrance, had recovered enough of their wits to purposely act dumb. 'Suspects are choosing to remain silent, Guv. I am arresting you both on suspicion of receiving stolen goods, specifically the Crown Jewels. You do not have to say anything but it may harm you defence if you do not answer, when questioned, something which you later rely on in court. Anything you do say may be given in evidence.'
One of the gentlemen broke his silence only to say 'Please tell me you haven't arrested the *Houdini Gang* too? If he thinks we've been involved in his arrest he will kill us! Big blond bloke – looked like an extra from a war movie.' The other man looked on in disgust at his accomplice's brazen cowardice, to which he simply continued. 'C'mon man he was scary strong, you felt the van rock when he punched it. He'd tear us apart.' His voice warbling with the vibrato which only fear could induce. 'Got a bit of a drama queen here Guv.' Killen remarked, as they led the two suspects out. Hayes half smiled, there'd been no description of anybody to do with the accepted *Houdini Gang* crimes before, but something made him take note of that flippant description. Why did it ring a bell?

Ruedrav'tor waited patiently for The Oracle to finish his ritual. The cycle of education was almost complete. War had shown him many strange things, acts of heroism, honour, vindictiveness and cowardice he could not have imagined previously. Now knowledge had provided both the answers and created more questions than he'd ever realised could be. The place The Oracle had helped him access, the world within his consciousness, the space between spaces, allowed Rue to think through many things in a matter of moments that would've occupied many hours before. It was because conscious was weighed down, anchored by the physical world, the old sage had explained. In the place between places, only consciousness could exist, physical matter and energy were not a part of its construction. It was unencumbered by the rules and laws of the physical realms. Understanding it was the key to traversing it and journeying to the myriad realms that made up the Multiverse. And this was the frustration he felt. He could feel, see, and taste many numerous worlds from the vantage point of the realm of consciousness. He could also sense the Nexus, he was sure of it. But the one realm he sought the most, the universe of the Nemesis, eluded him.

Calmly Ruedrav'tor opened his eyes to see the Oracle had joined him, dressed only in a loose fitting white linen tunic top and trousers.
'My attire surprises you, mighty protector?'
'Very little surprises me now, wise one. But how you still manage to make your way to my side without me realising your presence sooner does so.'
'That is the final lesson for you. For as the consciousness you possess can pass into the Nexus, so can you appear to be as only consciousness in our world. Only by switching off the impact of your physical form in a physical realm can you pass through the ethereal to another physical world.' As with much of the teachings, their simplicity resonated well with the ex-Warrior. '... the device, the portal, allows you to use it. Like a bird, you need to fly between realms through it; it is not in itself flown. It allows you to fly with it.'
'So how is this done?'
'That is the essence of the lesson today. It is not learnt, it is discovered. A skill you have yourself to master, no-one else can help. The answer already lies within you. You need to ask the right questions to find the right answers.'
'That... makes sense, somehow. Is that why I cannot find where the Nemesis come from? I have searched many times from the void, seen things that make my heart sing and my soul cry, but never what I seek to understand most.'
'It is. The question cannot be answered as they are not from anywhere. They simply are. The place between places is everywhere and nowhere at all. Exclusively and simultaneously. Their realm is essentially no place at all.'
'They are consciousness. Unencumbered by the physical worlds.' Rue thought out loud.
'And as such, wise in ways we cannot comprehend, yet lacking in many things only a physical being can understand. They play at life and death because to them, it has no meaning. They do not pass through our world as we do on our journey. They merely engage it and others similar to it. Like a child. They know what things are but often not what they mean. A little knowledge can be a dangerous thing. This is a truth throughout the multiverse but not necessarily in the space between spaces, and not for the Nemesis. They, like all children, crave most what they do not

have. The physical form. That is what drives their actions if not what drives their ultimate goal. But they are not born of our worlds, so they do not fully understand what it is to be of solid flesh and bone and not just thought and will. They view themselves as ascended in some way, that indulging in our realm is some kind of primitive pleasure yet it is our very mortality that allows us to understand the value of existing. I believe that, ironically, the Nemesis will never be truly happy because of this. Finality brings clarity, means certainty.'

The old man's words rang around in Ruedrav'tor's head, both in this world and the time between times. The quietly spoken tones adding somehow to their significance, like a reassuring whisper from his father before a particularly hard task was to be attempted. That analogy brought out the next and last question he had for the Sage, knowing his journey now lay purely in his own hands.
'So what happens to us when we reach our end? Do we pass to paradise or do we became part of this, this Nemesis?' The wise old one thought long and hard about his answer.
'I have not yet discovered the truth of that fully. But I do not fear my end. And nor should you. Every piece of our universe is recycled or transformed; waste is merely a subjective term. With all I have seen and learnt, I know that my consciousness would not simply dissipate come that day. Physical entropy would appear to only be the manifestation of leaving this realm for another. Where my soul will go? That is the greatest adventure I will undertake but one I am sure I have done many, many times before.'

The night time sky in Central London was low and heavy. The bright lights cast dabbled patterns across the clouds, causing them to look a little bit like clouds of milk mingling with tea in a clear glass mug. Sam sat in the privately-run coffee bar at the foot of the exclusive apartment block where only a few short days ago she'd spent the night with Luke. She'd made her excuses at the office, a migraine, and had to admit to herself she'd felt pretty emotional as she walked away from their building knowing it was the last time she'd see any of her colleagues. In the fullness of time they'd undoubtedly see her image again, somewhere along the line she'd be in the news, even if it was simply as a missing person. There were certainly quite a few of them she would happily never meet again but, even so, the finality of it all weighed on her for quite a while. The lack of notice, the swift change from all the trappings of a normal life versus the new life she was about to embark on was surprisingly traumatic. The phone conversation with Grimes seemed to point to a similar seismic shift from his point of view too. It seemed that despite the fact that such a change inevitably had to occur once they had chosen this path, neither had adequately prepared for the abrupt disconnection of the lives they had previously known.

'Would you like another Latte, Madam?' asked the barista in a slightly concerned tone, seeing that Sam was miles away, lost in thought. She answered positively.

'Best make that two.' It was Grimes, dressed casually and looking very tired. He bore the look of someone who'd rarely worn anything other than a suit in the past ten years.

'So this is really it?' he commented as he settled into the armchair 'The end of an era.'

'It sure is.' Sam felt compelled to lighten up the mood. 'Wonder if they will ever make a film about us?' Grimes let out a deep and hearty roar of laughter.

'If only they knew the half of it!'

'Are we ever going to meet the other members of Luke's team?' The naïve validity of the question kept him in an amused state of mind.

'Samantha, my darling, I very much doubt it.'

She looked down into her empty cup. 'So where do you plan on going?'

'I know where I will be starting. Venezuela, then wherever the roads and my passports take me. South America is still the place to go if you want to disappear from view, and enjoy doing so.' Pausing to take note that she had not removed her eyes from the China mug she held in her lap. 'And you?'

'I haven't decided yet.' Her answer caused Grimes' brow to crease. 'If I could give you some advice? Only rely on yourself to make you happy. You can call all the shots, especially now, despite what Luke said. Don't let yourself be defined by someone else. You have the ability to be as free as anyone can be, now seize it for yourself!' Sam looked up as the two coffees arrived.

'Thanks.' It was not clear to whom she was addressing her gratitude to. At that moment, the distinct sound of a vibrating mobile phone could be heard.

'Yep?' It was Dyer on the other end of the line, calling from a payphone at a service station once more. 'OK, we are waiting at the foot of your building so see you in half an hour or so.' He put the phone down. Ordinarily he'd have destroyed it there and then but now he figured a few hours would make little difference. In fact, there was bound to be a stretch of beach where he could dispose of the device once he'd finished the first leg of his trip to start his new life. That would be very symbolic.

Desmond sat in the quiet solitude of the meeting room he often used at the back of the private members' club. Discretion was a byword for their service and only here did he know with one hundred percent certainty that he could conduct his business completely privately, unobserved, uninterrupted and without being snooped upon. With the door locked and a trademark glass of port at hand he could commune with his Masters. *The Nemesis*. Like his uncle before him, they had looked over him, protected and guided his career, ensured he wanted for nothing. All for a small, small sacrifice. His Obedience. Total and unwavering loyalty. Acting on orders when given no matter how innocuous, strange or disagreeable he may have found them to be. *The Nemesis* had even taught him how to deal with such petty things as a conscience. Techniques to disassociate oneself from the rudimentary morality that conventional society operates by, whilst not appearing to live outside the normal, established order of things. The change in perspective this gave him was, paradoxically, a very useful trait to learn and apply in gaining the trust of those who might otherwise have been unsure of unwittingly aiding him in doing his Masters bidding. Desmond gave a final tweak of the door handle to be sure the scene was perfectly set before speaking out loud the words to alert them that he was ready and waiting to meet. The words were ancient, spoke in a tongue long dead to the rest of humanity. Spoken deep and low like a humble prayer.

The ambient temperature in the room began to drop by about five degrees centigrade and moments later he became aware of a presence behind him.
'Is that you, Ancient one?' he felt the answer more than heard it. As if the sound was generated within his skull rather than from behind his head where the hot breath of his companion was generated. The hands placed on his back feeling as if they entered his body and rested uncomfortably onto his ribs and spine.
'*Things are not going as we had wanted. You know that we do not like it when we are not in control, little one.*' The words causing a sensation that was mildly painful to ripple down his back like a trail of hot oil. '*Are you taking your responsibilities seriously?*'

'Yes I am. As always, I am your servant. But our tool has proven to be somewhat… erratic. He is not completely predictable; it is not clear what truly motivates him.'

'The boy is not the problem. He serves his purpose with little direct influence from us. When the time is right, we will whisper in his ear to push him to our conclusion of his work. That is not the cause of our concerns.' Desmond was used to feeling uneasy in their presence but that did not make the experience any less unpleasant.

'Then how may I serve you best?' The ambient temperature had reduced enough to cause his breath to mist in the air, as well as a thin layer of smoke like moisture to occupy a chest-height stratum across the whole room. It fluctuated and pulsed slightly as The Nemesis responded.

'You do not have enough influence on The Organisation to be able to serve us as you should. It is under the illusion that it has an independence and a duty to its country that does not align well with our needs. You have not gained the trust needed, blinded by your own arrogance and self-importance. You have forgotten what we have taught you, that to give orders is the last resort and not the first course of action.'

'I, I will double my efforts to be more in control of the situation presently. I will just need a little time to figure out how, so as not to be suspected.'

'We do not have the luxury of time in your realm. The tide is on its way. The scene is set. We will deal with the immediate issues through the one called Dyer. To us, his motivations are not a concern; we will exert our influence directly. You will continue to do what we need in parallel and not concern yourself with our activity. We are sure you will seize the opportunity to extend your reach when it presents itself.' And with that, their presence evaporated into the air. For a few short moments he held his breath then realising he still could, he let out a long, low sigh of exhaustion. As time passed, the after effects of communing became more and more pronounced and debilitating. It was a small price to pay to be so close to those who had real power, he surmised.

Hayes and Killen had certainly enjoyed the journey back from Stamford, despite horrendous traffic and the anticipation of the undoubted outstanding paperwork pile, which would probably be of biblical proportions by now, waiting for them back at the office. Okay, in the grand scheme this was a small victory for the law but each small victory was worth a moment celebrating. As the initial jubilation had tailed off to a calmer, light hearted mood, his

thoughts returned to the vague description given at the arrest of "a big blond bloke". It took about five minutes of silence to allow Philip the time to remember.
'Shad Thames.'
'Sorry Guv?'
'Shad Thames. Scene of that horrific murder of a young lady where she was "torn in two". That's where I remember a description of someone seen near to the crime scene, acting weirdly. A tall, blond or fair haired man. Well built. Acting agitated as he walked along the south bank. I remarked at the time to the Super it smelt a bit of a strange one, the way she was killed, made me think of all the odd stuff we have seen investigating these crimes.'
'You think *the Houdini Gang* were behind that murder?' Killen winced as she said it, momentarily forgetting his dislike of the moniker they'd been given.
'I think there is the possibility that the poor girl was murdered by someone involved in the crimes we have been investigating. Tenuous link it may well be but a possibility.'

The phone rang suddenly with the pre-programmed caller ID showing it was their base.
'Hello.' Philip answered, allowing Killen to concentrate on her driving.
'Hello, sir? I thought you'd want to know we've just received some information on one of the pre-bought mobile phones we have being monitoring? It was turned on about an hour ago and the network has just notified us that it has also received a call. I am e-mailing you the location we believe the device is now located at. What would you like us to do?' Hayes opened the message on his smartphone to see where the device was located.
'We can get there in about forty minutes, can you get SO19 engaged and mobilised that quickly?' SO19 are the Specialist Firearms unit, a pretty wise precaution given some of the recent events surrounding the investigation.
'Probably not sir, not without it being a fully identified and recognised threat or need. Hard enough with all the senior officers in one building to get them involved in a speculative deployment but none of your chain of command are in your offices this evening.' His grey blue eyes rolled into his forehead in annoyance at the inconvenience, despite the fact he probably would have guessed it was an almost impossible task, given the circumstances.

'OK, just get a small team to travel there and meet with us at the site. We have a very loose description of one of our targets so there may be a chance of an arrest. We'll assess the risk once there but suggest protective vests will be in order.' Pausing to consider a little further his gut feel. 'And see if you can get someone looking at the CCTV footage at Grantham services for a tall blond man approaching the van driven by our latest guests of her majesty's wonderful residential facilities…'

Chapter Eleven

The Boss joined them on the sleek, black motor yacht. It was undoubtedly the best transportation to get them through the centre of London swiftly and relatively inconspicuously despite its slightly opulent and outlandish air. As he took up his chair he took a swig from his portable thermal coffee mug.

'Have you been keeping up to date with your silicon intake?' He asked Steve, sounding more like a dad nagging his four year old than the head of a covert government security operation.

'Yes, finding the supplements surprisingly tasty.' At that, Gmitrowicz signalled for them to embark on the short journey across town.

'Now, this is a very complex situation. There will inevitably be civilians in close proximity, I have the back office seeing if we can get as many evacuated as possible under the guise of a suspected gas leak but at this short notice we are bound to miss a few.' Jane turned towards *The Boss*, expecting him to interject. He did not need a second invitation to do so.

'The main objective remains unchanged. To neutralise the threat Dyer represents. Today he has taken the step we all feared he would and has become a severe and active threat to the security of our nation and the rest of the world to that end. We cannot allow him to escalate his activity further. He must be stopped whatever the cost, whatever it takes.' And with that the big man drained the last of his coffee, slamming the mug down a little too enthusiastically, causing the outer casing to slightly distort as a result. Steve felt the injector gun in its holster.

'A diamond to cut a diamond.' He murmured. *The Boss* smiled ruefully, aware of the sentiment and dread that mumbled statement carried.

'Indeed Steve. It may take you to act without any tools or weapons. After all, your entire body is now the most effective and self-sufficient weapon in the world. To serve our nation and protect its citizens. A vow of sorts we have both taken, no matter what it takes.'

It seemed that the whole of West London had been super glued into one endless traffic jam. Well, it was the middle of the rush hour and the proximity of Christmas meant the situation was somewhat exacerbated. Therefore only a few minutes had to pass before Dyer's wafer thin patience became completely eroded and an alternative method of getting across town popped

into his head. Because surely the whole beauty of driving a stolen car is that you don't really care about where you leave it, as you won't be needing it again. Just to be sure that it would cause the maximum disruption, providing an excellent diversion, Luke decided to ram as hard as he could into the car in front causing a chain effect of collisions ahead. The young man in the vehicle which he had just impacted, early twenties most probably, leapt out on to the tarmac in a full on fit of road rage, shoving Dyer who had also exited his car as he did so.
'You really shouldn't have done that.' Swiping at the driver as if he was a particularly irritating fly and sending him arcing over the traffic and crashing into a bus shelter on the opposite side of the road bringing out horrified gasps from those who witnessed it. Dyer nonchalantly got out his permanent mobile, looking at the map app to work out the most direct route from where he stood. Satisfyingly for him it was straight over a row of three storey shops and flats to his right so he grabbed at the chance of another dramatic exit leaping onto the roof and then out of sight of the terrified onlookers.

The trail of destruction across West London quickly became widespread and varied. Now that the thought of causing diversions had occurred to him it easily and rapidly escalated in to a spree of wanton carnage. The Icy cold wind rushing by his face only heightened Luke's senses. From his rooftop vantage point he could see intricate detail, every brick, slab and exposed edifice in a circular range of fifty miles around him. He could hear the babble of all the humanity that occupied that space too. Whilst standing at the top of the small tower block his attention was drawn to a young teenage boy, probably around thirteen, screaming abuse at his computer game, distraught at losing on whatever game he was engrossed in. Dyer pulled out another small coin from his pocket and flung it at the flat screen television to which the boy was physically addressing his tantrum, causing it to explode in a gloriously dramatic technicolour cacophony of sparks and smoke.
'There, now you have something to scream about.'
As Luke leapt off the building, he picked up the merest vibration from its left-hand side. It felt slightly unstable. Turning to look back at it he could just about make out a tell-tale hairline crack on a section of the load bearing part of the structure, approximately two thirds of the way down. In the garden in which he'd just landed was a very ostentatious statue of what appeared to be a prancing horse. Beaming like all his birthdays had come at once, Luke pulled the overgrown garden ornament from its foundations,

took careful aim then launched it tracing a low, long, curving trajectory precisely into the newly identified area of fragility. There was a brief delay then, with an almost exponentially increasing velocity, the left-hand side of the building collapsed in on itself, dragging the opposite side down on top of it, like a carefully set up and choreographed tower of dominoes.

'He's near, that way. About ten miles. And he's enjoying himself again at the expense of others.' The sudden proclamation catching Jane a little off guard, checking her phone to see if there were any alerts from the programme monitoring the available CCTV in the area. At that moment a message blipped up, the system had picked up the highly unusual event of a tower block suddenly collapsing within the area it was monitoring.
'Oh dear god, this has just come through.' Showing the screen to *The Boss.* He looked at it, snorting in the winter air and breathing out a massive cloud of steam. It conveyed, far more eloquently than mere words, how he felt. The steely determined look remained on his face. "Seven hundred and Fifty Million pounds of investment on monitoring software looks like an extravagant, redundant and unnecessary investment too…" She thought to herself as she turned to face Steve.
'I can only get a rough sense of him, it's not that accurate.' Seeming to respond and answer her unspoken reflection. Her phone vibrated once more, a message to state that Dyer was only about seven miles away from his flat now. Conversely, they were about a mile away.
'He ought to be arriving just after us.' Maybe technology was more accurate and predictable after all. Just.

The rather dramatic final leap across the river brought shocked gasps from people who were going about their daily routines of heading home along the windy south bank of the Thames. Dyer, somewhat theatrically, smoothed his short and hardly ruffled hair, repositioned his coat then opened the door to the Café where Grimes and Sam had been sat waiting for some time.
'You're a bit late.' Grumbled Grimes, as he extended his hand to shake.
'Yes, decided to take in a few sights by foot, it may be sometime before I get to see London again.' As the two men exchanged pleasantries, Sam stood up, her attention taken by the sudden flurry of hurried activity outside.
'What's going on out there?' just as an official looking man entered the Café.

'Sorry, can everybody please follow me. We have a serious suspected gas leak and need to evacuate the surrounding area immediately.' The trio glanced at each other a little bemusedly. Luke took in a deep sniff.

'Something smells funny about this,' pausing a moment 'or rather it doesn't smell at all.'

'What are you thinking?' Grimes understanding that the pun was fully intended, that Dyer would be able to detect even the merest abnormal amount of gas in the air.

'I think we need to get into my apartment to grab what we need right now.' And with that he led the way out of the café towards the entrance hall of the apartment block, forcibly swatting aside a couple more officials who tried to stop them.

'Was that completely necessary Luke?' it was amazing how quickly Grimes has become somewhat flippant about his colleagues' abilities. Samantha however was completely dumb struck. She'd never seen someone dispatch grown men with such ease.

'Was that karate or something?' she blurted squeakily.

'It was definitely something.' He retorted, flashing a cocky grin as he held the door open for them to follow him in.

With the benefit of hindsight, deciding to travel across the centre of London rather than around the ring roads had proven to be erroneous. They were probably six or so minutes from the location where using mast triangulation the team had calculated that the mobile phone had been activated. Thankfully the forward party were a little nearer. Hayes drummed his fingers impatiently on the dashboard mounted airbag cover just in front of him, mumbling discontentedly to himself. Killen leant her head against her right hand, which was supported by her right elbow leaning on the driver's door frame. A message buzzed on Hayes' mobile phone.

'Shit! I don't believe it.' Looking to face his companion. 'The immediate vicinity is sealed off due to what was initially a reported serious gas leak, but, as there has been a suspected terrorist incident in the past half an hour so SO19 and Counter Terrorism Command have taken over, even our guys cannot get in. Damn it!' thumping the airbag cover with a full-blown punch this time. The irony of the situation, bearing in mind his earlier conversation, simply adding to his frustration. At that point, the phone burst into life once more, this time it was Jenkins calling him directly. 'Hayes?' he confirmed it was him.

'Are you on your own?' the question took him a little by surprise, but he quick wittedly raised his fingers to his lips whilst he replied. 'Yes Ma'am. Why?'
'Have you heard about the tower block being completely destroyed this afternoon? It understandably has the corridors of power on full blown panic alert. The current CCTV footage of the incident we have our hands on is a little inconclusive, but there is definitely a concern that the way the block has been brought down is highly unusual. The conspiracy theorists will have a field day with this.'
'What's so unusual?'
'No visible flame or flash of an explosion. There was some sort of impact, but no evidence thus far that any incendiary explosives were used. Seems highly unusual so I naturally thought of you.'
The comment made Hayes give out a chuckle laced with a small amount of schadenfreude.
'Has anyone claimed responsibility yet, Ma'am?'
'No, no-one as yet.'

She paused, it was hard for him to tell why, but after the conversation he would reflect that maybe Jenkins was considering whether she should make her thoughts known or not. 'The thing is, I've had one of those cryptic conversations regarding you again, in light of this recent happening. I don't know what the agenda is here but someone somewhere seems to think you'd be a good fit to be seconded into running the investigation.' The cogs in Hayes' mind whirred momentarily.
'That's both massively irregular and somewhat of a departure from your previous conversations… I guess I should be flattered.'
'Off the record, I don't like it at all. We're being played here and I have no comprehension of what the game even is, let alone its goal. The inference is that the *Houdini Gang*, whoever they actually are, might be involved. I'll admit the fleeting impression that something inexplicable may have caused this tragedy did cause that thought to occur to me also. However, we have, with no disrespect to you Philip, many good officers in the right place and departments to handle the team investigating this incident. It will probably take years to reach a conclusion too. I've been asked to get you in for a meeting in my office oh seven hundred hours tomorrow. I'm sure that in today's politically correct way you'll be able to make a choice but…'
'But the wrong choice will mean a fast track to retirement no doubt Ma'am.' He glanced once more at his secret companion on the call, who was completely confused by the whole exchange. 'Maybe that's what they want?'

'If I know you Philip, that's probably an incentive to take the opportunity. See you bright and early.'

Jenkins cut the call, leaving the occupants of the car to mull over what had just been discussed. The traffic continued to be completely grid locked.

'You know, Killen, I sometimes think that the crimes we have to solve are put there to stop us using our skills trying to work out what goes on further up the chain that shouldn't be.'

The horizon seemed to stretch to infinity from the vantage point the Pyramid provided. Over the city, a large Starship slowly lumbered to its berth, covering roughly three square miles of the conurbation with its immense shadow. For all of the travel he'd partaken in, the sight still made him a little awestruck. The marvel of their ingenuity, the resources of the realm in which they lived conquered and controlled to fulfil their will. The power of a galaxy harnessed and manipulated. Ruedrav'tor placed a palm firmly on the trapezoidal shaped craft by his side. In comparison, it seemed an insignificant inconsequence. Looked barely capable of flight let alone much else. How much he'd learned from The Oracle. "Let the Obelus *not be underestimated. It can pass through the eye that links all realms and move to any point of anywhere you wish, once you have mastered your own thoughts, mighty warrior." Indeed it could. The secret he'd learnt well, now his to command. You did not fly the* Obelus, *through it you flew the multi-verse itself. Everywhere and anywhere moved around you, not the other way around. Even the mighty Starship, which bent space-time like putty, still had to move under its own power too. The* Obelus *brought those points you wished to visit to you. As such, the normal laws of whichever realm you wished to visit did not constrain you. Only your own thoughts and feelings could do that.*

He took one last look at the world he'd fought so long and hard for. The beauty of its purple sky. The magnificent quad-wings flying majestically along the river valley below the mountain range in which he stood. Next to him they would look enormous, monstrously proportioned. From here, with the backdrop of the Starship and city they seemed rather small and insignificant. 'I am ready to see just how small we all really are.' He thought out loud. Then, in his great hand he grasped the crystal sphere that allowed him to communicate with and to guide the Obelus. *The Sphere was the one true constant he'd learnt, all natural worlds were but balls of rock, ice or gas. Entering the craft, the globe begun to glow, cycling through many phases of colour and light, until finally settling on a mix of mostly blue, green, white and sandy brown. The outline of a strange alien world made sharp and clear. 'So this is where the Nemesis are most vulnerable?' For that was what he'd asked the Obelus to help him find. The mighty warrior sat precariously on the chair inside. It seemed to be more suited to the Oracle's peoples' frame than that of the warrior classes. No matter now. The journey was about to begin. He closed his eyes and prepared to move all of creation to his desire and will. The power he had at his disposal in such a moment was lost on him. Only the cause was of importance, not the means or his potency at wielding it. That was after all why the Oracle had entrusted this mission to him. Ruedrav'tor possessed a truly balanced perspective.*

With somewhat uncharacteristic tentativeness, Dyer slowly opened the door to his apartment. He could not hear or smell anything untoward in the lobby or lift as they approached it but, with all the theatrical shenanigans going on outside, there was every reason to remain vigilant. *The Organisation* was undeniably on to him with far greater accuracy than they had managed previously. Satisfied that nobody was waiting in hiding for them, he entered closely followed by Grimes and Sam. All three sat on the furniture in the large, open-plan living space at the centre of the accommodation.

'So this is it. The last time we meet to plan our joint operations.' Grimes sat back somewhat imperiously in the armchair he more than amply occupied. 'We are no longer going to be *the Houdini Gang*, scourge of the Met police. Inspiration to a generation of Grifters and budding professional thieves everywhere.'

'Indeed, it is the last time we shall meet in this country, or be hemmed in by its boundaries.' Turning his predatory stare to Sam. 'Where are we going first?' like a CEO asking their PA what the first appointment in their busy schedule was going to be. The presumptive nature of his request not surprising Grimes at all, Though Sam's response was not one he'd anticipated.

'I got us tickets to Brazil.' Pulling them out from her jacket pocket as proof. 'From there we make our minds up on what happens next.' If ever a sentence had more than one meaning, then this was it. Grimes looked at the pair of them, his disapproval of any future liaison written so blatantly on his face that it may as well have been a twenty-foot-high road sign. Then a fatalistic huff and shrug, it was, after all, a hopeful gesture on Sam's part to buy a second ticket but not exactly one of comparative great expense, almost as frivolous as buying someone a chocolate bar whilst getting yourself one. He sat forward once more.

'Well, maybe we will bump into each other on the Amazon or the beach in Rio. My dear, if you would please be so kind as to let me have the cards and paperwork associated with my accounts, I can be on my way and begin the rest of my life.' Samantha obliged, pulling an enveloped simply marked "a" from her handbag. Her gaze not leaving Luke's at all.

'Thank you young lady. It has genuinely been a pleasure doing business with you.' Starting to raise himself from his chair as if about to leave. His exit was abruptly halted as Dyer leapt up in an instinctive and unthinking manner. Sam noticing that the speed at which he did so was far quicker than should be normally possible.
'What the hell is that?' he asked out loud as he sped into the bathroom. His head spun with giddying speed as he scanned the whole room in fractions of a second before fixing on the toilet itself. Kicking the porcelain bowl clean off the ground, causing water to erupt like a fountain Luke smashed his hand into the waste pipe and pulled out a still part functioning micro-bot, covered in the detritus it had encountered on its hellish journey through the subterranean sewage network. 'Damn it, they know where I live! Grimes, they know where I live!' Discarding the device as he re-entered the room he'd just vacated.
'Who knows where you live?-' Sam's question immediately followed by the sound of shattering glass and window frames as what at first appeared to be some kind of projectile turned out to be a man, who rose slowly from the crouching position he'd landed in.

The figure was dressed in black from toe to tip, topped off with balaclava, which did its job well enough to disguise the look of surprise on Fletcher's face as he looked around the room.
'What the hell are you doing here?' he exclaimed, the comment making everyone else in the room forget that they should be spurred into some kind of action at his arrival. It was Sam's turn to look even more surprised now.
'Steve? Is that you Steve?' sitting back down again, finding the last few moments ludicrously overwhelming in their own right, let alone when combined with all of the dramatic build up that had occurred over the past few days. Steve took off the mask, ignoring the frantic questions and orders being beamed into his ear via it.
'You two know each other?' Dyer's tone one of a mixture between questioning and contempt, then addressing Sam directly. 'You're a plant? You're working for *The Organisation*?'

'What Organisation?' irritated by the accusation, ignorant as to how much risk of harm she was now under because he suspected her of such treachery. Her stare now firmly fixed on Steve's face.

'You're part of the *Houdini Gang*?' Questioned Steve, listening briefly to his inner voice, filling in the gaps for himself. 'Of course, you'd be perfectly placed to organise the money side of things.' Relaxing a little as he thought it through. 'I'm guessing you have no idea *how* he has been pulling off these crimes, do you?'

'I have no idea how you just got into this room!'

'Well I think you're about to witness some action that will both give you some answers and some more questions.' Dyer stated turning to face his other partner in crime. 'Sorry big guy I have one more thing I need you to do for me.' Grimes momentarily looked calm until he saw the return of the trademark maniacal smile. He knew he was powerless to avoid what was about to happen. Luke grabbed him squarely by the shoulders and tossed him like a ball at his still distracted opponent. The very audible sound of bones crunching and flesh tearing causing Sam to gag as if she was about to vomit. 'I think you could still be useful.' As he lifted her one handed from the chair, leaping out of the conveniently placed large hole where windows and frame had once been.

Steve took a moment to feel for a pulse on Grimes. None evident, unsurprisingly, as his body resembled a mangled pile of clothes and rubber, all stained in the blood spurting from various injuries caused by the force and sudden, juddering halt of collision. He felt the *sil-adrenaline* gun in its holster and pulled on the balaclava as he leapt out in pursuit of Dyer, who had already made it back across the river once more, with Sam thrown over his shoulder like a cartoon burglar's swag sack. He could hear her panicked breathing and it didn't take someone with his *en*hanced intuition to figure out how she was feeling right now. Steve could however clearly see that her knuckles were white with the pressure her hands were applying whilst hanging on for dear life as Luke bounded from roof top to pavement and back again.

'He's got a hostage.' Barking the information down the communications link to Gmitrowicz, sensing that it was vital for her to know the full facts.

'Ok, keep in contact with the target and let us know if that situation changes.' Jane then shouted to a colleague to back off, the reason why becoming immediately clear to Fletcher as a drone diverted overhead and hovered with some menacing purpose over the Thames beside them, keeping in tandem with their movements.

'Unless that thing has syringes for bullets it's nothing more than an over grown gnat.'

'It packs enough of a punch to distract our *wayward child*, giving you enough time to administer "The Cure" Steve.' It was at that moment he noticed that said *wayward child* had momentarily paused atop a Victorian end of terrace house. There were a number of school age children in the street just below and it became instantly clear that this was a stalling opportunity for Dyer, who almost petulantly kicked at the chimney stack to send the bricks spraying out over the street below. Fortunately Steve had already anticipated this move, sprinting, so as to almost disappear with the rapidity of his movement, and grabbing, swiftly but carefully, the intended victims up in his arms and delivering them safely out of the range of the now obliterated bricks and mortar, as they rained down onto the street. The subject of his pursuit had however gained enough time to be out of sight.

'Target is heading…'

'North East, I know I can feel him.' Interrupting the proffered information. 'Take it you have him on visual still from the drone, maybe it is more useful than I'd presumed.' Thinking to himself that he should at least sound grateful for the back-up. 'He's about half a mile north of the river now, though he is rather conveniently continuing to keep more or less relatively parallel to the river's general direction. We are not too far behind the chase.'

'Understood.' Slipping slightly on the roof slates as he landed awkwardly after another hundred foot bound closer to the path Luke had already taken.

He could make out their silhouette through the murky ambience of the semi-residential environment through which they sped. The high rise edifices of Central London standing out like an enormous replica of Stonehenge in the distance before them. It was obviously where Dyer was headed. The grand stage on which he would paint his next magnificent performance, no longer hampered by a desire to remain unknown and unseen. The spontaneity of the escape had him worried for Sam's safety. Psychotics tendered to have little regard for another's worth as he'd so ably demonstrated when he'd utilised his now former business partner as a distraction moments ago. Fletcher doubted that he'd have any less remorse in utilising her in a similar fashion when it suited.

'Do you have any idea who the hostage is in relation to our man?' He decided not to acknowledge the question, instead he had an idea.
'Can you get our gnat to buzz him? I think he has something in mind that involves getting a wider audience to his one man show and would like to not let him get to the middle of the city if we can.'
'Sure, leave it with us.' Jane turned to her colleague at the on-board camera screen and control panel. 'Let's get in front of him and force him to slow down by making a nuisance of ourselves. Don't get too close, however, his reactions are considerably quicker than yours.'

'That's it, good… aim for the tall towers. Where everyone can see you.'
Dyer was unsure of whether it was his own deluded subconscious talking to him or if he'd completely lost the plot as a result of the past few days' dramatic twists and turns and developed a split personality. All he knew is that the compulsion to head towards Central London was intense, so much so he could almost feel an energy nudging him back on course if he deviated from it by design or by necessity of the way being blocked ahead.
'They will all know of you by the time today is through.'
And that "thought" appealed to him very, very much. Why had he allowed himself to be so furtive, so secretive? He could have ruled, he knew that, He'd thought about it so often. Now was the time to do so. Lay siege to the houses of parliament, demand the respect and power he deserved. The woman's nails dug into his shoulder like claws, they'd have drawn blood even through the clothes on a normal man. Their dull but fluctuating pressure brought him back into the here and now just in time to draw his attention to something hovering menacingly ahead of him. The tell-tale flash of automatic arms fire ensued and Luke bounded effortlessly to the left avoiding the impact of the bullets by what seemed a lengthy margin of time.
'Excellent, that toy could do some serious damage if it follows you where we want to go. You could make them make themselves look foolish. Don't destroy it like I know you want to, encourage it to keep up with you.'
The fleeting heavy sensation in his head cleared again and he resumed his relentless journey across the increasingly high roof tops stretched out before him.

'Careful with the firearms, we don't want any friendly fire incidents on the streets of London!' Jane glanced over at *The Boss*. He seemed somewhat subdued and in thought. In fact, she was surprised he'd not already commented on the use of the Drone's arms before she had. 'Sir?' the direct address took a moment to sink in and then the Big Man turned to face her. 'At this rate of progress Dyer will be hitting central London in about three minutes.' He showed that he'd heard the information with a gentle nod.

'He's headed for Parliament Jane. I can sense it.' Steve's tone conveying the inner concern he felt at what that might entail. Gmitrowicz gestured to *The Boss,* suggesting he should make a call on his "hotline" to notify *the Civil Servant.*

'Try to get the drone to divert him, delay him. Steve, how far away are you from *Wayward Child* now?' In the background she could hear the rush of the wind interjected with the staccato crunches that his landings made upon the masonry on which they occurred.

'About twenty metres.' Throwing a lump of prefabricated concrete like a hand-grenade sized mortar shell as he answered, sending it whizzing by Dyer's ear as if to remind him of his pursuit. It smashed into the large mirrored windows of an office block on the Kings Road, which was where they now found themselves. Luke looked up at the tower and decided to scale it, avoiding the trail of bullets from the nearby drone that continued to try and distract him. Thousands of shards of glass rained down on the street below, causing a large number of civilians to be unintentionally injured.

'Hey, easy with the trigger, there are too many people to go freestyle with it.' Inside he was predominantly fearful for Sam's safety. She was breathing a little less rapidly than before, maybe her adrenaline rush had subsided but her fear of heights was certainly not going to be helpful to her right now.

How the hell had she managed to live such a double life, all this time they'd been together? Why had he not suspected anything was wrong? Okay, he had not possessed his *en*hanced intuition before but he had always been able to perceive that something was not quite right normally, why not this time? Dyer had reached the top of the office block now, setting Samantha down as he worked to tear free a mobile network aerial to use as a makeshift javelin. Steve caught the projectile with ease, tossing it with precision to one side, safely onto a nearby flat roof.

'Too scared to fight me hand to hand, Luke?' figuring that, although dangerous due to his unpredictability and aggression,

he was also more vulnerable when riled, and that it may offer an opportunity to shift attention away from Samantha long enough to enable him to rescue her.
'Not yet, there will be time for you to deal with this pawn later, when more eyes can see your worth. Keep that in mind. Go to where the power lies first, to where they rule.'
The voice having the desired effect of calming the bubbling, boiling temper within to a gentle and more controlled simmer. More automatic arms fire came in, hitting Dyer square on the shoulder, hurting no more than the annoying flick of an ear would but causing him to momentarily rock back on his heels. Steve seized the moment to pounce, traversing the twenty feet across a sheer wall of glass towards his target, only for Luke to recover his balance, grab his hostage and jump up and out into the now pitch black night sky.

Seething with rage, the atmosphere within the car was decidedly uncomfortable. Killen daren't make eye contact with Hayes for fear of what his reaction might be. She could feel the direction of his stare weigh heavy on the air around it, almost like two columns of lead pointing out from his eyes and smashing all in their path. Despite being involved with cordoning off the area, SO19 had not been able to gain close enough access to the area due to a serious gas leak, reports of which now coming through that it had caused an explosion at a nearby residential block, completely destroying at least one apartment. Philip hazarded a guess it would be in some way linked to their objective but whether they ever managed to find that link or not, it would be ultimately too late. The café, it was confirmed, had been completely evacuated. The back office were trying their best to access any CCTV in the surrounding area but thus far to no avail. Their best hope would be the instore CCTV. It was the Tower incident all over again. The frigid, unnatural silence was cut apart by the abrupt and warbling ringing of the hands-free phone. It made the hairs on Hayes neck bristle with the static-electricity that his mood had discharged into the atmosphere.

'Killen.' The relief of another person to communicate with barely disguised in the tone of her voice.
'Social-media is going crazy.' It was one of DI McCarthy's team, in their course of investigative work they found social media to be a great tool in helping them trace links and patterns that may not otherwise have been so obvious. This time it was a much simpler connection. 'The hash tag Spring Heeled Jack has just burst into life once more. Tons of mobile phone footage showing dark

outlines of figures leaping from roof top to roof top, across roads as well as smashing walls and windows. They're leaving a real trail of carnage, starting more or less from the Thames near that gas explosion. I've plotted the sightings and they are headed back towards the West End or the City, fast, by the look of it.' The news made her forget that she'd been avoiding looking at her companion. Fortunately, his interest had piqued enough to cut down on the off-putting effects he was having on the general environment he occupied.

'Shall we try to get back over to where they are headed?' Her green eyes expressing an eagerness to be anywhere but here, stuck going nowhere fast.

'Hmm, where are they now?' Philip considering how unlikely it was that they would be able to catch them as he asked.

'Last picture is on the Kings Road according to the GPS stamp on the digital photograph, bystanders hurt by falling debris about a minute ago. Seems like two of them again and rumours of a drone tracking them and firing on them too!'

'That cannot be true, no-one would authorise a drone attack on British soil, besides why they would use one on anyone other than an identified terrorist or other major security threat.' The obviousness of the statement catching her up, causing her to stop talking and turn the car around, hidden lights and siren bursting into life as she did so.

'Looks like we are on our way. Keep messaging us with updates on location.' Hayes paused as he looked at the map on the dash mounted monitor, which shared the relevant posts plotted on to a map. 'Reckon they'll hit the West End any minute now, we may get there in time to view the aftermath.'

'If there is a drone in the air chasing these two down, we needn't bother trying to get a helicopter up there, Sir?' Killen's question phrased and communicated to indicate that no answer was really necessary.

'Knowing these two, a chopper following them would just be another handy asset to use to cause mayhem. They're out of control, completely against the character of what...' pausing to search for an alternative phrase but none were forthcoming, so he carried on with his original thought, 'what this *Houdini Gang* have demonstrated in their actions previously.'

'I know people see things they want to see, Guv, but do you really think there is a drone chasing them?'

'Hmmm, they'd be shot down by now I'd have thought... though they seem to be able to dodge almost everything else that has been thrown at them so far. But if they are the ones behind the

Tower Block destruction, that, tallied with all of their other obviously potent and dangerous tools, makes them the biggest threat to national security out there, enough so for whoever authorises such things to take the unprecedented step of authorising the use of one on home soil.' The deep furrows of thought seemed almost agricultural in size across his brow. 'Unless… unless we have got this slightly wrong.'
Killen turned to face him directly momentarily as they had reached a less treacherously busy road as they progressed, lights casting fragmented shadows like momentary individual pictures sprayed onto the dark street scene backgrounds. 'What do you mean?'
'What if only one of these individuals is our target? What if the other is one is simply trying to do what we are, capture him?'
'But how would he have the same tech as the *Houdini Gang* possess?'
'Because it's the *Houdini Gang* who possesses the same tech as they have. Tech that is secret and military in nature. Of course, this is a rogue agent cell, a renegade group of some description. It's why we've been so subtly but successfully blocked and tripped up at every turn.'
'If that is true, it'll make the new job offer even more complicated.'
'Agreed, it will be a big ask… Quite a challenge. I'll need someone I can trust to help me in the team, be my eyes and ears. Any group who can exert the kind of influence and covert control we've, *not* seen, being seemingly demonstrated here, are almost nailed on to have someone on the inside lurking around.' Smiling at his companion to emphasise how unsubtle a hint that was.
'Guess I better be in the office bright and early too then, Guv.'

Amid the chaos, Gmitrowicz was still occasionally monitoring the potential Tachyon activity around Fletcher and *The Source* with some interest. The readings could probably best be described as almost metronome like in pattern, a short, sharp and regular pulse of activity not unlike a homing beacon signal would look if you measured its pulses in a similar fashion. The interesting point was that neither "signal" appeared to be in sync with the other. It was almost like two radio wavelengths existing at the same time but not interfering at all with each other. However, this was not the most surprising reading. She'd taken the liberty of installing a Nano-measuring device that could look for any signs of potential Tachyon activity being generated in the vicinity but not directly attributed to Steve. Jane was in particular trying to understand why the previous records had not shown similar results for Dyer, so in reality the device was installed with the expectation that nothing would be picked up. This was the surprise as the monitor showed a couple of spikes, randomly spaced and consistent with the traces previously observed and associated with Steve and *The Source*. And they were extremely powerful surges too.

The Boss looked over her shoulder at the traces on the small screen in her hand. He still carried a slightly distant look in his eyes. He then spoke, almost a thought out-loud but for addressing her by name. A volume as close as he ever came to a whisper.
'Jane. Do you ever question why we do what we do? I mean, why we are needed, why we operate in such a unique way?' The question, clumsily worded as it was, drew her attention away from the immediate tasks in hand.
'The secrecy is necessary, the cause is national security, the world is a complex place. With that in mind it makes perfect sense to me.' No question spoken but her tone conveyed her unspoken thought, why did he ask such a ridiculous thing?
'Something Desmond said to me once… like you say, the world is a complex place. And as we know,' adjusting his gaze towards the mobile command centre, watching the continued pursuit of Dyer from both Steve's and the drone's perspectives. 'It's hard to be completely certain that the facts are what they seem. I guess we can only concentrate on doing what we believe is the right thing.' Pointing to the large screen. 'Looks like the team will have to work overtime covering over the cracks in our façade after this evening is through.' The screen showing that they had reached Sloane Square and that the internet was a buzz of activity although thankfully nothing so clear as to show exactly what was happening, or who was involved.
'If Dyer is headed to Westminster, we should be arriving soon after at the riverbank there.' Gmitrowicz paused to receive some information from one of the other members of staff. 'And our airborne mobile unit should be there presently for us to utilise if necessary.'

The first-class lounge at Heathrow Airport was the very paragon of understated opulence. Clean, clear and crisp design. A quiet, almost serene atmosphere with more attentive serving staff than many a five-star hotel. And he would know. Being the kind of connected businessman he was, Bahajoub had experienced many places on many deals. News of the suspected terrorist attack in West London completely destroying a residential tower block dominated the twenty-four-hour news channel being shown

on the large and impressive TV screen to the far right of the room, but the coverage was interspersed with unconfirmed reports of numerous sightings of strange figures traversing across the roof tops of West London, headed towards Central London. The captions read *"Houdini Gang on the run?"* and the fact that such a story that would normally be centre stage was almost a foot note this evening showed that you could never quite predict what might happen next. It struck him as the kind of day in politics where they'd say "it is a good day to bury bad news". He wondered if the stock markets would use these events as a good excuse to sell off also, flush out the smaller investors or the more weak-willed, creating an opportunity for the powerful to buy back in, having taken some profits.
'Funny how they do not seem to have connected the two stories, don't you think?' Bahajoub turned to face the person sitting next to him. She was strangely familiar but he could not place a name to the face, or indeed recall if they had actually met, exactly where and when it would have been.
'Ahh, do you see a conspiracy theory.' Smiling as he spoke, it was after all his instinctual cloak to mask how he actually felt.
'Mr Bahajoub, I am surprised at you. Why would I talk of theories, when I am only interested in the facts?' perfectly manicured hands deftly removing the curtain of wavy hair away from her face so that eye contact was uninterrupted.

'I am sorry, but you have me at a slight disadvantage. Please forgive me but I do not remember your name?' forever the polite gentleman.
'If only that was the sole disadvantage you have.' She smiled, a calm and pleasant smile that seemed as unthreatening as the words seemed menacing and foreboding. 'Not to worry, such pleasantries are unimportant in the big scheme of things.' Breaking their eye contact to look once more at the screen to the side of them. 'Have you ever wondered why so few people fully understand what a strategy is?'
The obscurity of the question causing his smile to morph momentarily into a thought filled grimace. 'Hmmm…' Unsure of quite what to make of his new lounge companion. 'Not really, I have always suspected that like so many subjects, most people are ignorant to the importance of such things or simply believe they have no need to understand it. Much like politics or science. People are happy to be led rather than take part, content that something is done for the right reasons.' The last comment made her chuckle.

'Maybe you are right. What is it the English say? Ignorance is bliss? Well, there is a certain truth in that. But often not knowing the big picture is the very thing that makes understanding strategy impossible. And I am sorry for that.' Her companion not taking the opportunity to reply, merely taking a moment to sip his tea and resume eye contact. 'The art is to let the foot soldiers feel like they understand the strategy when they do not. Take a business that is trying to achieve a position they desire. The sales person may think they understand more than most what is needed, what the strategy is. They are goal driven so they must know what the ultimate objectives are, surely? Funny how they are probably the ones who are most expendable when things start to go wrong.' She stood up, elegantly. Through instinct and manners, Bahajoub tried also to stand and suddenly became aware that he could not. 'You have been a great salesman for our cause, Mr Bahajoub. I thank you for that. However, I am sorry to say your services will no longer be required. Please enjoy your retirement.' And coldly she walked away, as he felt the paralysing effects of the poison traverse up his torso and his consciousness, swiftly and inexorably, fade away.

Soil, grass and concrete sprayed across Parliament Square. At such short notice, it was not possible for the security forces and the police to effectively evacuate the vicinity so a ring of cars remained to witness the spectacle of one, then two dark figures landing with force in the middle of the small green, one that had seen many protests and political interviews take place over the years. Dyer had managed to successfully bend a nearby signpost over Sam, trapping her and preventing her from running away whilst he was otherwise occupied. He and Fletcher were presently joined by the ominous outline of the drone over-head, followed by fire-spark trails of gunfire aimed solely at Luke. Steve seized the initiative, pulling out the Sil-adrenaline injection-gun as he leapt purposefully toward his target. As they collided, he tried to swiftly press its tip towards Dyer's thigh, only for Luke to react just before the device could properly engage, swatting it into the distance.

'Excellent, that was his best hope of defeating you. You have the upper hand now. Use it.'
'I intend to.' Luke's thinking out loud causing a moment's pause as the two foes eyed each other for the next move. 'Here to save the people, are we? Well let's help you to prove your worth at it.' Grabbing a nearby motorcycle, rider still mounted and throwing it to effectively distract him, then taking the opportunity, whilst

Fletcher's attention was diverted, to throw a small coin at the drone overhead. The coin pierced the outer shell, disintegrated the motherboard within and clear cut through the other side of the fuselage as the robotic device began to immediately plunge towards the gathered crowds on the streets below. Meanwhile, Steve had successfully managed to catch the motorbike and rider cleanly and safely set them down on the other side of Parliament Square. The sudden cutting out of the drone's engine caught his attention. 'Shit!' was his unthinking response as he sprinted across the square in a blur, clambered instantaneously onto the roof of a lorry and caught the stricken object just before it would have crashed and exploded into a fireball that would have cost many lives. At that moment, his built-in earpiece sprang into life.

'Steve, do not engage the target until I give the go ahead.' It was *The Boss* barking his orders with his usual authoritative air. The command did take Fletcher somewhat by surprise, but the soldier in him knew to trust his commanding officer implicitly. 'Give the go ahead to fire at the target at will, in controlled bursts. No more collateral damage please.' And with that the small team of armed personnel, *Organisation* personnel that had been hastily drafted in to engage with Dyer as soon as they had guessed his destination, began to fire short, sharp and accurate bursts of bullets at him. Luke stood nonchalantly, waiting for them to hit his skin and stay there ready to be propelled back. Except this time they did not. They tore into his flesh and caused searing pain. The bullets were diamond tipped, and there was a practical reason for only firing a few at a time. Not even *The Organisation* could afford many of these bullets and indeed only possessed the few they had managed to get manufactured in the short time since the Tower attack that had initially inspired Jane to commission them in the first place. Distracted and giddy from pain, he dropped to his knees then instinctively, Sil-adrenaline flowing through his veins continuing to heighten his senses and abilities, Luke managed to dive powerfully into a storm drain and disappear from the range of the armed unit.

'Cease fire. Steve, over to you he is weakened momentarily. Make it count.' With that Fletcher burst into action, but he did not immediately pursue his quarry down below the streets of London. Instead he first grabbed one of the weapons from the armed personnel then stood motionless momentarily. 'If I am equally matched in my speed and reactions, maybe I need to trust my instincts to get a better advantage?' He thought to himself, eyes closed trying to feel where Dyer was. Faintly in his mind's eye he could "see" the bright pinpricks of light where the people around him stood and the one below the ground, moving relatively sluggishly for someone who'd been enhanced. In a matter of nanoseconds he had spotted the next storm drain along from where Dyer stood and crashed through it into the under-street rain sewer, about thirty feet in front of his opponent, who was gaining strength rapidly. He took aim and pulled the trigger, and two bullets left the gun in what appeared to be slow motion to both individuals. Their budget had not stretched as far as Steve would have hoped for and he found himself immediately out of ammo. The projectiles traced their path towards Luke, who had regained enough of his equilibrium to dodge the first completely and to only be glanced by the second on his left deltoid.

'You need to fight him where they can see you, not here in the darkness. Buy yourself time to recover.' The voice was beginning to irritate him but Dyer couldn't disagree with its guidance though. He spotted a weakness in the fabric of the storm drain ceiling between them both. The Victorian infrastructure also affording him with a ready-made missile with which to target the weakness, a loose brick just to his left. In a sweeping movement he clawed at the masonry, tossing the brick with enough force and accuracy to cause the desired effect, a chain reaction bringing down a section of the drains ceiling creating enough of a distraction and obstacle to allow him to reverse back up the passageway unpursued. As he ran with ever increasing efficiency, he began to check his wounds. It felt as if any bullets that had made contact had fortunately not remained within his body.
'The exit is just there, time to take this back above ground.' That was enough, his patience with his new found "inner voice" already tested to the full.
'I am not going up right where I entered, they might still have some effective bullets left in the other guns. Now piss off and leave me to figure this out whatever you are.' He could hear that the blockade was proving to be even more temporary than he'd initially thought it would be. The next manhole cover was about a hundred metres further down the shaft. That would get him back to approximately where he'd left Samantha "securely restrained". She would be useful in getting away from any further potential attempts to shoot him.

Fletcher stopped clawing at the remaining debris that still blocked his progress, 'Sam!' he thought out loud. Getting a sense that she was where Dyer would be headed to. He spun around and headed immediately back up the point of entry he'd created a

matter of moments earlier. Luke was prising back the makeshift clamp under which Samantha had been trapped since he had placed her there. Their eyes made contact for the briefest of moments before Dyer bounded once more into the London Skyline.
'He's on the move again, away from parliament though which is a small blessing.' Steve muttered to the control centre in general via his integrated comms-link, sprinting at lightning speed along the road to catch up.
'Thanks, we have him on the cameras.' Jane replied as she and *The Boss* boarded the large, unmarked and heavily armoured helicopter that performed the ultimate in mobile command function. 'We will be a safe distance behind you both.' Large boulder-like lumps of concrete and rubble rained down on him as he continued to pursue Dyer. Wherever he could, he tried to intercept or divert the path they took to minimise any civilian casualties but unfortunately he soon resigned himself to the fact that the best way to reduce the risks was to focus solely on removing their root cause. Recognising a small side street that joined the loop of the main road a little further on, Steve made a split-second decision to divert down it, hoping at minimum that it would bring him a little closer to his goal. The move caused Dyer to slow momentarily, confused as to what had caused the sudden loss of his shadow. This allowed Steve to emerge ahead of him and climb up onto the roof of a tower block that was immediately in his path. They stood a matter of a few metres apart, facing each other like two old time actors playing the lead roles in a spaghetti western.

'Put her down, gently, Luke.' Pausing to gauge his reaction. 'There is no need to add her life to the list you have created over the past few days.' *The Organisation's* Helicopter making a low, rhythmic droning noise just to the west of where they stood, about the same height up as they were.
'What a very military attitude you have,' peering down at the chaos that had ensued on the street just below. 'A list? We haven't even started yet. It's barely a footnote.' Gripping a little firmer on to Samantha as she tried, unsuccessfully, to escape his grasp then glancing into the distance at the spot from where the thundering of rotor blades was emanating. The outline did not appear to be a standard military helicopter, meaning it was not an immediate threat to be urgently eliminated. 'So here we are. Face to face. Just the three of us. No weapons, no robo-sniper in the air. No diamond tipped bullets. Just you, me and Sam. Cosy isn't it?' thankfully for his own mental balance the voice in his head

seemed to have obeyed his request. Luke held his hostage very firmly by the back of the neck, almost like a game hunter holding up their kill for the camera.

'It doesn't take a mind reader to work out she has importance to you. Why? She's just a normal person. What does it matter if she lives or dies, in the big scheme of things?' Steve, bizarrely, felt himself relax a little. Right now talking bought him some time to figure out his next move.
'Meant, meant something to me.' Guessing that appearing to demonstrate a level of apathy may be the safest option for Sam right now. 'Make no mistake, I am fully focused on the task in hand. You and I both know one thing, Luke. If all else fails, fight fire with fire. Use a diamond to cut a diamond.' Pausing to adjust his footing to be able to more instantly react to anything his opponent may try. 'You ever faced a situation where you were not in the strongest position on the battlefield?' Dyer shrugged his indifference to the question. 'I thought not. That teaches you the value of life, what it means to be brave. What it means to be *human*.' Luke laughed whole-heartedly.
'Hah! Human? You and I are no longer part of that club.' – The voice returned once more.
'He is still encumbered with the weakness of his birth, use its biggest flaw, blind loyalty and compassion, against him.' Dyer's face flashed with both annoyance that his unwanted guest had returned as well as the fact that its counsel was undoubtedly once again very good advice.
'This ape is no more to us than ants are to her. Smaller, inferior, weaker. At best a pet, a plaything.' Holding her a little closer to the edge near to where they stood, Sam's last remaining shoe looping out and down to the street below. Steve could smell the terror her pheromones were irradiating. He stood fast, somehow he had to get Luke to let her go, she did not stand a chance whilst his grip remained steadfastly around her neck. Even over such a short distance her neck would be snapped before he could do anything about it.

'What is going on?' *The Boss* bellowed above the noise of the engine and blades, even though they were all wearing headsets to communicate with. 'Sounds like Steve is buying himself a little time to think. Dyer still has his hostage.' Glancing at the incoming message on her phone. 'Ahh, we have a complication. Facial Recognition has identified who the hostage is.' Gmitrowicz turned and showed the screen to her companion. He recognised her instantly from the file they had compiled on Steve before they'd initiated their recruitment of him. He sighed very audibly, thoughts rushing through his head of how he should react to this new information.

'Can we get this thing down near to where they are now?' His question seeming somewhat odd and counterintuitive to the doctor.

'I think not. The best place is where it picked us up from.' Jane could see that this fact did not surprise him but was an irritation nonetheless.

'Patch the feed from Steve's communicator into my headphones as well please! I want to monitor exactly what is happening.'

'You would think that I have done terrible things, sinned against people I loved, treated others as toys to play with. Used people as commodities and as extensions of my own satisfaction, thrown them away when they have displeased me. The weight of guilt should be too much for even our frames to bear. But unlike you, I am not connected to anyone else, to these people and their pathetic problems, their issues and emotions. I have grown from there, I have become more. I have embraced the fact that I no longer need to be anchored down by *humanity* anymore. It is how I have managed to evade your *Organisation* for so long. You are too weak minded and unimaginative to see the big picture. Nobody has told you the big picture and like a good soldier you can only obey orders.'

'You haven't grown Luke. It's not a process of some kind of greater evolutionary path that you have chosen to take whilst on your self-indulgent crime spree. You've shrunk, become smaller, small minded, self-deluded and weaker for it. You're merely a psychotic bully, a small boy trapped within an *en*hanced frame. I feel sorry for you...'

Whether Steve had meant for his words to snap him into a rage was not clear, but that was exactly what they did. Luke tossed Sam over the edge of the Tower block, out towards the sprawling streets below. Steve reacted almost before the move, letting his extra sense guide him without any question or pause. It was just as well, he only just managed to catch her, setting her down safely at ground level, the force of his landing creating an almost perfect set of rings of rippled concrete radiating out from where he stood.

'You'd better quickly get out of here. I won't be able to stop the more conventional law enforcement from...' His words stopped as he felt another wave of precognition kick in, reacting to it by pushing Sam to the side with enough force to carry her forty foot

away, just as several floors of steel and concrete came crashing down on his legs, toppling him over and crushing his limbs at a right angle. Moments later, Dyer landed just beside him.
'Never saw that one coming, did you?' Steve writhed in pain as he struggled to get free from the immense weight of the rubble, his legs threatening to fuse back together in the unnatural shape which they had been snapped into. 'I would kill you but actually, this is a far better punishment than I could have thought up. There is no way they will get to free you before your bones meld together, and the only person who could help reset them now is…well, me.' Dyer's look of absolute pleasure only served to demonstrate that Steve's words earlier were right. He pushed on the girder that stuck out ominously just inches from Steve's face, who could feel the movement both by touch and the waves of excruciating pain in his limbs. His heart was now beating so fast as to feel like a violently oscillating vibration deep in his chest.

The Boss looked on and around him at the bedlam that he was surrounded by. Only he was calm, because he knew he was the only one who could help now. 'Jane,' Firm, calm, controlled but also tinged with genuine warmth. 'This is your operation now.' he handed his smartphone to her like a precious family heirloom. 'I know that you will be a much more pragmatic leader than I ever was.' He smiled, Jane's troubled and confused expression loosened and was replaced a little cautiously with her own smile. She saw a glint, a glow in the big man's eye's she had always observed but never paid much attention to before. At that moment she figured out why they were so bright despite his age. *The Boss* tore his tie from his neck with a swift tug as well as removing his headset and continued to bark his commands. 'All you need to know about *The Organisation* is on that phone. Guard it well. Do not let Desmond get his hands on it.' And with that, he leapt the impossible distance out of the command-copter towards both Dyer and Fletcher.

Through the fog of his tormented confusion, Steve felt someone else approaching them, rapidly. The surprise caused him to momentarily forget the pain, allowing his strength to increase enough to move the rubble a little further from his legs. The look of surprise on his face caused Dyer to stop his inane babbling and respond with a faintly quizzical look of his own. Just as the approaching dim blur in the night sky became a large shadow with a familiar outline.
'Nice to see you again, Luke.' As *The Boss* swung a sledgehammer of a punch straight onto Dyer's jaw, launching him

hundreds of metres back into the air towards and over what remained of the block he'd just torn the top off of. 'Looks like you could do with a hand son.' In unison they heaved the tsunami of twisted masonry back enough to enable Steve to pull himself free, his legs now able to mend and fuse back to their original state. 'No time to explain, we still have our *wayward child*'- Steve pushed *The Boss* to one side as an incoming Dyer shaped missile hurtled in, dispersing and disintegrating rubble like a meteor striking land. He emerged from the smoke moments later, brushing down some fire that had settled on his left shoulder.
'Well, well big man. Been holding out on us have we?' The crazed grin firmly re-established across his face. Steve, stumbled a little, the effects of continually forcing his legs to re-break whilst struggling to be free had left him weak and in need of rest.
'What's the point of working for a secret organisation if you can't keep any of your own?' The old man's gruff voice added a rich texture to the intended irony of the statement.
'What is this now? Sending a man to finish a boy's job?' Goaded Luke mockingly, attempting to provoke a reaction.

They both started to circle each other slowly, like two has-been boxers reduced to sparring in an all-out bare knuckle fight in an abandoned warehouse on the wrong side of town.
'Shame that being buried alive seems to have left Steve a little weak at the knees? Together I am sure you'd have both been too much for me. You should have acted earlier *Boss*. Too little, too late.' It was true; Steve was in no real position to help him out right now. *The Boss* stood still.
'You were always irritatingly over confident. I'd forgotten how much it annoyed me. What you fail to understand though is...' his words temporarily stopped by Dyer's lunge towards his throat. The big man caught his fist and crushed it effortlessly whilst he trapped Luke's head under his other arm. '..is I had to go through *The Process* the hard way. The brutal way, it made me the stronger for it. You know what they say – no pain no gain.' With which he sharply yanked Dyer's head forwards, leaving his body to slump to the floor like a robot that had suddenly run out of charge. *The Boss* turned to face Steve, slowly dropping to his knees as he did so, letting Luke's decapitated head roll awkwardly away from him. Steve leapt to his side, both of them wobbling a little as if disoriented by spinning too much.
'The doctor... the original doctor said it would be suicide to use my full strength once more... <cough> I always hated it when he was proven right.' Steve gently held his arm steady, keeping his body upright.

'You were the other connection, the one I couldn't fully see?' *The Boss* nodded his reply.

'*The Process* I took was crude, and painful. I nearly died, my heart stopped twice during the change. We… we didn't understand the effects as we do now… <cough> or have the technology to carry it out as effectively. Using a mix of Nano-bots to act like a virus rather than crudely incorporating it into a common existing virus was a touch of Genius by Jane…

Enduring *the Process* the way I did made me even stronger than you but for one fundamental weak…ness, my heart itself. As time passed, the additional strain on… it and the fact…<cough> the fact it had less exposure to the change took their toll.'

'Let's get you out of here; Jane must be able to do something to help…' The big man squeezed his arm as Steve started to lift him.

'Even if she could've before, my race is run now… You're all that is left of our *Organisation's* legacy now… use our gifts wisely. Be a man, not a god… Steve.' and with that, the light in his eyes finally faded and flickered off. Steve picked him up gently, as if he were a sleeping toddler and stood still, contemplating all that had just happened.

Chapter Twelve

The black void slowly began to illuminate with a myriad points of light, stretching out like a vast city as far as he could see. He would blink if he was able to but for some reason could not. As he began to recall what had just happened, he also noticed the unfilled space before him and a presence by his side. The Boss was never one to feel irrational fear, but had to admit to himself the entity made him feel more at ease with the situation.
'Mighty one, it is an honour to commune with you at last.' The words not so much spoken and heard as felt. Somehow in this place that felt natural. 'You wonder who I am?'
'I wonder where I am.' He responded, still a little awestruck.
'I am Ruedrav'tor, the Source *as your scientists rather coldly labelled my living cadaver. I am sorry we have not been able to meet in… in more tangible surroundings. This is, I think you would call it, Limbo. I am sorry but as yet I have only had a few chances to practice the language of your fathers. This is where people of all realms come to choose their next path.*'
'What is that, that fireball just there?' as ever to the point even in such surreal circumstances.
'Who, rather. The lights represent all the people in all the multiverse, at all times. That is Steve. He cradles the body you last inhabited. He burns so brightly as you are still connected to it, and to he.' The big man turned to where the presence seemed to be and gazed on the face of Ruedrav'tor alive with expression for the first time.
'It all looks like Las Vegas, and we are standing on the edge of the neighbouring desert.' Turning once more to face the blankness.
'Your people have the gift of being able to see things the way that makes most sense to you. I thought it a defect at first. Now I understand the strength it brings you. We are on The Edge. The whole of everything, every-time, everywhere lays within. Most who stand where we do simply enter and traverse it to the next existence, with no say of what will happen next, nor any recollection of being here. I guess that you, like I, have been given the freedom to choose.'
'To choose what?'
'Where and when you go from here. Normally the life before effects the next step. But rarely do we get to think about where it may lead. Even rarer are we able to remember this experience or the last life lived. Very few get the chance to stay, or even go back.'

The Boss *sat down, dangling what would be his feet into the seemingly endless abyss just beyond* The Edge. *He felt the hand of Rue on his shoulder.*
'Reality needs strong ones like you in so many realms, at so many times. You were the mightiest of us all, fighting through The Process in a world not quite advanced enough to deliver it well. Your essence from this point has been forever transformed. Wherever you will go you will be a force for good more powerful than any of the Nemesis have encountered elsewhere.'
'Nemesis?'
'That is what the ones you have long suspected exist are called, Mighty One. And their will is hard to oppose, to risk to fight the opposite side of. One person has never thus far managed by themselves to completely alter the path they had planned. It took millions upon millions in my home realm to sacrifice themselves. I sense that, even though it may not feel like it, you have dealt them with a very significant blow. They had not anticipated your move. It has weakened their position just as they sought to ramp up their interference and influence. With the one called Dyer they could have wreaked havoc on your world unopposed, were it not for Steve and for you working together, being prepared to give all unselfishly. But the Earth is just one skirmish in the battle that rages around everyone you can see from here-' *pointing to the infinite number of lights behind them.* 'and every-time you cannot.' *Once more facing the void of* The Edge.

'So, I should move on and not return? What if the Nemesis finds another way to create a replacement Dyer? You say it was working together that successfully defeated them. Steve is alone now.'
'Not for long. You have chosen wisely with both your successors. And I will soon face the same choice as you. To return or move on.' *The old warrior stood tall, facing full on to the void ahead of him.* The Boss *could not tell if his sheer presence was a true reflection of his physical self but it was one that filled the space beside him with its magnificent stature.* 'The Obelus *took me to your home for a reason. The Oracle taught me many things, opened my eyes to what was clearly hidden from me for a reason. I cannot risk wasting that learning by starting another existence now. Steve will not be alone.' *The big man stood up beside Rue, barely reaching his shoulder height.*
'Fletcher will get Doctor Gmitrowicz to end the artificial stasis you have been kept in?' *Noting the small arc of electric like light*

extending from the fireball to Ruedrav'tor like a network cable.
'You and he have already met, here before?'
'Not quite but, more or less here. I only regret that we could not have shared such a gift, but we are merely immortal souls set to wander from one existence to another, without knowing what the next one may bring, or why the current is as it is.'
'Well, personally, knowing how the story ends somewhat takes the fun out of the ride.' *Extending his right hand out to shake with the old warrior's, who looked momentarily puzzled at the gesture.* 'I have a feeling we will meet again, though whether we know it to be so is not so clear. Give Steve my best regards. It will be good to have the vitality of youth once more and fight this unseen enemy armed with the prior knowledge they exist.' *They shook hands firmly, a grip that would have crushed all but the hardest minerals between their palms in their respective physical realms.*
'Use your knowledge wisely, Mighty One. The Nemesis will not underestimate you so next time. Be careful who you share this wisdom with. Remember, together we are more powerful than they.'
They smiled, bid each other a determined and mutually respectful goodbye and with that, The Boss *took a stride out and over* the Edge *into the void, on to the next "now". Ruedrav'tor sat back down, cross-legged, taking a final chance to enjoy the unique pleasure of meditation in the space between spaces. His next such contemplation would be gained from the vantage point of the physical realm, of that he was sure, in a strange world he had yet to fully experience.*

They sat in the debriefing room in the Shard, the cloud that had shrouded the sky like a thick insulation earlier that night had cleared, providing a dramatically beautiful vista as a back drop. The emotion as much as the physical exertion had left both of them exhausted, mentally and physically depleted. Jane twiddled the last thing *The Boss* had handed to her in an unconscious motion. Like a witchdoctor using a golem or a voodoo doll whilst trying to invoke some ancient incantation to revive the dead, or contact a long-lost ancestor in the spirit world. Fletcher sat up straight, head inclined backwards, eyes facing the ceiling deep in thoughts of his own. He then half chuckled with a certain amount of bitter sweet emotion in his tone.
'Least I know who's been having a swift cup of my coffee when I've not been looking.' *Facing forwards and smiling wistfully at his colleague.*
'I wonder if…' *Gmitrowicz's hand moving on to the crucifix around her neck, in a subconscious sign of nervousness.* 'I wonder who

else knew about him. If Desmond was privy to his data, knew him from before.' Steve gentle rolled his head left and then right as if chewing the thought over metaphorically.
'That thing's probably the only chance you will have of ever finding the answer to that question. Assuming the IT bods haven't received an order to remove any "unwanted" files from the powers that be.' He was alluding to the fact that the tech team *had* just managed to extract and delete the last of any clear or good quality video files of his and Dyer's last chase from not only social media sites but any device that had been in the vicinity, or indeed ones which were downloaded to network back up or file transferred into the wider cloud at large. It was decided that it was better to fuel any conspiracy theorist paranoia than add credence to their views with evidence, or, at minimum, reduce the risk of a positive identification of one of Luke, Samantha or Steve. 'The funny thing is… I don't feel like we've completely lost him.' Standing up and walking over to the window to drink in the view. He could clearly see the scene of carnage that had been left behind them.

'I have a request, Jane.' She looked up at him, silently waiting for him to continue. 'Can you tell me if *The Source*, if Ruedrav'tor can be awoken.' Turning to meet her gaze.
'I guess I can arrange that, now. Though the risk is…'
'There is no security risk, I can assure you of that.'
'That is reassuring to hear, if a little harder to accept that you speak with any true knowledge either way.'
'Your faith is important to you, doctor, isn't it? I can tell you have seen things that both back up and dismiss that faith in equal measure. I can't even explain how I know it to be true but I can tell you it is. Ruedrav'tor deserves to be conscious, to be free from his imprisonment. He is key to the future.' Taking the seat by her side. 'Surely you can feel it too? All of the events of the last few days? This is bigger than just a rogue soldier with *en*hanced abilities going a little mad and running amok? There is something profound going here. And we are in the centre of it, whether we choose to be or not.' Jane acknowledged his insight.
'I am a scientist, Steve. I look to understand, to define. If what you are telling me is that *The Source* is the key to us uncovering more of the truth, the facts, then I agree we must revive him. But let's get some rest first. We will travel there first thing.'
Gmitrowicz stood up and proceeded to leave the room, halted only when Steve begun to speak once more.
'You know what his last words were to me?' shaking her head in response. 'Be a man, not a god.' He was visibly choked by the

memory. 'I will try to be what he has taught me to be in the short time I have known him. To honour him that way. To honour all the brave men I have had the privilege of serving for and alongside.'

Jenkins sat in her office re-reading the hastily put together briefing on the events of the last forty-eight hours. There was immense political pressure being placed on the senior leaders of the Metropolitan Police to get results and quick. National government, European authorities and the not insignificant influence of the Mayor of London were all in play here. Financial markets were in melt down, globally with all of the main indices being suspended until later that morning. This was about as big as it gets in terms of profile and pressure. What she felt was a strange sensation.

The fact that she and one of her team members had been singled out to lead the taskforce to bring whoever was responsible to justice did make her extremely proud. Pleased at the recognition of their skills. This was counterbalanced with the sorrow and horror at all of the death, destruction and pain that was the aftermath of these events. And fear. That was a purely natural and expected reaction. But fear of the unknown, of the change in the social environment wasn't the only feeling that churned her stomach. What unnerved her most was the nagging feeling that it wasn't just the criminals, the terrorists who were acting nefariously here, an apprehension she had expressed to Hayes previously. Maybe she was seeing problems where they didn't exist, but the relatively long list of stakeholders involved in the governance of the project, especially the names she did not recognise from Whitehall added to her sense of nervous unease. Hannah took off her spectacles and rubbed at her tired eyes, the early morning, following what little sleep she'd managed to grab that night, leaving her feeling a little bit jaded to say the least. At that moment there was a knock on the door and Hayes entered the room.

'Morning, Philip, please have a seat. I take it you have had a suitable think about the proposition of running the new project and the expanded team?'
'Indeed, Ma'am, I have. And I would very much like to do it on one condition. That I get to hand pick and personally vet all members of the team.' Setting his stall out early, perfectly aware that he would not get carte blanche over the whole unit. His superior did not react to his demand in any way that he would

have expected. She simply looked down at the pieces of paper in front of her that lay on what was otherwise a clear and faultless desk top. After a few moments she looked up, handed a single sheet of A4 paper to him and sat back a little in her seat.

'That is the proposed structure of the team. You'll note there are quite a few positions already filled. And that the role you will be fulfilling carries an acting DCI title.' What he noted with some surprise was the number of positions not filled, more than he would have accepted as a compromise in terms of recruiting team members. Definitely a role for Killen in there too, with a similar acting up promotion as well. It would at minimum make it potentially easier to figure out who, if anyone, he could trust and, more importantly, who he could not.

'And what is to happen to the investigation that I have been running up until now?' Avoiding using the obvious moniker!

'I think we all agree privately, if not publically, that these crimes are almost certainly linked. Along with the murder on Shad Thames you have identified. How we will report on the results of any success your team has will be another matter for discussion at the appropriate time.' She leant forward and spoke in slightly more hushed tones.

'And for both our sanity's sake I suggest we have the odd review in the privacy of my car from time to time.'

Fear bubbled under the calm exterior that he was exuding that morning. It was relatively unusual for him to be in Whitehall so early in the day but then again, it seemed it was the season for unusual happenings. For Desmond, the one thing he feared most was the wrath of the *Nemesis*, having been informed through his sources that Bahajoub had died suddenly and unexpectedly at the airport whilst heading for the "much needed" holiday he'd suggested, reminded him that people very rarely got to retire peacefully from serving the overlords. Undying devotion and servitude was more of an indication of the actual means required to stop serving them than anything else. More or less stating the terms and conditions of the employment contract than simply stating the desired sentiment of loyalty. Travelling in that morning the civil servant had felt relatively safe in his chauffeur driven car, trusted employee at the wheel and the incredibly heightened levels of security leading him to believe that even *they* would not try to do anything untoward so openly in the public gaze. Not today anyway. But here in the relatively sparse, quiet echelons of the government machinery in which he worked, that probably false sense of security had completely evaporated. Outside of his immediate sphere of influence there was always the uncertainty of who else may be engaged with the *Nemesis*, who else may be even more in the know than he.

Desmond surmised often that this culture of fear, uncertainty and doubt was the most effective means of ensuring people always tried to do their best for a cause, worried about what may happen if they did not do so, doubting that they were ever truly able to let something go unnoticed, or rest, if a task had not been fully actioned. All he could do was hope that his position in the very machinery in which he sat, and had done for many years, was enough to make it at least annoyingly inconvenient for *them* to remove him. The electronic blip of his intercom made him jump a little, becoming self-aware of the here and now and the fact he'd just spent twenty minutes staring at the same memo on the screen in front of him. His PA passed on the message, that the task force to look into the reign of terror inflicted on London in the last few days had its main members put into place. Made up of good, honest members of the police force, including a number of known quantities to him and the cause. Sitting back, the tension in his neck and shoulders eased a little, but the uncomfortable feeling acted as a continued reminder of what it felt like to commune with the *Faceless Ones* and that he would never, ever be able to live free from their stare.

The news on every means of communication was dominated by the two major incidents of the previous day and the associated stories. The total number of lives lost was estimated at over fifteen hundred and rising, many of the victims being elderly, mothers and children in particular with regards to the first residential tower block. "The Grim Reaper" was probably the most apt newspaper headline, with some articles and agencies choosing to take a different angle to gain readers and viewers by focusing on "Conspiracy nuts blame Victorian bogey man for twenty first century terrorism", alluding to the few remaining pictures in circulation showing the chase across the roof tops of West London, along the Thames and the West End and linking it to the tower block's destruction. Social media and the rest of the web echoed both sentiments, but mostly commented on the horror and shock caused and felt by the occurrence of these tragedies.

The fact that the death toll was so high, making the day the single worst loss of life event since World War two in Britain, brought the United Kingdom together in a single mood of mourning not seen since the death of Princess Diana. It would be a very long time before London in particular would be operating under anything approaching a business as usual mind-set, and it would be many months before the physical scars placed upon it would be removed. Fact was the emotional ones may never be truly healed. Against such a backdrop, along with their own personal sense of remorse and heart ache, Gmitrowicz and Fletcher travelled up to *The Organisation's* Facility in Rendlesham. There were noticeably more police and military presence visible at major locations in the City and the surrounding areas as well as generally on the roads, travelling to and fro. The reality was that all this activity was pretty much too little too late, but to not react publicly this way would only have drawn more awkward questions and created an even greater sense of foreboding within the public at large.

In the familiar setting of the massive, cavernous underground secure level they were joined by a number of *Organisation* science personnel. Whether it was the fact that physically as well as operationally they were somewhat removed from the day to day happenings in general society whilst on a weekly shift down here or not, their controlled exuberance seemed very much at odds with Steve's own mood. Doctor Gmitrowicz soon also cracked what resembled half a smile after a brief one to one chat with a colleague. In the furore of what had happened she had not been monitoring activity from the unit or its main occupant as she had previously.

'Your colleagues seem very noticeably hyper this morning, Jane.' His tone barely hiding his disapproval at their emotional, noticeably jubilant state.

'With some good reason. *The Source*.' She mentally checked herself. 'That is *Ruedrav'tor*, appears to have taken a turn for the better. Vital signs seem to be increasing rather rapidly. A sharp turnaround from the previous few months' decline. And all indications of possible Tachyon activity seem massively heightened too. It is the kind of mystery that gets us excited, especially when you are held captive in the middle of a long shift in this place, cut off from all external reality.' Her last comment drawing half a chuckle and a wry smile from Fletcher.

'Reality...' he repeated. 'Whatever that is?'

They entered into the room where Ruedrav'tor's body lay in state like a latter day incorruptible saint on display. Both could see visibly that the living tissue vessel was in a far more radiant state than it was only a matter of days before.

'Has this improvement occurred since we started reversing the induced state of coma?' Turning to ask her colleague as he entered the room.
'No Doctor Gmitrowicz, the vital signs began to improve yesterday evening, whilst you were, -' Pausing as he remembered what had just occurred back in civilisation above ground, 'whilst you were operational.' Steve placed a hand gently on the shoulder of the old warrior. He could feel the energy of life coursing through it like a mix of static electricity and the coarse vibration of a base speaker at a rock concert. It caused him to smile properly for the first time in hours.
'When will he be fully awake?' Jane looked at her watch and opened her mouth to answer, just as they both felt something and looked with a sense of trepidation and expectation on to Ruedrav'tor's face as his large almond eyes blinked open and his head turned to face Steve.
'We truly meet, at last.'

Printed in Great Britain
by Amazon